HEROES FOR GHOSTS

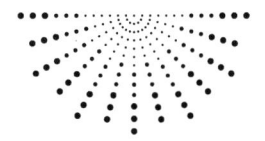

ALSO BY JACKIE NORTH

The Love Across Time Series

Heroes for Ghosts

Honey From the Lion

Wild as the West Texas Wind

Ride the Whirlwind

Hemingway's Notebook

For the Love of a Ghost

Love Across Time Sequels

Heroes Across Time - Sequel to Heroes for Ghosts

Holiday Standalones

The Christmas Knife

Hot Chocolate Kisses

The Little Matchboy

Standalone

The Duke of Hand to Heart

HEROES FOR GHOSTS

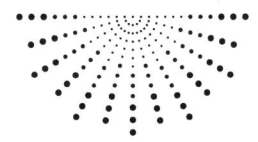

JACKIE NORTH

Heroes For Ghosts
Copyright © 2018 Jackie North
Published June 20, 2018

All rights reserved. No part of this book may be reproduced, distributed, or transmitted in any form or by any means, electronic or mechanical, including photocopying, recording, or any information storage and retrieval system without the written permission of the author, except where permitted by law.

For permission requests, write to the author at jackie@jackienorth.com

This is a work of fiction. Names, characters, places, and incidents are a product of the author's imagination or are used fictitiously. Any resemblance to people, places, or things is completely coincidental.

Cover Design by Jay Aheer, Simply Defined Art

Heroes For Ghosts/Jackie North

ISBN Numbers:

Mobi - 978-1-94-280904-3
Print - 978-1-94-280905-0
Epub - 978-1-94-280915-9

Library of Congress Control Number: 2018947775

For all those who know that love is love...

And to Wendy...
So many gold crowns, so, so many

IN FLANDERS FIELDS

In Flanders fields the poppies blow
Between the crosses, row on row,
That mark our place, and in the sky,
The larks, still bravely singing, fly,
Scarce heard amid the guns below.

We are the dead; short days ago
We lived, felt dawn, saw sunset glow,
Loved and were loved, and now we lie
In Flanders fields.

Take up our quarrel with the foe!
To you from failing hands we throw
The torch; be yours to hold it high!
If ye break faith with us who die
We shall not sleep, though poppies grow
In Flanders fields.

~~ John McCrae

CONTENTS

Chapter 1	1
Chapter 2	9
Chapter 3	17
Chapter 4	25
Chapter 5	31
Chapter 6	39
Chapter 7	45
Chapter 8	53
Chapter 9	59
Chapter 10	69
Chapter 11	75
Chapter 12	83
Chapter 13	93
Chapter 14	99
Chapter 15	107
Chapter 16	111
Chapter 17	119
Chapter 18	123
Chapter 19	131
Chapter 20	135
Chapter 21	143
Chapter 22	153
Chapter 23	163
Chapter 24	171
Chapter 25	177
Chapter 26	183
Chapter 27	191
Chapter 28	199
Chapter 29	205
Chapter 30	211
Chapter 31	219

Jackie's Newsletter	229
Author's Notes About the Story	231
A Letter From Jackie	233
About the Author	235

CHAPTER ONE

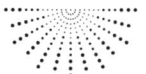

A mortar shell exploded at the far end of the trench, spraying black debris that slammed into the mud and sent up the acrid odor of burnt tar and hot, damp earth. Stanley hunkered down with mud up to his ankles, his backside pressed against the broken end of a mortar gun, his hands on his helmet as his body shook with the force of the blast. He tried to stem his tears as Lieutenant Billings stabbed at the radio with a bit of metal wiring to see if he could get it to work again. Between the mortar rounds, the radio responded with squawks and low pitched shrieks and then went quiet.

If the radio had been even six feet to the left, it would have been safe from being torn apart by the shell that had directly hit the trench mid-morning. And if Bertie, Isaac, and Rex had been on the other side of Stanley when that shell had hit, then they would be alive. Then he would have had someone to worry with, someone who would bolster his courage so he could respond to Lt. Billings' earlier request.

He missed his friends, but he wanted to be brave for them now. Lt. Billings needed a volunteer to run across the trenches and the misty, frost-bitten fields to contact the major in charge to get the final message for retreat. The battalion needed a retreat or all of the 200 men were going to be smashed to bloody bits and their families would not hear from them come Christmas.

It was horrible. Stanley wondered how he ever imagined that signing up and shipping off would be an adventure worth having, something he could tell everybody about back home. There was no way he could convey the tragedy of it, the futility of a radio that didn't work, of trying not to look at the bodies of his friends that were currently beneath a tarp for decency's sake.

Whether there would be a break in the shelling so that they could be buried was anybody's guess; the way it had been going, they would likely get frozen in place, spattered with mud and bits of shrapnel, and nobody would be able to bury them till spring. By which time, the war would be over, or they'd all be dead. Or both.

Stanley was shaking all over, and told himself it was because he was trying to warm his body up, but that was another futility, a lie he could barely hold on to. The Germans were coming closer with each passing hour. The shells were louder and more on target, and soon they would die. All of the battalion's efforts would come to nothing, and Stanley would be another body beneath a tarp, and nobody would have the energy to bury him.

He would become part of the landscape, part of the stretch of brown mud and red blood, decorated with torn limbs. The uniform he wore so proudly would turn into the tattered remnants of desire to do good, to fight for one's country, and to keep families and children and grandmothers safe. At least that's what the recruitment posters had stated, and behind every one had been the American flag, rippling with patriotism and an overwhelming urgency.

Stanley had signed up alone, but had soon met his three friends during training. They'd stuck together, sharing the burden of fear, bolstering each other up, proud to fight and do right. Only it was wrong, so, so wrong because what was happening seemed to be for no reason at all, and everything they did as a battalion felt like they were merely going through the motions.

Men kept dying, though the sudden silence across the top of the trenches indicated that the Germans seemed to have let up for the moment. Which left Stanley alone with Lt. Billings, and on the verge of blubbering. He was shaking with the effort of not crying, though his face was hot with tears he kept having to blink away as he tried to focus on what Lt. Billings was doing.

"The wire goes under," said Stanley with a croak. "Under on the left."

"Oh, yes?" asked Lt. Billings. His voice was gruff.

He didn't look at Stanley, all of his attention on the radio. He moved the wire as Stanley had suggested, and while this brought a sound from the transmitter, it ended in another ineffectual squawk.

The worst of it was that Stanley had previously thought the radio was too much in the open and ought to be moved, just in case. He'd not wanted to step on Lt. Billings' toes, though, as the lieutenant had only just taken over from Colonel Helmer, and had not said anything.

Helmer had been the worst commander anybody had ever seen, and the muttered comments among the enlisted men had almost grown into a roar. Though Stanley might have given him some leeway, due to his age, Colonel Helmer had taken the coward's way, run off in the night, and had not been heard from since. With the tenseness among the men, Stanley hadn't wanted to point out that the radio was in harm's way. It might have been seen as a challenge to the order of command, which was the last thing that Stanley wanted to do.

He'd refrained from talking about Helmer, and had generally kept his mouth shut. But if he'd not done that, if he'd given into his natural proclivities to think with his mouth open, they might have a radio now, might already be in an officially sanctioned retreat, and Rex, and Bertie, and Isaac would not be dead. They'd be beside him as they all scuttled to the rear of the battle and clambered into trucks to be taken to somewhere a bit safer than where they were.

It was all his fault, then. All of it. His lungs felt as though they were running out of air, and his belly dipped so hard he thought he might shit himself in fear. The only thing for it was to do something so that it didn't get worse. And that meant answering Lt. Billings' question from earlier that morning.

"Sir?" asked Stanley, though he realized that his voice was too soft to be heard. "Sir?" he asked again, more loudly this time.

"It just sparked," said Lt. Billings, completely focused on the radio. "If I move that wire again, I'm going to fry this fucking thing."

Stanley scrambled up from where he was, his boots slipping on the mud as he surged forward to land on his knees at Lt. Billings' side.

"Sir, I'll go," said Stanley. "I'll take the message and bring the code back."

Lt. Billings' hands froze in the midst of what he was doing, and then he slowly turned his head. The lieutenant's eyes were red-rimmed, and his face was be-grimed with smoke and mud that seemed to have pushed its way into his skin. He didn't smile as he looked at Stanley, and his expression was grim.

"You might not come back," said Lt. Billings. "In fact it's a death sentence. Do you want that?"

Lt. Billings was so unlike Commander Helmer in every way; Stanley knew that it was a death sentence, so Lt. Billings, not one to suffer fools, was making sure that Stanley knew exactly what he was getting into. A zigzag run across a field of dead bodies, horse carcasses, guns, gouged earth, and barbed wire, all the while dodging bullets and shrapnel and mustard gas.

"There's no other way," said Stanley. He wiped his hand across his upper lip, and took a hard breath, feeling his metal ID tag like a circle of cold ice in the middle of his throat. "You said so this morning. If we don't get the order to retreat, we're all going to die. Right here in this trench."

He did not add that they could retreat anyway, without the order, and save a whole lot of lives. But Lt. Billings was a seasoned army officer, and while he might take it upon himself to take control of a battalion that was currently officer-less, it was not in his makeup to call such a command without a direct order.

Stanley could try to convince Lt. Billings to overstep his authority, but that would only get everyone irritated, and as they were all so edgy already, it would be the worst way he could contribute. The best thing for him to do, besides throw himself on a land mine, was to step up and volunteer. It wouldn't bring his friends back, but it would give their deaths meaning. Or would it? At any rate, it would be better than sitting with his ass in the mud watching Lt. Billings mess with equipment in a way that was probably making it worse.

If only Stanley had spoken up and told him to move the radio. If only Stanley had told his friends to sit someplace other than where they had. If only Stanley had been born at a different time, and had missed this stupid war entirely. One hundred years ago or a hundred years from now, it made no difference to him. But he was here now, and he needed to do his best for the sake of his friends' memory.

He stood up and made an ineffectual pass at the front of his wool sweater vest. He winced as his fingers touched dried blood, the source of which he didn't want to identify, but which had been the spatter from Rex's head as it exploded. Rex would have gone with him, big and silent and close as they crossed the field of battle to carry the message.

"I'll go," said Stanley.

Lt. Billings stood up too, though he didn't reach out to shake Stanley's hand. Stanley was glad about the lack of the gesture because that would have truly meant that Lt. Billings did not expect him to return, but was only sending him out because there was nobody else who would go.

"Find Major Walker," said Lt. Billings. "Give him half the message, and he'll know I need the other half. He'll tell you what that is, and when I have the whole message I can call retreat. Tell him I sent you, you got all that?"

"Yes, sir," said Stanley. His heart was thumping in his chest, threatening to push its way out, and his knees started to knock together. "I'll bring the message back, I promise."

"It's a foolish thing to make such promises," said Lt. Billings. He shook his head, and looked down at the busted radio before looking up at Stanley. His expression was so deep and serious that Stanley knew he was going to die the minute he stepped out of the trench. The alternative, however, was to stay in the trench and watch while his friends' bodies froze in the mud, taking his heart with them as they became one with the earth, and that he could not bear.

"Here's a canteen and here's your rifle," said Lt. Billings. "You might need to kill some Krauts, and you won't believe how thirsty you can get when you're running hard, terrified enough to piss your uniform."

Stanley took the canteen and looped it over his neck and shoulder, then hung the rifle across his chest in the other direction. He wasn't exactly armed to the teeth, but he had a pouch of bullets and could give somebody a run for their money. After that, he'd be out of bullets and dead in a ditch somewhere.

He couldn't think about that now. He needed to go over the top and start running. The major would be in a trench at the back of the field, at least that was the general idea in most battles.

"That way, right?" asked Stanley. He pointed over his shoulder with his thumb.

"More over that way," said Lt. Billings. "Straight across and then over. He'll be in the right quadrant. You won't see any flags, but it's going to have more sandbags and look a damn sight tidier than where we are now."

"Yes, sir," said Stanley.

He straightened up and gave Lt. Billings the most efficient salute he'd ever managed, out of respect. Then, not allowing himself one last glimpse at the pile of bodies at the end of the trench, he pushed his way past the three soldiers who were manning a Howitzer that was almost out of shells, and climbed up the ladder.

Stanley slipped at the bottom rung, and was tempted to call it done then and there. For the memory of Isaac, Rex, and Bertie, and all the others, he made himself go up and up till he was standing on top of the ridge, looking over the dip in the earth that ran next to the ruined castle and the small cottage whose roof was half gone.

The sprawl of barbed wire along the top of each trench was intertwined with the dark flags of smoke that twisted and moved as though it was alive. The sun was a smudge through the brown and black haze, and the smell of hot oil and human excrement shot itself into his lungs with his first breath. The air was cold and it seemed as though frost speckled the air like little bits of diamonds made half yellow by the smoke from fires and the general exhalation of despair and gloom and death. Stanley watched a shell explode a hundred feet to his left, turned the other way, and started running.

The idea was to get out of the line of fire, for that was where the major was to be found. The easiest way was to follow the line of trenches, to run inside of them, along the bottom, and make his way there. He started to run, his canteen bouncing, his rifle banging into his thigh the whole while.

At the edge of the trenches were the round tops of helmets. Beneath those glimmered the exhausted, tired eyes of soldiers who saw him go, who knew where he was headed, and who had no hope that he would make it. A few soldiers stood up and fired beyond Stanley to draw enemy attention away from him when he had to cross over the top of a trench to get to the next one. The shots zinged around him anyway. If he slowed down, he was going to take a hit, so he kept low in the trenches and kept running.

His boots slipped as he headed down a small hollow, and he almost fell to his knees as he went up the other side; it was like trying to run up a waterfall, only this one was of mud, with bits of shell and hunks of rock. Just as Stanley got halfway to the top, he heard the high-pitched pop of a canister as it opened, and even before he smelled the bitter tang, a yellow cloud of mustard gas descended around him like a blanket of pure poison.

He brought his hand to his mouth, and staggered to the top of a trench, and though he kept his breath shallow, he felt his lungs collapsing, and fell to his knees, coughing up spit, his hands in the mud, his eyes closed. The yellow swirl filled his brain until there was nothing left but an empty ache and the sting in his lungs. He barely felt his head hit the mud and then sighed, thinking that it would be good to stay right where he was, for what did it matter anyhow? And then it became blackness, so, so much blackness.

CHAPTER TWO

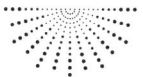

Devon checked his notes, which he kept in a suitably old-fashioned canvas notebook, and continued typing on his laptop. It was always easy if he just started and kept typing for a good solid hour. That way, he didn't have the time or brain energy to doubt his own ideas. Besides he was on the tail end of the project, so there was no shifting to another thesis now, no changing themes. No going back. Soon the miracle of the grant would come to an end, and his time in the cottage near the little French village of Ornes, where once the brave 44th Battalion had met its sad fate, would come to an end as well.

He paused to consult the chart that the university's meteorology department had emailed him, though he didn't really need to. He had it memorized, as well as the other five spreadsheets, and the 15 colored charts that indicated the weather over the course of the battle. He'd picked this one battle because his advisor had told him to focus, which would help keep the thesis from going all over the place.

It was slightly amusing to know so much about a single event, but it was a little sad, too, with the futility of it all. The lack of supplies, plus the terrible rain that had remained positioned over the small valley, made life in the trenches a living hell. The men in the battalion had all been young and inexperienced, fighting and dying without having much effect on the overall war, which had ended three years after the battalion had met its fateful demise.

Devon pulled up Google and entered *WW1*, which the search engine finished for him, as he'd entered the term so many times that he and the search phrase were practically on kissing terms. He didn't even have to capitalize it, though he did, out of respect. Then he clicked on *Images*, and scrolled through what came up.

It was always the same, hundreds and hundreds of black and white images of battlefields. Some of the images were streaked with the dust that was on the camera lens when the photo was taken, others scratched, some sepia toned. Then he typed *soldiers*, and pressed enter, and sighed as the familiar array of pictures of World War I soldiers displayed before him.

The young men who had fought the war had had no idea what they were getting into. At the beginning, it must have seemed like a lark to join a war as their uncles and grandfathers had. But the brutal conditions in the trenches, the lack of technology to coordinate efforts over vast tracks of land, not to mention the flu pandemic, all of that had been bad enough. To Devon, the worst of it had been the innocence that had been destroyed.

If he really wanted to torture himself, he'd entered *American doughboys* in the search field, as the nickname would bring up hundreds of pictures of young American soldiers fresh-faced and ready to ship out to war, but his heart wasn't in it this morning. He couldn't bear to see them, not when he was writing about the lack of bullets, the bad food, and the cold front that had lingered over the area for weeks, making the boys cold and damp and miserable.

He was fascinated, however, with how they looked, though it wasn't always good to let himself give in to his obsession. He loved their American faces, sweet and innocent, their eyes full of adventure. Their hair was typically greased back in a jaunty way, as if they assumed that once they got to the front that there'd be more Macassar oil and mirrors available so that they could check their look once they'd applied it.

So he didn't do more searches. Instead, after writing a few hundred more words, he got up and stretched, and thought about making some coffee. The French had the best coffee he'd ever tasted, smooth and silky; even the regular stuff was miles better than it was in the States, though maybe that had to do with the lack of haste in which the French drank it. Though that was only in town, as there was nobody in the cottage to watch him whip up a cup in his French press, and then to stand there drinking it black, hoping it would wake him up so he could finish his stint for the day.

Or maybe he should just go for a walk now? Anything to take him away from the dull task of replicating spreadsheets of data into small, manageable tables. He hated working with tables, and never could remember how to get them to break between rows instead of across them. Besides, it was good to step back from his obsession every now and then so that he wouldn't be so much the mad grad student who couldn't think of anything else other than doughboys or coffee rations, or canvas tents, or canvas puttees, or canvas-covered canteens with lift-the-dot fasteners, which had been invented in the Civil War, or before that—

With a shake of his head, Devon put on a pair of sneakers that would instantly mark him as being an American, but he wasn't going into town, only across the fields. Then he grabbed a sweater and jacket, and after he'd bundled up in layers, went out into the misty afternoon. He could leave the door unlocked, and usually did, unless he was going into the village or would be gone for a while.

Back home, he was lonely, just as he was now, mostly because he was always involved in his work. But also it was because nobody else he knew was doing a master's thesis on how weather affected the battle of the 44th Battalion outside of the village of Ornes. Nobody from his college days could understand his passion for the subject, let alone take the time to listen. He bored everybody he knew within moments of meeting them, and his loneliness had grown.

At least in France, he could imagine that he was alone because there was nobody around; the grant that he'd received had included a stipend and use of a cottage that had once stood at the edge of the trenches that the 44th had dug. The cottage was a mile from the village, which had a compact but thorough museum and history center about the war. Most academics, however, preferred to study the area that had been closer to the Western Front. That was where the Battle of the Somme had been fought, and which, incidentally, was closer to Paris, where all the amenities of life could be found, according to one of his very few fellow students.

Devon had been to Paris, of course, you couldn't come to France without going, and it had been wonderful in a lot of ways. In the end, though, Paris was just another city like Denver, big and crowded and noisy. He told himself he was here, in Ornes, because he preferred the quiet countryside, which he did. Except now that the field stretched out before him, the cool rain falling, he couldn't decide whether he was contented or lonely. Perhaps both. So he began to walk.

The air was fresh on his face, and a keen wind kicked up as he clambered up one of the mounds of earth. The edges of the trench had been dug long enough ago that they were softened by time and covered with a carpet of green grass. He was high enough that he could look across at the cemetery, which occupied the flat valley at the edge of the trenches. It was dotted with white crosses, ten rows of twenty, two hundred and one in all. There was the memorial at the far end with an inscription to the over 200 brave men of the 44th Battalion who'd lost their lives.

Some days, he liked to go all the way around and stand in front of the memorial. He liked to admire the marble carved to look like American and French flags, crossed across their flagpoles. Beneath the flags, the stone was meant to look like mourning swags, but which, especially in the rain, usually looked like cold stone that couldn't possibly reflect, let alone empathize with, the condition of being mortal and dying in a strange country far from home.

Today was one of those days where he didn't think he could bear it. Instead he faced away from the memorial and looked out over the acre or so of earth, the rippled rows of lush green corduroy where once the battlements of barbed wire and old railroad ties had fortified the trenches and kept out the enemy.

The wind was in his face now, but it whipped the cobwebs from his thoughts and allowed him to just look and see and not take mental notes. To not think about what would happen after he finished his exams, oral and written, to not think about what it would be like to be an associate professor whose days and nights were so focused that he would get paid for feeling bad about American doughboys. He felt bad for all of the young men, even those who had been among the enemy. The war had been a stupid, foolish rush for power, as all wars were, only this one had been tragic beyond belief. Had there been any benefits? Few, very few.

Devon shook himself and strolled along the top of a trench, his hands in his pockets, his sneakers growing damp with each step in the wet grass. With his head down, he tried to imagine that he was a young soldier, perhaps on watch in the middle of the night, or when dawn was just breaking over the edge of the battlefield.

There might be the smell of coffee, or the mournful, faraway sound of voices as the men woke up and prepared for another day of fighting. What would that coffee taste like? Who would his friends be? What was his rank? How did he feel about the shovel he'd used to dig the trenches he and his buddies were now hunkered down in? Where was the shovel, and did he have blisters from using it?

These were the thoughts that really drove him, really interested him. He wanted to know what it had felt like to be a doughboy, to really be one. Only this was the path that led his thesis advisor to roundly scold him for getting distracted from the main point, and which had driven off his more casual friends and the guys he met with on the weekend to go running or to go to the bar.

One friend had actually told him that gay guys weren't supposed to be as geeky as Devon was, which seemed a rather limited view, not to mention rude. For who was to say? Devon liked guys, but he liked burying his nose in a book and spending hours in the library. He also enjoyed walking around, like he was now, pretending he was somebody else.

He stopped and saluted an imaginary commander on watch so that he could be relieved of his duty and go get something to eat. There would only be bully beef and tea, and maybe some sugar, if he were lucky. He'd eat with his pals, and together they would make jokes about how hard the biscuits were, and laugh in the face of danger. Then maybe they'd stack shells so they could be used in battle, firing at the enemy.

In truth, though, Devon's imaginings always turned away from actual fighting and ended with an image of him in a circle of soldiers, one of whom was bending to light a primus stove so they could make some hot tea. That was the moment that always drew him, that huddle of soldiers, their faces lit by some imaginary light as if in a painting, joined together in adversity, strengthened each by the other. That's what he really wanted to be a part of, and what he always felt he'd missed out on.

Which was foolish because the price to pay for that was being involved in the war where the possibility of dying, probably needlessly, was almost one hundred percent.

Devon reached the far end of the field where the trenches ended and dipped down as though fading away as they turned into a blacktop road that led to the village. The edge of the field was marked by a copse of trees that gave the whole area a solitary feel. Standing there always felt as though he was miles from anywhere, though only a single mile separated Devon from the small village with its shops, and museum, the patisserie that sold mostly sweet things, and the one that sold mostly daily bread, and the string of restaurants, of which there were surprisingly many for such a small place.

He turned and started walking back, trying to resist the impulse to take off his shoes so that he could connect with the earth. Truth be told, his real desire was to touch his skin to a flake of dust that somebody from the war had touched. He kept his thoughts from the idea that he might one day find bone, or blood-darkened earth caked around a bayonet because it had been over a century since the fateful battle, and surely all of that had been dug up by now. But the image was a vivid one, so he took off his sneakers and socks anyway so he could at least stand there and think about the doughboys in this one little moment, and pretend that he was one of them.

Which, as it inevitably did, led him to lie down in the wet grass along the slope of a trench, his arms and legs spread wide to absorb as much of the energy of the place as he could. He also felt that if he held still enough, he could absorb the memory he was sure the earth held, an idea that he'd never shared with anyone because they would not believe him. Worse, they would make fun of him, and while he was a steady sort of person, this one thing, this tiny part of his heart, was one he could not bear to have broken.

With the soft rain falling on his face, he looked up at the sky and thought about being a soldier. He breathed so slowly that he became almost still. This was one of his favorite moments, when the cottage seemed a faraway place that he might have made up in his imagination, and technology was farther away than that. Where the world was only the sky above, the green grass beneath, his breath misting in the cool air, mingling with the breath of soldiers, his beloved American doughboys, from years past.

He ignored the fact that the dampness was soaking into his clothes, and that soon his spine would feel like it had been fused to the earth in one long column of ice. In another minute, he would realize how foolish this was and rise into consciousness. He needed to come back to reality, go back into the cottage, change into dry clothes, and put another two good hours into his thesis. Then he could have something to eat, another cup of coffee, and then he could pull up Netflix and do his very best to watch something other than a movie or documentary about World War I.

CHAPTER THREE

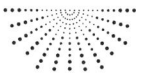

S tanley surged up from where he had fallen, his eyes wide open, his hands out in front of him. Instinctively, he reached for his rifle, wondering why he'd not pierced himself through the heart with his bayonet when he'd fallen. He clutched at his canteen to make sure the metal lid was still screwed on so he didn't lose all his water, which he'd need to keep from being dehydrated because he was just about to piss himself, just like Lt. Billings said.

His knees were soaked, and he was cold all the way through, as though he'd been in a block of ice. He reached up to touch his head; mud caked through his short hair fell in damp clumps. He stepped forward with jerky movements and a sense of what-the-hell? Before him were row upon row of white crosses across a green, frost-tipped field. At the far end was a larger cross, also white, and he saw the stone swags that he thought were meant to represent a flag or funeral bunting, and squinted.

Where were the trenches? If he drew his eyes along the edge of the field in the right way, he could see the top of the most recent one he'd been running along, but that was impossible. The sun was coming over the trees with bright, gold shards, cutting through the chilly morning, sending fog up from the earth, dressing the air with wisps of ghost-like tendrils. They would soon grab him if he didn't move, except he couldn't because the mustard gas had been all over him, and he'd fallen and maybe hit his head. Was he unconscious and dreaming? Or had he died and was he a ghost?

There was no war. There was nobody, no soldiers, no barbed wire, no smoke and, noticeably, no sounds of mortar shells exploding. No shouts of command, no cries of despair, no movement. There was only stillness and the white crosses across a green field, the edge of what could have been a trench. A sky full of frosty, jagged clouds as the blue began to break through. Larks singing somewhere in the bare trees.

Over the rise, he thought he saw the roofline of the cottage so that, at least, was familiar. If he moved toward the center of the crosses, which was eerie as hell, the cottage came fully into view. Stanley knew he had to get to a high point so he could figure out where he was, and started running.

The movement jarred his head, and his lungs felt seared with the gas, the burning taste in his mouth that made him want to throw up. His heart was beating so fast, but he couldn't stop running till he made it to the edge of the field and got closer to the cottage. A moment later, he could see the ruin that before had been only a pile of stone with one wall, but its carved frame against the sky like a broken hand reaching for help was now an entire, well-tended building.

Stanley had only one moment to wonder why or how such a ruin had been repaired so quickly when he tripped over a body on the ground. Thinking it was a dead body of a soldier whose face he did not want to recognize, Stanley pushed his rifle away from his body and rolled as he fell. He braced his elbows and pointed the rifle at the body as it sat up, one of the living dead.

His arms were shaking and his breath came in heavy jerks, sweat rolling down the side of his face. He wiped the back of his hand across his forehead to keep it from getting into his eyes. Gripping the rifle again, tighter, he pointed it at the man, and wanted to shout.

But what would he say? He needed to figure that out before he started blabbing, as that would be the sensible thing to do. And then the words spilled out anyway, all in a rush, as they tended to do when he couldn't put the brakes on them.

"Where did the ruin go? Where are the bodies? Where is the mud—where is the fucking war?" He was almost screaming when he stopped, mouth open, gasping for air.

The man on the green grass leaned back on his arms to support himself. He didn't seem the least bit worried that Stanley was pointing a rifle directly at him, though he was frowning, as though confused, which of course he would be because where in the world was his uniform?

"Where did you come from?" asked the man, his dark brows lowering. He looked cross because Stanley had left a streak of mud across his shirt when he'd tripped over him. Moreover, the shirt was a white button down one that Stanley hadn't seen on anybody since he'd enlisted.

Nobody had enough soap to keep something that white. Everything soldiers wore was designed to disappear into the earth, to blend in with the countryside where the fighting was. Yet this strange fellow was wearing the white shirt and those blue jean dungarees that farmers wore.

In spite of the odd clothes, the stranger drew Stanley's gaze to him in the way that Isaac always did. He had long legs and looked incredibly fit and healthy, as though he'd not gone hungry one day in his entire life. He was not clean-shaven, but looked only a few razor swipes from being so, with his dark hair, the color of ink, cut away from his face. He was handsome even though he was frowning, and he squinted at Stanley, as though with displeasure at being disrupted from lollygagging in the grass. Which begged the question, what was he doing without any shoes when there was a war on?

"I'm asking you again, where did you come from?" asked the man.

"From the 44th Battalion," said Stanley, incredulous that the man didn't already know this because the soldiers in his battalion been all around him only moments ago. "From the 44th, can't you see the bodies? Can't you see the trenches?"

Stanley's voice rose to a high shriek and then warbled away as the man got up, feet bare in the grass, a continued scowl on his face.

"Those trenches are from World War I," said the man with a snort, as though Stanley was a little foolish. "Why are you wearing that getup?" asked the man. Then he stopped. "I'm sorry, did you say the 44th Battalion? Are you role playing or something?"

Stanley didn't know what role playing was, but it was obvious that the man didn't think very highly of it, and thought even less of Stanley for participating in it. Stanley decided to do what he did best, deny. Which is what he'd been doing since the war started, deny that it was that bad, deny that he was terrified as hell all the time, deny that it was the worst thing imaginable.

He tightened his fingers around his rifle and held it firmly in front of him, elbows planted in the cold grass. The grass was so wet that in spite of his wool uniform, he was going to get soaked through. And then he'd get pneumonia, and then he'd die. At least he'd be with his buddies, at least he'd be with his Pa, who had died before the war began, and before Stanley had enlisted. That was a sad tale Stanley had barely been able to share with anybody, though there wasn't much point, as everybody he'd met had a sad story of their own.

With nothing to lose, Stanley pointed the rifle at the man, tightened his shoulders, and crooked his finger to pull the trigger. But the man was quick, even in bare feet, for he reached down and with both hands on the stock below the blade, twisted the rifle sideways, and jerked the whole thing out of Stanley's hands. Stanley's whole body went hollow with shock, his breath leaving him in a gasp.

He thought that the man was going to shoot him. Instead the man opened his palms and lifted the rifle close to his face to examine it.

"This is a museum quality piece," said the man, sighing softly, his eyes alight. "Where did you get it? Did you steal it?"

"No," said Stanley. He got up and reached for the rifle, but the man pulled it out of his reach. "It's a Winchester 1912 and it's mine, it's *mine*, I got it when I finished basic training. It's mine because they gave it to me to kill Germans!"

"Why would you want to kill Germans?" asked the man. His eyes were a flinty green, and he scowled briefly at Stanley, his dark brows drawing together. "Do you think we're at war with them?"

"Yes, we are!" shouted Stanley, lunging for the rifle, for it had been drilled into his head since the day he'd been given it that it was his most valuable possession and the main thing that would help him survive and win the war. "Because the Kaiser attacked! Because Americans couldn't stand by and watch while—"

"Yes, I know all of that," said the man as he backed away from Stanley, shaking his head. "But that doesn't explain why you're digging your heels into the dirt like it's going on right now. Or why you're dressed in a uniform that ought to be in a museum, just like this antique rifle."

"It's a new rifle," said Stanley, reaching again. "And it's *mine!*"

"I doubt that," said the man. He cradled the rifle along his arm and stroked the stock gently, running his thumb across the place where Stanley had scratched his initials. "Why on earth would you damage such a fine piece by carving your name in the wood?"

"I did that so I'd know which one was mine," said Stanley, confused by the man's care with the rifle. "In case a shell comes, in case I drop it, in case—"

"Why do you keep talking like there's a war on?" asked the man.

"Because there is!" Stanley shouted this at the top of his lungs and barreled forward in a desperate surge of energy, hands out, shoulders braced, reaching for his rifle.

At the last minute, the man stepped back and braced his feet, holding the rifle pointed forward at Stanley, with as much grace as anybody Stanley had trained with. Stanley was about to be pierced by the bayonet end of his own rifle, and die at the hands of a man who insisted there was no war but who handled the rifle as if he'd been born to carry it.

Reaching for his rifle, Stanley slipped on the wet, slippery grass that was shockingly cold on his hands. He tried to roll into a defensive ball as he'd been taught, but instead slid to a stop, face down, splayed out, ready to be sliced into pieces.

That didn't happen, even though Stanley's ribs hurt from the fall, his lungs ached with trying to get enough air, and his throat was tight with trying not to scream piteously for mercy. He was going to piss himself in another minute, and then he'd be dead, and all of this would have been for nothing.

"Can I help you up?" asked the man. "Come on, I'm not going to hurt you. I just don't want you hurting me."

Rolling on his back, Stanley expected to see the rifle aimed right at his heart, but though the man held the rifle at the ready, his right hand on the stock, his left on the barrel below the blade, he did not move into position to shoot or anything. Instead he looked at Stanley with his brows drawn together, an expression of concentration on his face.

"You're not from around here, are you," said the man, as though puzzling it out. "And you're not French."

"No, I'm not," said Stanley with some force. He didn't hate the French, though their language sounded like babble to him, and the gestures they made with their hands confused him. He was rather fond of the cheese that he had tasted, but he was an American and he needed to make this calm stranger understand that. "I'm an American through and through."

"Okay, then," said the man with a laugh as though Stanley had said something funny. "But get up before you get soaked and catch your death."

"*You're* in bare feet," said Stanley, accusing and pointing at the same time.

"Yes, but I'm going in the house now, and you can come, too, and dry off. Then we'll figure out where you belong."

The man reached down, extending his hand to Stanley. He was muscled as all-get-out, as though he'd trained for a war he professed was not going on.

Stanley was sure he was going to get yanked with some force, as the man was taller than he, and broad through the shoulders. Instead, the man took Stanley's forearm in a firm grip and then gently pulled him to his feet.

For a moment, Stanley was close enough to see the little black specks in the man's green eyes, and the line across his cheek where his five o'clock shadow ended. The curve of his smile. The white teeth that pressed against his lips.

Stanley turned his head because he'd kept his secret this long, though Isaac might have started figuring it out only days ago, days before he died—

"Hey, kid," said the man as he let go. "I'm not going to hurt you. I just want to help you."

"I'm not a kid," said Stanley rudely before he could stop himself. "I'm nineteen and I'll be twenty next year so stop calling me a kid."

"Okay, okay," said the man.

As Stanley moved out of reach of the man's grip, he could see that the man thought Stanley was funny. This wasn't surprising, as that was the reaction of many of the guys in the battalion, except for his buddies, and Lt. Billings, as the latter viewed everything with serious eyes.

"You can laugh all you want," said Stanley. "I don't care. I just want to get back to my battalion and continue my mission, and see if I can save some lives."

"Which battalion did you say again?" asked the man, a quirky smile playing across his mouth as though he meant to humor Stanley.

"The 44th, or can't you see my stripes? This badge?" Stanley pointed to his uniform, which would have told anybody with any sense where he belonged. "Lance corporal, second class gunner, in case you didn't know."

"I *do* know," said the man, though his words came out more slowly. "You did say the 44th Battalion, right? And are we talking about the Battle of Ornes? That battalion was wiped out, and the village was too. I mean, there's people living there now, but it's more like a bedroom community—"

"What do you mean wiped out? All of them, *all* of them? Nobody was saved? How could you *know* that?" asked Stanley. He knew he was screaming, but couldn't stop, a sense of panic rising in his chest so hard and fast that he thought his heart would stop.

"Because of the records," said the man, somehow calm in the face of Stanley's agitation. "In the museum in Ornes, where I've been doing the research for my—don't you see the crosses, don't you see the memorial?"

"Yes, I see them," said Stanley, though his voice warbled and his breath was coming in such short bursts that his vision was going black. Round circles began to block out the cloud-draped sunlight, and the only thing he could focus on was the man's green eyes. "But I don't understand—"

He was falling to the ground, and the wet grass was about to embrace him. If he could just stay low and catch his breath, slow his heart, he could figure out what was going on and get back to his battalion. He'd return without the code needed for retreat, but at least he'd be with them, his commander, his friends, with people he knew, when he died.

CHAPTER FOUR

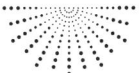

The man caught him, one arm scooping around Stanley's waist, the other holding the rifle at a distance so Stanley couldn't grab it. Or maybe so Stanley wouldn't collide with it, he couldn't be sure.

Exhaustion pulled at him, and for a moment he was held against the man's chest, which was so warm and broad, Stanley wanted to wrap his arms around it and press his cheek to it and fall asleep forever. Which of course, given Stanley's luck, wasn't what happened. Instead the man steadied Stanley on his feet, and turned him around so he could see all the white crosses, row on row. At the very far end, near where the grass sloped up in an echo of the top of a trench, was a large monument.

Stanley had seen it before, but now he had to really look at it. At the top of the monument was a white stone cross, and below the cross was a large bronze plaque. He couldn't see the words, though he could see that they were faded, as though weather and time were trying to erase them.

"That's the monument to the Battle of Ornes," said the man. "There's another one at the edge of where the village used to stand, an old metal sign saying what happened here. All of the soldiers were killed, and their bodies buried beneath those crosses. Some soldiers were identified and some were not. You have to understand the battle was almost a century ago, so wherever you belong, it's not with them."

"But I just came from there," said Stanley, his mouth trembling, and he was so cold the only spot of warmth came from where the man was still gently holding him. "I was running and the mustard gas came down—"

"That's what that smell on your uniform is," said the man. "I thought it was, but couldn't think why—"

The man stopped talking so abruptly that Stanley turned to face him. His mouth was tight like Stanley was lying to him for the worst sort of reasons. Then he shook his head and tugged on Stanley's arm.

"Listen," said the man. "Let's get you inside and out of those wet clothes. I'll make some calls and see where it is you escaped from."

"Can I have my rifle?" asked Stanley, though he wasn't surprised when the man pulled it out of reach.

"No, you may not," said the man. "But tell me your name, so I know what to tell *les gendarmes* when I talk to them."

"You're going to have them arrest me?" asked Stanley, his voice rising to a sharp point. "I haven't done anything!"

"No, not arrest you," said the man, shaking his head. "But I'm going to start with them, and see who else I need to talk to. Okay?"

Stanley knew that he could turn and run, though where he would run to and what he would find when he got there was beyond him. Somehow he'd been taken out of the war and was now in a place that looked familiar in only the vaguest of ways.

The color of the sky, now darkening with clouds, seemed the same. The shapes of the trees, the tall oval ones that he'd never seen back home, spindly with only half of their brown and orange autumn leaves still clinging to the thin branches, were familiar. The roll of the earth, the trenches now hidden by green grass flecked with frosty rain, had shapes that looked like a memory he kept trying to recall, but which kept being subsumed by the landscape before him. He was not on the battlefield, except that he was.

"Come on, kid," said the man as they walked toward the cottage. "Why don't you tell me your name."

"Tell me yours first," said Stanley, thinking at the last minute that if this were some sort of trick by the enemy, he'd recognize the German accent hidden in the man's voice, and take off running.

"My name is Devon Foster," said the man. "I'm a student at DU working on my master's thesis. And you?"

Stanley had no idea what any of what the man—Devon—had just said meant, except that he was a student at a school somewhere, and that there was not a trace of any accent in his voice. In fact, he sounded like someone from back home.

"DU is the University of Denver," said Devon, as if sensing Stanley's confusion.

"Denver, Colorado?" asked Stanley, his voice high pitched again. His throat hurt, and he could hardly believe what he'd just heard. "I'm from there, I mean, I'm from Harlin, Colorado—I was going to go to farm school, but enlisted instead—how could you be from Colorado?"

"Because I was born there," said Devon. "So we have Colorado in common, it seems."

Devon smiled and Stanley could sense that Devon was trying to put him at ease, though he didn't know whether he should believe him or not. But the clouds were moving in overhead, and it was starting to rain. Either he could stand there and argue it out until he convinced Devon as to how wrong he was, or he could give in, give Devon his name and rank, and then go someplace warm.

It was pathetic how easily he was about to surrender, and he thought he should resist just a little while longer, like a good soldier. Except that Devon looked at him, and in that moment, he didn't look quite so fierce, and in fact, seemed concerned because his eyes were gentle and he let go of Stanley's arm.

"I'm Stanley Sullivan," he said, giving Devon a sharp salute. "Lance corporal in the 44th Battalion, second class gunner."

He didn't know why he'd given the salute, even if it seemed the right thing to do because Devon shook his head.

"If you're a soldier, where's your helmet?" Devon looked at him as if the missing helmet would prove that Stanley was wrong and Devon was right.

Stanley debated not telling him because Devon wouldn't believe him, and it didn't make any difference anyway. Besides, the morning's horror was too real, too recent, to talk about.

The shrapnel had come directly at him. He'd ducked just in time, the metal of the shrapnel clanging against the metal of his helmet, the brief heat of it against his forehead as the shrapnel skipped off the rim of his helmet and dug itself into the trench behind him—all of this came at him, and he found his mouth opening, the whole story coming out in a babble of words: the sound of the explosion, the smell of burnt metal, and the horrible realization that the majority of the shrapnel had just ripped his friends to shreds.

He was shaking so hard he couldn't stop talking, couldn't breathe. Just when he was about to start screaming, he realized that Devon had laid the rifle in the grass, in the rain, and was gripping Stanley's arms in his hands, firmly, but with kindness.

"Stanley," said Devon. "Stanley, listen to me. If there's a war going on, you're not in it, okay? You're not in a war—you're here in this field. Listen to how quiet it is? Can you hear the birds? Can you hear the rain on the grass?"

It was such an odd thing to say about the grass and the rain, but Devon's voice was low and continued in the same steady way for a few minutes. After the earth and the horizon of the trenches stopped rocking back and forth, Stanley found that he could focus again.

He had to stop himself from falling into Devon's arms to be caught by a warm embrace because it was sure as shooting that Devon would be horrified. He would then indeed call *les gendarmes*, except it would not be to find out where Stanley should be, but instead to have him arrested for being the sort of man who was attracted to other men.

"Better now?" asked Devon. He let go of Stanley, bent to pick up the rifle, and then pressed his hand in a broad circle in the middle of Stanley's back. "Let's go in the house before we get soaked."

"It's not a house," said Stanley, mumbling as he allowed himself to be directed. "It's a cottage. It was the caretaker's cottage for the church, only now the windows aren't bombed out and the roof isn't collapsing."

He remembered the cottage from when they'd dug the trenches in the summertime; it had been an intact dwelling then, even if the church that abutted it had been falling down. Within weeks of battle, the church had been shattered to rubble, and the cottage had been mercilessly shelled by the Germans, who used it to calculate the distance to the enemy.

The cottage showed hardly any of the damage now. The grey stone walls still bore evidence of having been chipped, though somebody had taken the time to patch the cracks, as some of the stone was less weathered than the others. The roof was dark grey slate rather than thatch, and the whole of the cottage sat in the green grass as though it had been gently and carefully planted there.

Devon opened the door and gestured with the rifle that Stanley should precede him, and it felt a bit like Stanley was under arrest. But Devon held the rifle at his side, and the interior of the cottage beckoned, so to get out of the rain Stanley ducked his head beneath the low lintel and went in.

The floor was of thick boards of honey-colored wood, and the ceiling was crossed by dark, time-worn beams. The walls were of the same grey stone, and though it should have been chilly, like the last time Stanley had been inside, it was warm. The windows had thick curtains that were drawn to the side to let the rain-grey light come in.

As Devon crossed the open space to the sturdy farmhouse table, Stanley followed him. He watched as Devon pushed papers aside, moved a thin metal box to a wooden chair, and then placed the rifle on the table.

"I'm sorry about the mess," said Devon. "I could use the storage room as an office, but the light's better in here, and it's closer to the food."

He jerked a thumb at the kitchen, where Stanley saw on the wooden counter evidence of tea things and a wrapped loaf of bread. Also on the counter was an entire bowl of fruit, including oranges, which Stanley hadn't seen since he enlisted.

His mouth began to water, but he just swallowed. He might be a soldier, but he wasn't one of the ones who marched in and demanded that they be served, as he'd seen some American and British soldiers do. As if the French owed them for not razing their village to the ground and should be grateful that they didn't put everybody up against the wall—

No. Stanley shook his head. Those were just stories soldiers told each other when they were attempting to distract each other when night came and the shelling hadn't stopped.

In the beginning of the war, the stories had been funny, laced with kissing and half naked women and sex, and it had been easy to join in and laugh at the right things. Stanley secretly replaced the females with an equivalent male. Of late, the fellows in the stories had looked a lot like Isaac, though Stanley had never mentioned this to anybody.

It was only recently that in the trenches the stories became more dark. In them, the soldiers were doing bad things, with the civilians the butt of the joke. Or the stories were about captured Germans, who always resisted torture by crying and pissing themselves, which only added to the fun.

"Hey," said Devon, and though his voice seemed to come from far away, the hands that directed Stanley to a chair were warm and firm. "Sit down and I'll make you some coffee. We'll get you fixed up and then I'll make that call, okay?"

"Okay," said Stanley as he sat down, saying the word like Devon said it.

CHAPTER FIVE

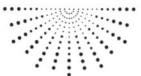

Stanley clung to the edge of the table, and watched as Devon went into the kitchen and did something to what looked like a metal coffee pot plugged into the wall. Stanley couldn't understand why Devon didn't put the pot on the stove, which was right there. Only the pot began to rumble in under a minute, and Stanley didn't have time to explain that he didn't want coffee.

Coffee in the trenches tasted like watered-down tar. There never was enough sugar in the world to make it taste good, but most days it was the only warm thing. If you drank too much of it, then you'd spent a good half hour afterwards squatting over a hastily dug trench, hoping you could get your pants up before another shell exploded.

Devon took milk from a sleek looking ice box that had an amazing wealth of food inside of it, and brought it and the cup of coffee over to the table. He pushed a bowl of what looked like brown sugar, and looked at Stanley, eyebrows raised, as if he expected him to take over.

"That's raw sugar," said Devon. "I was kind of on a health kick when I came to France and found that I liked it. Help yourself."

Stanley added sugar to the coffee and a splash of milk, just to be sociable. He needed to go along with it so that Devon wouldn't get angry and throw him out into the rain, which had started to come down pretty hard now, sheets of it falling outside the large, paned windows. But when he took a sip, the smoky smell of it hit him seconds before the taste did, and a warm sensation soothed his stomach, his insides.

"This is good," said Stanley, a little astonished. "But that's an understatement, this is really good coffee. I never used to drink coffee until I enlisted, and everybody drinks it, so I had to, you know? It tastes bad and it smells bad, but usually it was the only thing that you could drink because something happened to the water rations, and if you went to the village to get water from one of their pumps, they'd stare at you, and—well, I drank a lot of bad coffee."

"You like my coffee?" asked Devon. Stanley was surprised to be asked that, as if Devon were truly worried rather than fishing for compliments. Plus, he'd managed to follow all of Stanley's nervous chatter and dismantle it to its essence.

"Yes, I like it, it's good," said Stanley. He took another large swallow, and felt the energy moving through him. He leaned back a little in the wooden chair; it creaked beneath him in a homey way, though he knew he shouldn't be at ease. Until he knew what Devon was going to do next, he needed to be as alert as if he had been captured by the enemy.

"Hey, are you cold?" asked Devon. He took a step closer and looked about ready to place his palm across Stanley's forehead as if to check to see if he had a fever.

"No," said Stanley with some defiance.

"You're shaking like a leaf," said Devon. "Listen, why don't you get out of those wet clothes—I mean, uniform. You can use the shower, and I can loan you some clothes until we find out where you're supposed to be. Okay?"

Stanley wanted to shout that it was not okay, that he was *not* okay, as Devon seemed to want him to be. It was bad enough to be stuck in a muddy trench with a radio that didn't work, realizing that he was the only one who wouldn't be missed if his suicide mission went sideways.

It was almost worse to be stuck in a warm kitchen looking at an ice box that was about ten times the size of the ice box back home, and a stove that looked like a stove on the top, but that had a bunch of lights and switches Stanley didn't recognize. There was a metal box on the kitchen counter that Stanley had no idea what it did, and another metal box below the counter that was currently growling and churning as if it were about to birth something from inside of it.

The whole of the interior of the cottage was filled with half familiar, half bizarre things. Stanley realized how out of place he felt, and that he was shaking and sweating beneath his armpits, and freezing where his uniform was stuck to him, which was pretty much everywhere.

"I don't belong here," said Stanley, his lips numb. He wrapped his arms around himself, clutching at his arms, and looked up at Devon.

"You don't, and that's a fact," said Devon with kind eyes. "But nothing bad's going to happen to you. I won't call anybody until we figure out where you do belong."

"You won't have me arrested?" asked Stanley. He needed to be clear before he let himself come completely apart. "You won't call *les gendarmes*?"

"I wouldn't call them to arrest you," said Devon. "Look, I won't call them at all, okay? I'll call the local clinic and ask them if they know of anybody who's escaped the local loony bin, I mean—"

"I'm not crazy!" Stanley stood up, and knew he had shouted at Devon. His fists were clenched and he was probably pissing off the one person who had offered to help him. But he couldn't help it.

"I'm not crazy, damn it! I've just been in a trench watching my lieutenant trying to fix a radio that couldn't possibly work on account of the fact that it had been hit by a shell. I was up to my knees in mud and the blood and brains of my friends who had been torn to pieces only this morning and who are now very dead. The whole battalion is going to die and I can't help them because I got hit by mustard gas. So nothing is okay, do you *get* that?"

Devon was silent for a long moment, and he looked at Stanley in a way that seemed to suggest he might be starting to take Stanley very seriously.

"You honestly think you're in a war," said Devon. "Don't you."

Stanley nodded, a sharp jerk of his chin.

"And what year do you think it is?" asked Devon. "The 44th Battalion was wiped out in early November, 1917. And you think you're back then?"

"I *am* back then," said Stanley. "I mean, that's now, right now. It's November 10th, 1917. I was talking with my lieutenant about our ruined radio. Then I was in the bottom of a trench, trying to get to the top of it when the mustard gas hit me. And now I'm here."

There was sympathy in Devon's eyes, as though he'd heard every word Stanley had just said and felt the tragedy of Stanley's story keenly in his heart. Devon opened his mouth like he was about to ask Stanley more questions to get more details about the battle, but he held up his hands, as if resisting the urge.

"Hot shower and dry clothes," said Devon, pointing at Stanley. "Then food, then we'll talk. I have something you can wear, okay?"

"A shower?" asked Stanley. He stood up, thinking that Devon must be wealthy to have such a contraption and share it so freely. Back home, most people in his neighborhood had tubs. Coming into the army, Stanley had taken showers with the rest of the men upon enlisting, but it'd had been a long time since he'd had warm water to wash with.

"Oh," said Devon. His smile was genuine and his eyes lit up. "If it's 1917, most people didn't have showers, did they."

He seemed to want to go on with this discussion, and Stanley could see that for some reason Devon was really knowledgeable about the year 1917, but was keeping himself from asking any more questions. Instead, he gestured towards a closed door that was just past the kitchen.

"Feel free to use all the hot water you want, and I'll get you some clothes. But could I look at your uniform while you shower?"

"You want to look at my uniform?" asked Stanley, thinking that it was nice to have someone on his side in this. Devon's eyes were kind when he looked at Stanley, and wanting to look at Stanley's uniform wasn't too much to ask, was it?

"It's for my master's thesis," said Devon. He dipped his head and looked up at Stanley like a little kid. "I'm close to finishing up, but I'd really like to take a look to see how close the stitching is and whether the buttons are really sometimes made of wood wrapped in leather."

"They used to be," said Stanley before he could stop himself. "Now they're just made of wood because leather is hard to come by. My helmet used to have a leather strap, but the rats ate it, so now it's a strip of canvas. But then my helmet shattered."

"When the shell hit you and your buddies," said Devon. He nodded as though he was remembering that Stanley had told him something that was a fact, rather than something that Stanley had fabricated. "Okay, okay. Let me get those clothes."

Devon went through a door that was off the area where the table was, and soon came back with a folded bundle in his hands. Then he pointed to the bathroom where the shower presumably was, and handed Stanley the clothes.

"Give your uniform to me and I'll hang it up so it can dry," said Devon.

Stanley could see by the look in his eye that Devon was looking forward to going over the uniform with a fine-toothed comb.

"You going to take that off, too?" asked Devon. He pointed at the ID tag that sat in the hollow of Stanley's throat, looking a little eager, as though he wanted to examine it up close, pleased at having found such a fine specimen to write about in his thesis.

"No," said Stanley. His hand clutched impulsively around it, the cold metal cutting into his palm. "I never take it off. It'll identify me when I die."

"Got it," said Devon, putting his hands up. "Why don't you just take that shower. It'll get you warm, and then you'll feel better."

That was never going to happen because he was in a strange place where there was no war. He was in the future, or at least he seemed to be, though he didn't know what year it was. He was also far enough away from the year 1917 that the war he'd just been in was a faraway notion, worthy of study and nothing more. Nothing to fear, nothing to be concerned about. Besides, the air in the cottage was warm, and Devon seemed to have plenty of everything.

"Here," said Devon.

He opened the door to the bathroom, which looked different than the rest of the cottage; there was no trace of old stone walls or a time-worn wooden floor. Instead there were shiny tiles, white alternating with blue, and a shiny white toilet, and an enormous shiny white tub. The fixtures, the taps and the drains both, were silver and were also very shiny.

Devon flipped on a switch as they both went in, and everything gleamed so brightly that Stanley had to blink.

"You know how to use a faucet?" asked Devon.

"It's 1917, not the dark ages," said Stanley. "We have bathrooms, same as you."

"Just checking," said Devon with a smile, seemingly unaffected by Stanley's rebuke. "Hot water's on the left, cold is on the right. Soap's there, and the shampoo and everything; towels and washcloths hanging there. Holler if you need anything, and don't forget to give me your uniform, and be careful when you unwrap your puttees, okay? Don't tear them."

"I'm not going to tear them," said Stanley, which was only the truth, as the leg wraps were the only part of the uniform that were sturdy enough to withstand rough handling. Devon seemed obsessed, though if that was the price Stanley had to pay for a bit of food and shelter, then so be it.

Devon went out of the bathroom, leaving Stanley alone for the first time that morning. He quickly shut the door and pressed his forehead against the door, trying to breathe slow breaths to calm himself.

Finally the draw of having a hot shower was too much to resist, so he got out of his uniform. He took special care when he unwrapped his puttees, and placed everything in a neat pile outside the door. Then, stark naked, he figured out how the hot and cold water worked, and that the curtain needed to be inside the tub. Grabbing a clean washcloth, he stepped into the stream of deliciously hot water.

He hadn't had access to hot water since the summer, and had made do with a basin of cold water with a thin sliver of soap, no washcloth, and only a flap of canvas to dry himself with. He and Isaac and the rest had made jokes, as if the whole thing was a lark, and that had made it better. Having friends had made everything better, and until that morning, he'd actually thought they might all make it out alive.

Only Devon had told him that everybody had died, and the white crosses row by row on the green grass attested to that. It might be true they had all died, which meant that Isaac was buried beneath one of those crosses. And if that was true, was Stanley really in the future? Had he left the war behind? Had he died, or was he still alive, and this was all just some trick of his brain?

It wasn't good; the questions slammed into him as though the Germans were aiming their guns at his head. He needed to focus on where he was, and not on the bizarre things happening all around him, or he would go crazy, just like Devon thought he was.

Except even if Devon thought he was crazy, he was trying to help. He'd been nice to Stanley, and his movements were slow and careful. Devon's hands were warm and his eyes were the most beautiful green color that Stanley had ever seen in a man. He had long dark eyelashes, and a strong jaw, and whiter teeth than anybody back home.

Was this all it took to get Stanley to trust him? To get Stanley to feel a pull on his heart, his soul? Maybe it was. Devon was not flashy and vibrant in a way that Isaac had been, but he was steady, and he made Stanley feel safe in a way he'd not felt since the war began. Since his Pa died. Since forever.

Stanley closed his eyes and put his head beneath the stream of hot water, and scrubbed himself hard all over. His hip and ribs on one side felt bruised from when he'd fallen, and there were traces of the bitter mustard gas in the back of his throat. Stanley washed the bruised places gently, and gargled with the hot water to wash the taste away. Maybe Devon would give him more coffee and, if Stanley asked nicely, maybe Devon would give him an orange for his very own.

CHAPTER SIX

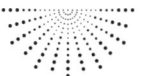

After Devon showed Stanley how to use a shower, he stepped out and was a little surprised at how quickly the door was shut behind him. He did not believe, not even for a minute, that Stanley was who he said he was. By all the laws of physics, it was impossible that he'd come from the year 1917. Of course there was always quantum string theory to explain it, but that didn't help because Devon didn't know much about that. But how could Devon resist the idea that Stanley said that he had come from the war, the very war that Devon was writing about?

His obsession was about to kick in, and hard. Stanley said he was from 1917, and though it was impossible that he was an American doughboy, he looked exactly like the sepia-toned images that Devon had been staring at for years. He was Devon's dream come true, a fantasy come to life.

Stanley had the same haircut as the soldiers in those images, a haircut that lacked only a sweep of Macassar oil to groom it into place. Stanley's smile was sweet, though his face was drawn thin by hunger. And though his eyes had an expression that told more of experience than innocence, there was still a brightness to them, an eagerness.

Devon knew he had to watch himself, or the thing his advisor had always warned him about would happen, and Devon would lose focus on his thesis to fall head over heels for Stanley based on who he appeared to be, rather than who he was.

Just then, Stanley opened the bathroom door, dropped his uniform into a brown and tan puddle on the floor, then quickly shut the door again. Devon barely saw the flash of the ID tag around Stanley's neck, and didn't let himself stare. Didn't let himself think about Stanley in the shower, as that would be rude, and wouldn't help Stanley at all. To distract himself, Devon picked up the rifle from where it was propped against the wall and carried it to the table so he could look at it.

Stanley could have gotten the uniform from a re-enactment place, and scoured the internet for the gear. However, he would have had to sell his soul for the rifle and bayonet combo, as they were collector items. At the same time, the bayonet was attached to the rifle with the original heat shield and bayonet lug that looked, beneath the mud, new enough to have come from the factory yesterday. In fact, it *had* probably come from the factory yesterday.

It had probably been one of Devon's old college buddies who had hired Stanley to play Devon for the fool, and flown him to Ornes, France, just for this one joke. Though, at the same time, Devon couldn't think of anybody who would pay that kind of money just to make Devon laugh at the cleverness of it. Because it was clever and highly detailed, and, yes, a little bit cruel. Even if Stanley weren't real, he was the very image of a World War I doughboy, the spitting image, a sepia-toned photograph brought to life.

His hair, shorn close to fit beneath the helmet, was dark and might have a little bit of red in it. His face still had the roundness of youth, but that had been sculpted away by a lack of food, the harsh conditions in the trenches. His eyes were the color of whiskey, enormous, like the ones in the images of doughboys returned from the war, the expressions of hope removed—

Devon stopped himself. Stanley was no more a doughboy than Devon was. He'd been paid a handsome price to play a joke on Devon. That, or he was an escaped lunatic who only thought he was in the

Battle of Ornes, and who thought he was now in the future. It was all very confusing.

Devon picked up his phone from the kitchen counter and looked up the number for the local council office, and tapped in the numbers. The village of Ornes was so small that it was likely that the council offices were closed, but to his surprise the phone was answered, and a French voice greeted him and asked him what he wanted.

"Is there anybody reported missing from a local clinic for psychiatric care?" he asked in his halting French.

"The nearest facility is in Reims, monsieur," said the voice.

"That's great, but is anybody missing from there?"

"You would have to call them, monsieur, do you have the number?"

She rattled off the number, and then said good bye before hanging up.

It was rather French of her not to be overly curious, so he wasn't really surprised that she didn't ask why he wanted to know. If there had been somebody on the loose in the area, would she have told him? Wouldn't that type of information have been on a need-to-know basis?

Even after living in France for nine months, Devon was still mystified by the order of events when a car accident happened, or when your mail went missing. Or what you were supposed to do when you found a soldier from World War I on your doorstep. Except Devon hadn't found Stanley on his doorstep. He'd found him amongst the corduroy rows of grass-covered trenches that sagged beneath the weight of their crumbling battlements.

But where had he come from? Devon had walked around the trenches many a time. The best two ways to access the area was from the tiny dirt circle in the copse next to the road that served as a parking lot, and from the cottage. Devon had been standing on top of the trenches looking around, and had seen nobody on them. Had seen nobody coming, and as the memorial park was several acres across, he would have.

Had Stanley wanted to surprise him, which he had, he would have had to have been waiting in the trenches for hours. Waiting for Devon to come out of the cottage at some random time when Devon had needed a break from his work. He would have had to sneak up on him with all his gear clanking about him, but Devon hadn't heard a thing. Not a whisper, nothing. Just all of a sudden Stanley had been on top of him, arms pinwheeling, canteen spinning out.

Then he'd pointed his rifle at Devon. That had surprised him, but not as much as the fact that the rifle had been loaded and that Stanley's finger had been on the trigger. He'd really acted like there was a war on and his life was in danger and he needed to protect himself.

His whole body had been at the ready, though the look in his eyes told Devon in an instant that Stanley would rather not kill him. He'd stared at Devon and, in that pause, Devon had been able to take the rifle from him, thanks to self defense training back home and the fact that the grass was slippery.

Devon picked the rifle up from the pile of papers on the table. It was almost new, and there were initials carved in the stock, which was a crying shame because it would bring the value down, had anybody been willing to part with such a sweet piece. The bayonet had been recently rubbed with oil, though there was a coating of black dust along the blade, which could have been from the mortar explosion that Stanley had talked about.

The band to sling the rifle over your shoulder was made of canvas, not leather, and looked new enough to have been recently replaced. Which meant the rifle had seen hard work, and supplies were such that there was no leather to be found. The canvas would see more hard work, get worn through inside of a month or two, and need replacing again. All of this spoke to the conditions in the trench that Stanley had supposedly just been fighting in.

With a long pet, Devon put the rifle down and went to the pile of uniform and gear that Stanley had left outside of the bathroom door. Devon listened. The shower was running, but it was pretty quiet, as if Stanley was standing beneath the flow of water, pretending he was in a rainstorm. Which was what Devon sometimes did, though he never told anybody.

With the bundle in his arms, Devon went over to the couch and started going through the uniform, top to bottom, touching the trousers, the shirt. He ran his fingers along the seams of the sweater vest, feeling the warmth of Stanley's skin in the wool.

The uniform's jacket was so authentic that it was caked with dirt and smelled like iodine, which was a common disinfectant in those days, used for wounds and rinsing clothes. The dust-colored wool was marked with the stripes of a lance corporal, with a jagged line of crisp black thread to show where it had been sewn back into place after being tugged loose not too long ago.

The khaki colored shirt was a surprise, as American soldiers had worn blue denim, though this shirt might have been supplied by a nearby British regiment. There was no winter coat, which meant that Stanley had been braving the weather in only his uniform jacket. If it was November where he'd come from and the coat was standard issue, which it was, what had happened to it? At least Stanley had a sweater vest to wear, though it was thin and dusty as though it had recently come from storage.

The trousers were of dull brown wool, and the belt of brown leather, as were the boots, with the requisite 48 holes, with woven laces. At least the puttees, the canvas wraps for soldier's legs, were new. Devon ran them through his hands and folded them with some reverence, as usually puttees were the first thing to disappear from any uniform, being used for bandages or slings or just lost in the mud.

The canteen was a fascinating piece of work. It had military grade canvas wrapped over a metal body, with pull-the-dot fasteners that Devon recognized being from the original factory in Connecticut, which was the geekiest thing that anybody ever knew, and no proof of anything. The screw on lid was attached with a little chain.

Devon opened the canteen and smelled the contents; water had no smell, but the iodine that it had been laced with did. Iodine was useful for so many things, and, at the time, one of the few ways to purify water so as not to infect the troops with dysentery.

If the water *were* from World War I, and Devon took a sip of it, then it was likely he could become quite sick from whatever was in the water that Stanley's stomach was used to and Devon's most definitely was not. He tilted the canteen and poured water in his hand. It glistened and dripped like most water did when let out of its container, but it excited him to think that it had come from the battlefield only moments ago.

The uniform deserved to be treated with dignity, so Devon took everything into the bedroom and hung it up in the closet. He pushed away the other clothes on the rack so that the uniform could dry without getting overly wrinkled. The puttees he hung on their own hanger, and the boots he hung from the boot hanger that had come with the closet. The sweater vest he spread out on a newspaper on the floor; the wool was too thin to hang, and the newspaper would absorb the dampness from it.

The belt and the canteen he lined up against the wall, and the rifle he placed in the corner, although right away, the bayonet left a scratch in the paint, which made Devon wince. The damage was going to come out of his deposit for sure, but mostly he was worried about the bayonet, which he checked hastily, wiping the flakes of paint and also the black dust onto his hand. It smelled like gun oil when he brought it to his face. It also smelled like something else, like fire, as though it had come from an explosion of some sort. Or was his imagination supplying the rest of the story to Stanley's hastily donned costume?

CHAPTER SEVEN

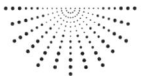

It was too easy to dismiss Stanley as a liar with the worst possible intentions. The other alternative was to imagine that Stanley was just plain crazy. Or maybe he was a troubled young man who needed more attention than the world could give him, and thus had come up with the idea of dressing as a World War One soldier who'd become detached from his battalion.

Or maybe Stanley was telling the truth. The uniform and the gear was hard to ignore, though, at the same time, it was not altogether impossible to get hold of articles with the dust of the battlefield still clinging to them.

Devon gave the trousers one last pat and went into the kitchen. He could still hear the water running and hoped the on-demand water heater could keep up. Meanwhile, he needed to get supper going, and find the bottle of wine to go with it in the vague hope that the wine would loosen Stanley up enough to tell Devon the truth.

To that end, he got out two steaks, the remains of the lovely potatoes au gratin that he'd bought from the French equivalent of a deli in the village, and made a quick salad. He set the table, and poured himself a glass of red wine. He used a jelly jar, as the real wine glasses had both broken when he'd first tried to use them, and he'd never gotten around to replacing them. Besides, jelly glasses worked just as well, if not better. They didn't hold more but were sturdier in the hand.

He washed his hands and prepped the steaks with salt and pepper, and realized that he was nervous. Part of the problem was that he'd been alone in the cottage for over half a year, and had spent a great deal of time in his own head, staring at his computer screen and writing. Sometimes he walked the trenches, but he was always alone. Having someone near like this was not the same as going into the village and greeting a stranger when buying bread, though after a month, the baker had warmed to Devon, on account of he bought so many pastries on a regular basis. No, it was more that having someone in the cottage made him realize how different everyone else was, and how solitary his life had been.

People liked being with other people, and Devon usually didn't mind being alone, even if it was lonely. Back home, his college friends had often chided him for this habit, and Devon had ignored them, though now it was impossible to ignore. Especially since Devon's dream of meeting a doughboy had come true. That is, if it *had* come true, if Stanley was telling the truth.

Devon wanted to believe because Stanley was a handsome American doughboy and it was hard to ignore how that pulled on his heart. But time travel *was* impossible. Which meant that Stanley was either a liar or crazy. Devon hated that either one might be more true than the other option. Though, if memory served him, there were several theories that time travel was possible. And, if he wanted to, he could take the time to open his laptop, bring up Google, and search.

Except that would take him down a very complex rabbit hole, which in the past always took him to YouTube, which would end with him at three o'clock in the morning, watching yet another video about five impossible images that shouldn't exist in photographs that could shock you. That or recipes involving potatoes, which he had not the strength to resist. Besides, he needed to stop going round and round in his own mind anyway, and just let everything play itself out.

As he took another drink of his wine, a lovely merlot that the wine merchant in the village had sold him, he decided he would watch Stanley and study him as though they were together in an experiment. Devon knew more about World War I than anybody except his thesis advisor, but that didn't mean there wasn't somebody who knew more than him. Which wouldn't be proof, only that Stanley had studied the era. But to what end?

When the water in the bathroom turned off, Devon's heart sped up. He tried to ignore the fact that his new guest was somebody he could actually talk to about his project, and who seemed interested. He must not forget that Stanley was probably a liar, he must not forget that what he should have done was call *les gendarmes.* He had, instead, called the council offices in the village, which had proven itself worthless.

In another minute, Stanley was going to come walking out of the bathroom in a cloud of steam, Devon's dream come true. He needed to make up his mind about Stanley, only he didn't know how.

Devon's mental version of an American doughboy had been more along the lines of someone who was eager to go and had not yet seen the horror of it all. Round faced and bright eyed and full of energy. Which was not what he got when Stanley came out, although yes, it was in a cloud of steam.

Stanley was wearing Devon's jeans that no longer fit Devon on account of the pastries he'd been eating since day one. The jeans hung low on Stanley's hips. The long sleeved grey t-shirt that was so big on him that his collarbones showed, and when he moved, was proof of how thin he was.

"Hey," said Devon in an effort to seem calm, rather than the fact that his heart was beating even faster and he really didn't know what to say.

Stanley was not the round faced boy going off to war for the first time, no. He was all angles and lines, his dark eyes the color of whiskey, his shorn hair a shade darker, his face pale, the skin pulled to the bone. If Stanley were troubled, then obsessing over him like this might make his delusions worse, so though he was hard to resist, Devon knew he had to try.

"How was the shower?" asked Devon, doing his best to sound normal.

"It was good," said Stanley, speaking in the way he had, as if all the joy had been drained out of him and he was doing the best he could to be polite. "I like your soap."

"It's French," said Devon. It felt foolish to be talking about such mundane matters when he wanted to be grilling Stanley about the war. As if he believed him, as if it were all true. "France has got a lot of great things, bread, soap, wine—"

Stanley had come to a complete stop near the wooden table that Devon had cleared his papers off of. In the middle was a bowl of fruit that had pears and apples and oranges. It had been Devon's goal to eat at least a piece of fruit a day, but that had gone the way of toast and butter, crepes in the village, and potatoes au gratin.

Stanley was staring at the oranges as if he'd seen Santa Claus, or a pile of gold, like he'd not seen them in *years*. Which, if he'd been at the front lines, was a very good possibility. But not proof. Maybe he'd been in a mental hospital, where fresh food was scarce. Or maybe he'd been on the run from the law, and caring for his health had been the last thing on his mind. Regardless, Devon could afford to make the offer.

"Do you want an orange?" asked Devon. "Help yourself while I cook the steaks."

"Really?" Stanley eyes were wide as he looked at Devon.

Devon wanted to smother him with reassurances, but it was important to stay cool. At least, it seemed like it was important to stay cool, to keep himself safe if Stanley turned out to be a con artist. But it was hard and growing more difficult with each passing moment because the things Stanley needed were so easy to give. Not to mention that those big eyes of Stanley's were tugging at Devon's heart.

"Sure," said Devon, swallowing. "Sit down, help yourself."

Stanley pulled out the chair and sat at the table, and when he picked up the orange, his hands were shaking. Devon drank his wine and looked away while Stanley peeled away the skin, though his eyes were drawn back so he could watch when Stanley ate the first piece.

His mouth was tender around the slice of orange, as though slowing the moment down to savor it. Except when he looked like he was about to bite into it, he shoved the whole thing in his mouth, cheeks bulging, eyes closed, dark lashes long on his cheeks. He chewed slowly, and Devon was easily able to imagine the burst of sweet flavors, the tang of it.

When Stanley opened his eyes, it was slowly, as though from a dream. It took a little of the shell shocked look away, the look of a man who had seen too much too soon, and shaded him a little softer, to that of a young man, a boy from home who had come to visit Devon while he worked on his paper.

"So you realize why I have a hard time believing this," said Devon, clearing his throat. "Time travel is just a theory, right, and not something that just happens." Then he laughed, thinking of his life of study and silence. "Well, not to me anyway."

"Nor to me," said Stanley. "As far as I know, I died and I'm a ghost right now." His voice trembled, and Devon felt bad for doubting him.

"That," said Stanley, as he took another bite of his orange, seeming to rally himself. "That or this is heaven."

Devon smiled and sighed inwardly, warning himself against the cascade of feelings in his heart, and how that smile made him want to be able to see it forever. Which was impossible.

"Do you think you died from mustard gas?" said Devon, making himself stay serious and focused.

He knew all about the terrible effects of chemical warfare, which was partly why he'd been dragging his heels for a while. The futility of war, especially when he'd gotten into the details of different ways that had been invented for men to kill each other, made it hard to be disciplined about writing.

Before he'd started his master's degree, in his mind the war contained images of bon voyage parties, and doughboys in hastily erected dining halls being served hot coffee and donuts, or was that

World War II? The fact that there'd been more than one world wide conflict always depressed him.

"Yes," said Stanley in a low voice, as though dragging himself from his own memories. "One minute I was running along the trench—"

"On the top or along the bottom?" asked Devon before he could stop himself because it looked like all of this talk about war was upsetting Stanley and Devon should really stop asking questions. "I'm sorry, go on, but mustard gas is most potent at a certain level. On the top of the trench, you're golden, except for the bullets. At the bottom of the trench, it can be safer from bullets, but you're more at risk from mustard gas. Plus the damp weather made the gas even more dense, so it really collected at the bottom of the trenches. Sorry. Go on."

"Sometimes I had to go to the top to cross over, but mostly I was at the bottom. Then, when I was climbing up the side of a trench, I heard the click over my head. It's a really tinny click, that means—"

"That means it's too late," said Devon, filling in the blank.

He wanted to ask about the sound of the mustard gas canister coming open, and whether it came down with a sound like wings falling or whether it was something else. How long you could breathe, really breathe, before the effect of it overtook you. What had happened to the gas masks for Stanley's battalion anyway? How had they gone astray when they were such an important part of a soldier's kit?

It would be unnecessarily cruel to make Stanley go over these details, whether or not he was delusional. More importantly, why was Devon staring? He tried not to as Stanley finished off his orange, but it was hard. Stanley was an American doughboy, Devon's dream, sitting right here at his table, eating an orange, dusting his hands as he finished. It must be that Devon was obsessed with doughboys, and that was why he was staring and not because of Stanley himself. Right?

Regardless, Devon wanted to sit at the table with Stanley and ask him questions, listen to him talk, and encourage him to talk about anything, anything at all. Then Devon could watch his eyes brighten, and his mouth move, and his hands make gestures in the air. It had happened from time to time, but then Stanley would remember the war. His features would fall silent, and his hands would fall to his lap, and all the joy would go out of him. It was difficult to watch, so Devon reminded himself not to poke for information about the war, but to talk about something else.

"So," he said, brightly. "Now that you're here, do you know what this is?" He pointed to the fridge, sure that Stanley wouldn't know, not if he really was from 1917.

"It looks like an ice box," said Stanley. "A really big ice box, but I don't see where the ice will go—"

He leaned from his chair to get a better view, and Devon waved him into the kitchen. Stanley got up and came to Devon's side, which was distracting, so Devon made himself concentrate on his little tour.

"You're right, only we call it a fridge. See?" With a sweeping gesture, Devon opened the door and presented all of the food inside, thinking that, as it was a French fridge, it was a little smaller, more compact, than an American one, but it still held a lot.

"Is that *milk*?" asked Stanley. "It's not in a bottle, but it's got a cow on it."

"You want some?" asked Devon. Without waiting, he got out a glass, poured milk into it, and handed it to Stanley. He wanted Stanley to know it was for him so that he wouldn't be able to try and pretend that he didn't want any.

Stanley got up, reaching for the glass with both hands.

The mistake on Devon's part was to stand so close while Stanley drank from the glass because his throat moved as he swallowed, and his eyes closed in pleasure, and the sleeve of the t-shirt fell away from his thin wrist, where the bones were pushing through. Devon wanted to take him, hold him close, and feed him till a flush came to his cheeks, and his bones weren't so stark, so obvious beneath his skin. But that would be pushing it, pushing too fast for someone who came from 1917.

CHAPTER EIGHT

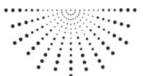

Just when was it exactly that Devon decided he believed Stanley? He hadn't, not really, mostly because it was impossible. Except he had decided to believe, in a way, because nothing Stanley had yet done or said jarred with what Devon knew about the era, and nobody knew more about it than Devon.

"And this," said Devon with a slight cough, "is a microwave."

He opened the door to the microwave, trying to see it through Stanley's eyes: a metal box with a window with a grid pattern in the door and a circular glass tray that turned on little rubber wheels.

"A micro *wave*?" asked Stanley, peering at it. "What does it do?"

"Well, it's mostly good for heating things up. Like an oven. You have ovens, right?"

Devon waited for Stanley to nod, though he didn't really need the conformation; ovens had been around since forever, he just wanted to be sure that Stanley was following what he was saying. He thought, in the back of his mind, that this was Stanley's own attempt to distract himself from the bigger problem that neither of them had brought up. Which was, if time had pulled Stanley to the present at a whim, as it seemed, could it then yank Stanley back to the past any time it wanted to?

This troubling thought was not what Devon wanted to be focusing on right now, so he grabbed a glass, filled it with water at the sink, and held it out to Stanley.

"Take a sip, cold water, right?"

"Yes," said Stanley. "Tastes metallic."

"That's because it's from a well, and then is filtered, here—watch this."

Devon put the glass in the microwave and turned it on for a minute, then when it beeped, pulled the door open.

"Now taste, but be careful, it's hot."

As Stanley took a sip, his eyes widened, and while Devon had thought that Stanley might freak out, instead he seemed pleased.

"How does it work?" Stanley asked as he put the glass down to peer into the microwave. He stuck his hand inside and felt around, then pulled it out. "It's cool to the touch, how did it *do* that?"

"Microwaves," said Devon, waving his hands in little circles as if that would explain it. "They move really fast, and get hot, and so heat up things around them? Something like that. It's not much good except to heat; we used to think we could cook with it, but you can't make the same crisp outside, you see? You can melt cheese, heat up cold coffee, melt butter, and stuff like that. Oh, and hot dogs, it's really good for cooking hot dogs."

"Hot dogs?" asked Stanley.

"I think it was called a frankfurter in your day," said Devon with a smile. Almost instantly, he remembered the faded photograph of soldiers just returned from the war enjoying hot dogs at Coney Island. Stanley could have fit so easily into that photograph—but it was wrong to let himself be drawn into a mere image when Stanley was standing right in front of him. Right *now*.

"I've had those," said Stanley, smiling back.

"We can also cook hot dogs by boiling them in water or grilling in a pan on the stove, which I'm sure you recognize."

Devon demonstrated how quickly the gas could be turned on and how big the oven was, thinking how different this must be for Stanley, how sleek everything was, how much of everything there was. As he showed Stanley the rest of the cottage, Stanley stuck right to his side, interested and focused on everything that Devon pointed out, the lights, the radiators, the doorbell, the porch light.

The fun really started when he showed Stanley his phone.

"That's not a telephone," said Stanley. "Telephones are tall with a little cone that you put to your ear." He gripped an imaginary phone that Devon realized must have been one of the old fashioned candlestick types, and put the invisible receiver to his ear.

"Yes, they used to be," said Devon. "But over time, they changed."

It occurred to him that he could pull up YouTube on his laptop and find a video about the evolution of phones, but would that be too much? Wasn't everything too much? Stanley didn't seem very interested in the phone, but then, why would he be when it looked like a slim metal box, so small and thin that there didn't seem to be anything you could do with it.

"Maybe we'll take pictures with it tomorrow," said Devon. "Like pics of you in your uniform that I can send to my professor for extra credit." This joke made him laugh to think of it. Stanley only cocked his head to the side, and it was easy to see that he didn't get it. Which stopped Devon from laughing.

"Okay, how about this? It's a laptop, a portable machine. There are different kinds, of course, but here." Devon opened the laptop, which sprang into life, the window instantly displaying a large mountain, sheered in half on one side. "I'm not up to date because I don't have time for updates, but what you could do on it—"

"What is it?" asked Stanley. His fingers twitched as though he wanted to touch it, so Devon pushed it toward him and watched Stanley trace the edge of it with his fingers.

"It's a computer—never mind. You type on it like a typewriter, and you can send messages with it, you can do research on it—"

It occurred to Devon that he could pull up all the pages he'd bookmarked about World War I and show Stanley how it had all turned out. Then he could show him sepia-toned photographs of soldiers in the trenches, in bunkers, standing in a row, beaming at the camera before they got shipped out. But that might overload Stanley's brain and his ability to get used to the present, not to mention some pretty graphic images could also come up, so Devon sat down at the table, and patted the chair next to him.

When Stanley sat down, Devon pulled up Google and entered *cute kittens*. Within seconds ten webpages were displayed. He clicked on *Images*, and hundreds of images of the cutest kittens anybody had ever seen showed up.

"Voila," said Devon with a wave. "Cute kittens, some of which are wearing spectacles." He typed *with spectacles*, and in an instant, all of the kittens were wearing glasses.

Fully drawn into the moment, Stanley smiled. He reached out to touch the screen, his fingers gripping the edges as though he was judging the width.

"Where do they all come from?" asked Stanley.

"People upload them," said Devon. The explanation might not be enough, but any gulf between him and Stanley seemed to vanish as they explored the internet together. "Tons and tons every day—"

"Yes, but where—how did they get *here*?" Stanley pointed at the screen and traced the edge of an adorable grey kitten wearing very serious black glasses.

"On the screen?" asked Devon, scratching his head. "I used to know this a bit better, but technology keeps changing, so this is what I know. You take a picture with your phone, or scan any image on a scanner, and then upload to a server, and then the server has it and you can look at what the server has. That's what I know."

"Okay," said Stanley. "I guess." He looked distraught, which maybe was because Devon was terrible at explaining or because he didn't understand any of what Devon had just said. Either was possible, but Devon didn't know.

"Listen, why don't we eat, and we can watch a bit of—" said Devon, then he stopped. If pictures of cute kittens were too much, then reruns of *The X Files* were way too much, not to mention the news, regardless of the source, or Facebook feeds, or any social media. Devon had stopped using most of them since coming to France, not because France didn't have them, but because he had so much work to do.

"We can eat and have an early night?" asked Devon. "Tomorrow, maybe, if you're willing, we could walk around the trenches and you could show me what you know. If that's okay."

"Okay," said Stanley.

Stanley didn't seem very enthusiastic.

"We don't have to," said Devon. He knew it was his responsibility to take care of Stanley, not to take advantage of him. Plus, while somebody else would have called *les gendarmes* immediately, Devon was here and nobody else was, so it was up to him to do the best he could.

"No, it's fine," said Stanley. "I should probably get the lay of the land anyway."

"Here, have another orange, and I'll get the steaks going," said Devon.

He got up and handed Stanley the last orange, feeling a little bit sad at the reverence with which Stanley took it. If anything was proof that he really was from 1917, his attitude towards oranges was one of them. Of course, he could be crazy, he could be a liar, or he could be a time traveler. Devon wanted it to be the latter, but that would mean Stanley had come through something horrific and would need the tenderest of care, the kindest handling. Which Devon could do, could most definitely do.

He turned on the burner, put the cast iron pan over the heat, and tried not to stare as Stanley ate his second orange.

CHAPTER NINE

Stanley ate his second orange while standing at the counter. Slice by moist slice, he worked his way through it, enjoying the sweetness on his tongue, the stickiness of his fingers. Not to mention it was the biggest orange he'd ever seen and the easiest to peel. As he ate, he noticed that Devon, who was frying steaks on the stovetop, was watching him eat.

Devon might have been laughing at him for enjoying the orange so much, and he'd not quite believed Stanley when he'd said he'd not had an orange since he'd enlisted earlier that year. In spite of this, Stanley felt comfortable and safe, and that feeling was growing with every passing moment.

Rain continued to fall outside the windows as the sky grew dark, and the cottage was filled with the smell of hot butter and salt. Those scents wafted through with the crispness of citrus and the sound of frying steak, and the war seemed very far away. If he never had to leave the cottage, never had to leave Devon, and could always feel the way he felt right now, he would be happy for all the days of his life.

"Here," said Devon, interrupting Stanley's reverie. "Sit down and eat this."

Devon brought over a platter with the steaks, and a bowl of sliced potatoes layered with cheese, which Devon had put in the oven to heat rather than the microwave, and which now bubbled contentedly in front of Stanley. There was also a dish of cut lettuce that glistened with olive oil, and though Stanley didn't care much for vegetables, he was going to have some, out of courtesy.

"You old enough to drink, soldier?" asked Devon, jocular even as he poured red wine from a bottle into two short glasses that looked suspiciously like old jelly jars. "Well, here you are anyway."

They sat down and ate together for a companionable while, each appeasing his hunger, both focused on their own plates, but it did not feel solitary. Every now and then, Devon would glance up at Stanley through his dark lashes, as if contemplating his presence at the table, or the truth of his tale. As Stanley drank his glass of wine, the taste of which curled like butter on his tongue, and ate the warm food, he grew more relaxed and felt more at ease. And began to feel that he might be safe here in the future, and that he would not get yanked back into the past.

Devon didn't look like he meant to throw Stanley out anytime soon, and had made no calls to *les gendarmes* in the hopes of finding out where Stanley had come from. Whether or not he believed that Stanley had come from 1917 was another matter, but for the moment, Stanley was safe, though in the wake of his earlier panic, as his body relaxed, the clamps in his brain relaxed too, probably from the wine. His mouth opened and words began to come out.

"I killed them, you know," said Stanley. When Devon sat up straight, his eyes wide and all of his attention focused on Stanley, he nodded. "I mean, I didn't *kill* kill them, but if I'd asked them to sit on the other side of me when that shell hit this morning, they'd be alive now. You know? But that shrapnel, it just cut through them, *tore* through them—"

"Was that the blood on your uniform?" Devon gestured to the bedroom where the uniform was stored, safely out of sight. "Did this happen in the trench?"

"Yes," said Stanley. He blinked at the remains of his supper and licked his lower lip, finding traces of salt. In that warm room with food in his belly, the war seemed far away. "It all happened so fast. One minute, Lt. Billings was standing there in front of the bunker, about to go up, you know, to get the lay of the land. He had a map in his hand to consult that I guess Commander Helmer had left behind—"

"Commander Helmer was the one who deserted?" asked Devon. He drank the rest of his wine in one large gulp and then waggled his glass at Stanley as if to ask him whether he wanted some more. Stanley nodded, and Devon poured them both more wine.

"He was the commander of our battalion," said Stanley. He was a little surprised that Devon already knew the desertion, but then he remembered that the last battle of the 44th Battalion was the focus of Devon's research. Plus, it was nice to talk out loud about his troubles because in the trenches you had to keep your doubts to yourself. "He deserted in the middle of the night, at least that's what we think, what the lieutenant thought."

Devon drank some of his wine as if to fortify himself against the fact that Stanley might be lying. Stanley drank as well, taking a large gulp, and almost choked, and Devon laughed at him. It wasn't a cruel laugh; there was sympathy in it, and Devon moved his hand in the air as if to wave the laugh away.

"Go on, the lieutenant had the map."

"And that was it," said Stanley. "He was standing there for just a minute, and the shells came. The Germans had been testing the distance for days, and Isaac and I—"

"Who's Isaac?" asked Devon, taking another sip of his wine, which made his mouth moist and red and Stanley had to jerk his attention away.

"Isaac was one of the fellows I met when I enlisted; we went all the way through basic together."

"What was that like?" asked Devon, in a way that told Stanley that Devon was about to get out a pencil and a pad of paper and start taking notes. His eyes had lit up, and he leaned forward. "Had they started training with gas masks when you came in? What kind of canvas were they made of? How did it feel when you put one on?"

"That doesn't matter," said Stanley. He felt soothed by Devon's interest, and the fact that Devon seemed entirely sympathetic to what Stanley had gone through. "We lost ours in transport anyway."

"I'm sorry about all the questions," said Devon. "It's just hard to deal with an obsession that nobody else can understand. Here you are with all that you know, so it's hard to stop." He looked down at his fingers curled around his little jelly jar of wine. "And I might be a little drunk."

"Maybe I am too," said Stanley, his heart warming to the idea of it, that Devon could feel comfortable enough around him, with a small dose of wine, to be himself. He tipped his glass to Devon's so they could clink a small toast because it was good to be able to talk about his fears and self-doubt, and Devon was a good listener.

"What really matters is that Isaac was my friend, and I let him get killed," said Stanley. "He was sitting right where I'd been sitting. It had started to rain, but my spot was dry and his feet were aching so I let him sit down. Right where I'd been sitting was where the shell hit. The three of them, they were nothing but pieces. Isaac was looking at me when he died."

"You liked him," said Devon.

"Yes, I liked him," said Stanley, and that was okay to say; a fellow could like another fellow without anything being read into it. "He was good to me, always giving me his chocolate, saying he never really liked it, though I knew he was lying because his eyes did this thing—" Stanley gestured near his own eyes, hands on either side of his head, swirling his fingers to describe what he meant. "They would twinkle, you know? How eyes can do. He was always so sweet to me."

"You were in love with him," said Devon. "That must have made it very hard—"

"I wasn't in *love* with him." Stanley sat up straight and shook his head. "We were just friends, buddies, you know."

"Oh, damn it," said Devon. He clenched his fists for a second, then spread his fingers out as if they'd just been smacked by a ruler. "I forgot that it was against the law to be gay in 1917." He looked at

Stanley with some sympathy, his brow furrowed. "That is, if we're going along with the premise that you really did come from then."

"It wasn't against the law to be gay," said Stanley, now completely confused. "We laughed all the time; Isaac would pretend to be very serious and I would make him laugh anyway."

"No, I mean—" Devon stopped, running his hand through his hair, making it messy. "Being gay's what we call it now when you're a homosexual."

Stanley knew what the word meant. He'd avoided thinking about it for so long, even in his own head, it was like a slap in the face to hear it said the way Devon said it. Casually, as if there were no sting to be found in it, no shame, as if he had no idea that the word was wrong and that to say it out loud was to bring unwanted attention.

"I'm not a ho—" Stanley stopped, his mouth trembling. He pressed the back of his hand against his lips. "I'm *not*, do you hear? Isaac and I were friends and that's all there was to it."

"Seriously, it's not against the law now," said Devon. "Well, in some countries, stupid, vile, backwards countries it is, but not here in France. Not in the States, not in England, not anywhere you might want to go. Like Iceland." Devon smiled like it was some big, wonderful thing. "Gays can get married in Iceland, you know. Australia, too."

The thought of marrying Isaac made Stanley go very still. The thought of marrying another fellow, someone like Devon, say—Stanley was warm all over and his heart was racing.

Devon was looking at him, his eyes wide open as though waiting for a response to his statement. Perhaps he was waiting for Stanley to admit who he was. To admit that he was a homosexual himself, as Devon had just seemingly admitted with the use of words like *we* and *you*. Stanley had to make sure, so emboldened by the wine and his own exhaustion, he dipped his head to look up at Devon, completely unsure of the response he would get.

"Are you—are you one?" Stanley asked. Then he added hurriedly, "You don't have to tell me if you don't want to."

"Yeah," said Devon, completely casual about it while he waved his hand over the plates as if they could confirm his statement. "I'm one of the quiet, stay-at-home ones. Too geeky to leave the house, too wrapped up in my studies. I barely qualify." He laughed, at the statement, perhaps, or at himself, or at the idea of being one kind of homosexual instead of another, as if it were all quite easy and natural and accepted. "I mean, there's all kinds; I'd be geeky regardless."

Stanley opened his mouth, but found that he could not articulate the whirl of ideas in his head, how it might have been if he could have told Isaac how he really felt. How it might have been to kiss Isaac on the mouth, to trace the little pencil scar on Isaac's chin with his thumb. To wrap his arms around Isaac and keep him safe. Except Isaac wasn't safe. He was dead, and Stanley was in the same cottage that, while building trenches, they'd taken breaks in to get out of the rain, to have a smoke, using bars of chocolate in barter like they were made of gold.

Swallowing, Stanley fiddled with his empty glass, swirling the dregs of wine around, red ribbons at the bottom of a jelly jar. He felt almost too warm in the heat that came from the white radiators along the walls. In Stanley's day, radiators were brown or black or tinged red with rust. If there were any evidence that he was in the future, it was that everything was so clean and orderly, and it was these thoughts that helped him stay calm instead of bursting into blubbering tears, like he so much wanted to do.

"I'm sorry," said Devon, his eyes grave and still. "Whether or not you came from 1917, you miss him, don't you."

"I never told him," said Stanley. He was somewhat shocked at his own honesty, but Devon had done nothing but be kind and sympathetic to everything Stanley had gone through, so perhaps he could be trusted with this. "It's nothing I could ever do, and he just seemed to like being my friend, so telling him would have ruined it. Maybe."

"Maybe," said Devon.

He got up from the table, grabbing the plates and bowls before taking them to the sink. He puttered around for a bit, doing ordinary things, making the moment seem as normal as it could be given the circumstances. Stanley sat at the table, too tired to move, still feeling shell shocked, as the fellows in the trench would have said. All he could do was watch as Devon brought to the table a little cardboard box with grease stains on the bottom.

When Devon opened the box, Stanley saw that inside were French pastries, crumbling and brown, flecked with delicate curls of frosting, the merest bits of sugar. He, Isaac, Bertie, and Rex had taken a trek into the nearby village when the frost had first hit the ground. It had been wonderful to walk in a foreign place with strange coins in their pockets, pretending that there wasn't a war on, and Stanley and his buddies had gone into a bakery, just like back home. Maybe that had been the same bakery the pastries had come from, though that was impossible, as Devon had said the whole village had been wiped out.

"If you really did come from back then," said Devon. "Or even if you didn't, maybe I could get you some help."

"For what?" asked Stanley.

"For the look on your face, the way you're remembering," said Devon. "I can see it in your eyes. I could find someone for you to talk to about it."

It was disconcerting to be looked at the way Devon was looking at him, in that focused way he had, but usually that had been when Stanley had mentioned something about the war. Now Devon was looking at him as though Stanley was what he was now studying and wanted to take notes about.

"You don't believe me anyway," said Stanley.

"I might," said Devon. "Let's just assume that you are telling the truth, even though time travel is impossible—"

"Is that what happened to me?" asked Stanley, more stunned than he'd thought he could be because he'd not considered it in those terms. "I keep thinking I'm just a ghost or something that shouldn't exist."

"I don't know," said Devon. He shook the box at Stanley and made the pastries rattle. There were three pastries and a grease spot where the missing fourth one had been. Stanley wondered whether they would each have one and split the remaining one, the way he and Isaac had done when they'd gone into the bakery.

"Have one," said Devon. "Sugar is good for shock, they say."

Stanley took a pastry, the nearest one to be polite, and bit into it, sighing at the taste of the sugar and the tender feel of the flakes coated with frosting. He ate it quickly, and watched while Devon ate his slowly. Then he realized he was staring and looked away. He was only a little surprised when Devon picked up the last pastry, tore it and held one half out to Stanley.

"Come on," said Devon. "Help me eat this or I'll need a new pant size."

Devon laughed at his own joke, and Stanley tried to smile as he took the half of a pastry, but it was hard. Devon was like Isaac in some ways, but in most ways he was different. He'd been so honest and open in admitting he was a homosexual, something Isaac never would have done, that it made Stanley want to be near Devon, to stay near him, and to talk until the sun came up.

But of course, they couldn't do that. Devon got up, laid his hand on Stanley's shoulder, and let it rest there, warm and heavy and solid.

"It's going to be okay," said Devon. "Whatever the truth is, it'll look better in the morning. I'll fix you up a bed on the couch, okay?"

Stanley looked up at Devon, who moved away. Stanley closed his eyes, thinking he'd much rather sleep where Devon was going to sleep. Where he'd be as safe as a bird in its nest, drowsy in the dark, hearing Devon's even, low breath, sweet as a lullaby.

It was exhaustion making him think this way; even if the whole world were homosexual—gay, as Devon put it—there wasn't a chance Stanley would have the courage to speak up, or that Devon might think that way about him. They'd just met, after all, and Devon thought that Stanley was either crazy or a liar, and neither was a good starting point.

Not to mention, Stanley felt wired and numb at the same time. As he got up from the table and pushed his chair back, he became dizzy. He had to stop right where he was, his hand on the chair back, the room growing dark and grey, speckled with white circles.

"Stanley, are you all right?" asked Devon, his voice coming from the darkness. In a moment, Devon was at his side. "You should sit down. Here, I've made up a bed, and left a glass of water on the end table. Here."

Stanley felt Devon's warm hands on him, and let himself be guided across the room. His vision began to clear, bit by bit, until he was standing next to the couch with Devon looking at him, his anxious eyes wide, and nothing but kindness in his expression.

Stanley reached out to clasp Devon's hand in both of his. He held Devon's hand for a good, long minute, using it like a lifeline, taking slow breaths to steady himself.

"Maybe I'll wake up and it'll be 1917. Or maybe I'll realize I'm not a ghost and didn't come through time, but I'm just a crazy person who knows too much about trenches and shell shock and what a head looks like when it's sliced through by shrapnel."

"Maybe," said Devon. "But you look ready to drop on your feet, so here—"

Devon guided Stanley to lie on the sheet that had been spread over the couch. Then, when Stanley's head sank into the pillow, Devon pulled another sheet and a soft, fluffy duvet over him.

"Do you want me to call someone?" asked Devon. "Do you want me to call a doctor? I'll do it right now, if you want me to."

"No," said Stanley. "Maybe if I get a good night's sleep."

Devon sat on the couch and took Stanley's hand. Stanley kept his eyes closed in case he was imagining their closeness.

"I think you're exhausted, regardless of anything else," said Devon. "But I want you to know that whatever happens, whatever the truth turns out to be, I'll help you. You can stay with me. I'll take you back to Colorado with me. We'll get you papers, whatever it takes, okay?"

Stanley sank into the moment. In his whole life nobody had ever offered to help him the way Devon was offering. In his neighborhood back home, or in the army, you fended for yourself, you did for yourself. You pulled yourself up by your own bootstraps. And yet here Devon was, being kind. Stanley had barged in on his life, and Devon had every reason to not believe him, to even be disdainful of Stanley's claims. But he hadn't, and he wasn't, and here he was making promises to be there for Stanley.

"Thank you," said Stanley, his voice coming out a half-whisper. "I'm sorry to be so much trouble, but I'm so tired."

"You should sleep," said Devon. He squeezed Stanley's hand, then laid it over Stanley's chest, and patted it. "I'm going to work a little more, but I'll be quiet. If you need anything, you just let me know, okay?"

"Okay," said Stanley, in such a small voice that he could barely hear himself in his own ears. He felt safe and warm and still, and if Devon were nearby, nothing bad could happen to him.

Before Devon had taken two steps towards the kitchen table, Stanley clutched his ID tag, closed his eyes, and fell asleep.

CHAPTER TEN

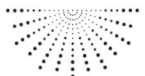

In the morning, Devon stood in the open doorway of the cottage, looking over the field in the pre-dawn's light. The morning's sunrise was the color of blood, streaked with dark blue, and though it wasn't raining, there was the smell of rain in the air. Devon's breath misted in silver sparkles in the front porch light. He snapped the light off, closed the door, and picked up his coffee mug from the counter.

If he got straight to work, he could make up for time missed the day before, but he didn't want to turn on the light and wake Stanley, who was still asleep on the couch. It might have been nice, the night before, to have Stanley sleep in the bed with him, as the bed was more comfortable than the couch any day. Besides, Devon could have kept an eye on him, rather than having to sleep with one eye open all night. Not because he was worried that Stanley would do something to him, but that he might suddenly disappear and go back to where he'd come from.

Devon had gotten up twice in the middle of the night to pad out to the living room to make sure Stanley was still there. Now he was tired. His eyes felt gritty, and he had a good hour's worth of work he needed to do before he could eat breakfast. In spite of this, he took a moment to walk over to the couch where Stanley was still fast asleep.

Stanley was curled up beneath the bedclothes, on his side facing the room, both hands tucked beneath the pillow. Asleep, he looked younger than he ought to have, given what he'd been through, and he still looked pale, in spite of the full night's sleep.

Devon wanted to wake him up and feed him and talk to him, and just be with him. It was as if Stanley's arrival, however ungainly, had opened the gate to Devon's heart. He wanted to open it wider, and to let Stanley in, to trust Stanley and share those secrets he guarded so close. But he needed to let Stanley rest. Perhaps later, when Stanley woke up, then Devon could say what he felt, if he were brave enough.

Doing his best to focus on his work, Devon started his laptop as quietly as he could. He found his notes by the glare of the screen, the wattage of which he turned down as low as he could and still see. After a quick swallow of coffee, he began transcribing his recent research about the weather, and how officers got first crack at being in the bunker when it began to rain. How the soldiers had to slog about in mud up to their shins, and how the food had started to be rationed because the roads were too muddy to get supplies through.

This was probably what had happened to Stanley. While the food shipments had not been delayed during the late spring and summer months, the supply chain had become strained when the cold front had moved in. The correlation between that and the occurrences of the flu were—

Devon stopped typing and pulled up the meteorology chart to double check on the actual temperatures, which would give his facts the heft that they needed to support his thesis. Which, he realized, as he always did at some point during each and every day, should have been about the futility of war because why—

He made himself stop from going along that line of thinking. It didn't do him any good, as he was too far down the weather path to turn back now. Plus, he didn't want to redo the thesis with another central point because he'd have to start from the beginning.

He already knew this subject so well that he'd be able to pass his orals easily, when the time came. Which would be in the spring, when he got back. Back to the States. But what would happen to Stanley when Devon left France if he didn't go with Devon?

Devon looked up and over at the couch, where the low grey hump attested to the fact that Stanley was still sound asleep in spite of Devon's tapping away.

The first and most obvious solution was to take Stanley with him, as Devon had promised. Stanley was an American, that much was clear, so maybe if they pretended Stanley had amnesia and had somehow wound up in France?

They'd give him John Doe papers to start with. There'd be a small media blitz with pleas for information about Stanley. His picture would be shown everywhere, shared on every station and social media outlet. Nobody would be able to connect him to the young man that he was, and then Devon would be able to keep him. Though, of course, if Stanley wanted to leave, Devon would let him go, just as long as Stanley was happy.

Devon was tempted to look up the records to see if Stanley was who he said he was. If he did find evidence of Stanley having existed back in 1917, he'd have to face up to the fact that it was real, that something paranormal had occurred. But that was all nonsense, wasn't it, and perhaps it was better to let the mystery continue, at least for now. Besides, he needed to finish his work for the day, especially if they were going to walk the trenches later, and then take pictures of Stanley in his uniform. That would be the fun part, so he needed to get the serious work done before Stanley got up.

It was nice having company in the quiet dark while the light beyond the drawn curtains grew brighter, and the room grew warmer as the radiators kicked on. It was nice to think about having breakfast together, and the pleasure he would get in feeding Stanley. Having someone around so he wouldn't be so lonely was nice, too. Which was a selfish way to be thinking about this, as Stanley, if he were truly a time traveler, would need to feel safe in the future he'd found himself in. Devon intended to do everything in his power to make that happen.

THE AIR on Stanley's skin was warm in a way that it shouldn't be because if he was in the trench and had fallen asleep while on watch, or while waiting for his turn at the latrine, the air would be cold. Should be cold. It was November, after all, and since the first of the month the rains had come, sweeping across the battlefields in chilly curtains, making mud of the earth.

The rain also cut through the mustard gas, and swept away the pall of smoke, but only for a time. When the rain stopped, the sky remained cloudy, and the vapor left behind by mortar guns and cook fires swirled up in the air and hung aloft at head height, giving every indrawn breath a choking, thick taste of smoke and bitter ash.

The air now smelled of freshly brewed coffee and the faint warm dust of toast. Instead of the sound of metallic booms from far away that were constantly coming closer, there was only a faint tap *tap tappety tap* sound. It was, yes, a little metallic, but it carried no threat, and wasn't scary to listen to at all. Instead, it was soothing in a busy kind of way, for it was continual and rhythmic, like something you could predict and count on.

Stanley opened his eyes, and was completely surprised to be looking up at the age-dark beams in the ceiling above him, interspersed with white stucco. The air was warm instead of cold or damp. When he looked over at the empty fireplace, he wondered at the source of heat and then remembered the white radiators. Then the whole of the night before came at him so fast that he sat up with a gasp, clutching the sheet and duvet to his chest, his hands spread, already short of breath as his heart sped up to galloping. Though he opened his mouth to speak, he could not utter a sound.

Across the room, sitting at the kitchen table, was Devon. He had been at work but instead of using a typewriter, it was on the flat part of a large piece of metal folded in half, with one half sticking up. The laptop.

Devon stopped typing the moment Stanley sat up, and though he was a little sleep rumpled, all of his attention, and those brilliant green eyes, were focused on Stanley.

"Are you awake?" asked Devon.

Stanley felt that Devon didn't know that he was afraid, and felt that he couldn't let Devon know that he was. Except Devon got up and crossed the room and was at Stanley's side. He even sat down on the couch, crowding Stanley with his nearness as he took Stanley's hand. Stanley wanted nothing more than to fall into Devon's arms and stay there forever, but he held himself back.

"Hey, Stanley," said Devon in a completely calm way. "It's okay. Do you remember where you are? Do you remember me from last night?"

"Of course I remember you," said Stanley, somewhat crossly at having been caught out being scared like a little girl. But he was shaking at the same time, both with fear at waking up in a strange place and with resisting the impulse to fling himself into Devon's arms. What would it have been like had he been born in Devon's time, where the strictures of 1917 had never existed?

"Are you okay?" asked Devon. "Do you want some coffee? I could make you some breakfast."

Devon seemed entirely more cheerful than he ought to be, considering that Stanley had barged into his life, taken up his couch, and had now interrupted his work. The coffee from the night before had been so delicious that the offer was hard to resist. Besides, looking at Devon, who was still holding Stanley's hand, made Stanley feel better than he ought to have, all things considered.

Stanley sighed, hoping that his dreams weren't shining in his eyes, as that was what had, very possibly, made Isaac withdraw. He nodded as he let out a breath.

"I'll take that as a yes," said Devon. He stood up, patting Stanley's hand with both of his as he let go. "You know where the bathroom is if you need to use it. I'll start a new pot of coffee and get some breakfast going."

Stanley shoved the duvet back and stumbled to the bathroom, which was a great deal easier than peeling back a half-frozen wool blanket that smelled of horse shit. Devon's bathroom, as well, was a veritable palace of white tile, and was clean and warm, making it easy to use. It was much better than using a latrine that was really a shallow ditch that left your ass hanging out in the air and offered no privacy whatsoever.

As Stanley washed his hands, using the sweet smelling soap and endless supply of warm water, which stayed the exact same temperature the entire time he had the tap open, he didn't want to look at himself, but he did. His eyes were like two burned spots of brown, with the usual dark circles beneath, and his cheeks looked as hollow as a flu victim on the verge of death.

His expression was the one Isaac used to tease him about, the one he always said made Stanley look like he'd been carved in marble, and which could only come unstuck with vast applications of hot coffee. Stanley had always tried to resist a response, to make the moment last, to make the tease more effective that way. Alas, he'd always broken into a smile, his whole face feeling buoyed up by laughter, which, when Isaac had been near and laughing in response, had warmed his entire body, his soul. Every time, he'd drawn away after the initial flirting. Both of them had.

Now Stanley felt like a bit of a traitor because the coffee that Devon was making—and Stanley could smell the half bitter, half velvet smell of it even now as the warmth of it seeped below the bottom of the bathroom door—would taste better than anything the canteen had ever served, better than anything he'd shared in a tin mug with Isaac.

Stanley looked away from the mirror and dried his hands; at least he wasn't leaving black streaks, on account of the shower he'd taken the night before. He looked at the tub, and knew that it would be too decadent to take another shower quite so soon. Besides, all of this was probably some wild fantasy his mind had dreamed up to take him away from the horror of the trenches.

Even he knew that time travel wasn't real. Maybe he was a ghost. Or maybe he was dead and dreaming as he floated his way up to heaven. Except that from behind the doorway, Devon was calling, and Stanley could smell bacon.

CHAPTER ELEVEN

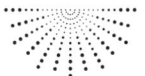

Breakfast consisted of perfectly fried eggs on a bed of buttery spinach, accompanied by as much crisp bacon as Stanley could shove in his mouth. There was toast, too, with soft butter and sweet raspberry jam, and Stanley ate all of what was on the plate.

Not once did Devon look at him askance. Neither did he suggest that it might be polite not to take so much, as there were other soldiers in line behind him, waiting for their share, because there weren't any soldiers waiting for their portion of food. Instead there was an entire loaf of bread, wrapped in clear plastic, waiting on the counter in case Stanley wanted more.

It seemed, actually, that in addition to Devon studying Stanley's every move as though taking mental notes in his head about the hungry bellies of young men and how that related to his thesis, he was studying Stanley for reasons of his own. As to what those reasons were, Stanley couldn't guess, but Devon's eyes were bright green and he was looking at Stanley as though watching something he enjoyed. And maybe there was a fondness in those eyes, as well.

Devon cheerfully made more toast, getting up to do this, wearing the same blue jeans that a farmer would wear. He padded around the kitchen in his bare feet like it wasn't a freezing November day outside, and he didn't have to worry about being warm.

"Here you go," said Devon as he put the plate of toast in front of Stanley. "You like the bread, huh? Don't worry about it. The first week I was in France, I ate a shit-ton of any kind of bread I could get my hands on. There's something about it that makes it taste amazing, not like the bread in the States."

Somewhat assured, Stanley ate three more slices of toast with butter and jam. Devon had one slice, and they sat at the table and crunched through their toast and drank their coffee. Though Stanley's belly almost hurt from being so full, his heartbeat slowed down and his throat wasn't so dry.

His eyes kept going to Devon's as they sat together. It was so simple, what they were doing. So many would find breakfast together too dull or stupid to call happiness, but Stanley did. He wanted to do it with Devon, being just like this, forever.

"What were you working on?" asked Stanley as he swept the crumbs from the wooden table and tipped them onto his now-empty plate. "I heard you typing on your laptop."

"That was my second laptop, if you can believe it," said Devon. "I dropped the first one on my second day here and had to get another one. Lucky for me I'm obsessed about backing up." Devon smiled at Stanley as though to get him to join in the joke.

"Backing up what?" Confused, Stanley shook his head. He could only picture an image where Devon was putting a large black typewriter with white keys up on a shelf, though why he would want to put something so heavy so high when he'd only have to take it down again was beyond him.

"Backing up to the cloud, for one, and my jump drive, for another, and—" Devon stopped talking and his eyes brightened up in the way that they did when he discovered a fact that he felt was wonderful.

"1917, right?" Devon asked. "You didn't have computers, you had typewriters, those great, enormous things with long spindly arms for each letter and white circles for keys."

"You mean an Underwood?" asked Stanley, for it was the typewriter his Pa had, and the kind they used at the enlistment office. "Everybody's got one of those, I think."

"Well, I don't," said Devon. "I don't think anybody does, unless they're into retro."

As to what retro was, Stanley had no idea, but Devon cheerfully got up and brought back his large piece of folded metal, his laptop. It was now bent in half and looked thin enough to break if you tried to unfold it. Unfold it Devon did, then he pushed back the empty plates and coffee cups.

Now that Stanley wasn't so tired, he could pay more attention to the keyboard. It didn't look like anybody could type on it very easily, as it was so flat it was almost smooth, with little square keys that were barely tall enough to break through the surface of metal. The top part of the metal that came away looked like a flat white window. When Devon touched a key on the keyboard, the whole thing lit up, showing a white space with black letters marching across it, row by row.

"I showed you this before," said Devon. He pushed the laptop a little closer to Stanley. "But there's more to it than cute kitties. You can type on it like a typewriter, and then you can keep writing or rewriting, as I often do." Devon smiled and seemed to be laughing at himself, welcoming Stanley to join in the fun.

"How does it work?" asked Stanley.

"The whole thing is portable," said Devon. He typed something on the keyboard and, across the screen, small black letters appeared. "Think of a document that's permanently available. When you're done working on it, you can put it in a safe place and take it out and revise it any time you want."

Stanley shook his head, though when he touched the sleek edge of the thing, his mind flared with a sudden desire to play with it, like it was a toy, which it wasn't. Besides, he was distracted by Devon's tanned forearms, his half-buttoned shirt, and the way he smelled up close.

Devon gestured with his hand that Stanley should give it a try, so he did. Except when his fingers touched the broad, flat area near the edge, the black line on the window jumped down on the white page.

Stanley pulled his fingers away, eyes wide and on Devon, worried that he'd broken something. He was always fiddling with things and breaking them.

"You didn't hurt anything," said Devon. "Look, see? I press this key, the Delete, and the cursor goes back to where it was."

"What about the part where you back up?" asked Stanley, even though he still didn't really understand what that meant.

"You push on here, and move the cursor. See that black line? That's the cursor. You move it to this icon—which is a picture of what the thing does—and tap. Watch it. See it blink? There. The document is backed up on the hard drive, and if I was really writing more than I'd want to risk losing, I'd use my jump drive."

Devon pulled out a very small silver stick that didn't look like it could do anything, let alone back up Devon's work. Thinking about all of this was making Stanley's head spin. Devon seemed to sense this and put the jump drive in his pocket and gently slapped the laptop closed.

"I've overwhelmed you, haven't I," asked Devon, though it was more a statement than a question. "That's my problem. My friends in the States say I'm obsessed about World War I and that I should get a different hobby or a boyfriend, but I'm in the middle of finishing my master's thesis, and either of those things would just get in the way."

Devon traced the edges of the laptop with his fingers and blew out a puff of air, seeming chagrined at his own failings. His eyes flicked to Stanley as if he wanted forgiveness for that or, at the very, least a little understanding. Which Stanley had in abundance because when he'd enlisted, he'd hoped to be assigned to the army's air force division so he could tinker with the cunning bi-planes that were being developed. Only they put him in the infantry, and he'd spent his days marching in mud watching his friends get killed.

That wasn't where he wanted his thoughts to go, so he took a long drink of his now cold coffee and swallowed and mentally shook himself. He wasn't a very good guest if he was going to wallow in his own troubles while Devon struggled in his mire of self-doubt. Devon, who had been so good to him and welcoming and who had the most beguiling tilt to his eyes when sad.

"Hey, I'm the same way," said Stanley with some forced cheerfulness in his voice. "My Pa always joked that I'd get so interested in something that I'd turn into it—"

"Your Pa?" asked Devon, his eyebrows going up, though not in that way that said he wanted to take notes for his thesis, but because he really wanted to know.

"He died from influenza," said Stanley quickly to get the explanation over with. "And then I enlisted."

"Did you enlist in 1917?" asked Devon, and at Stanley's nod, Devon nodded also. "That was before the pandemic of 1918."

"The pan-*what*?" asked Stanley, completely alarmed at the thought of the flu spreading that far, that fast. "A pandemic?"

"I probably shouldn't tell you this, what with time travel paradoxes and all," said Devon. He got up with his laptop tucked under his arm and put it with his other papers that were stacked in piles at the far edge of the kitchen counter. "Because if you go back into the past, you shouldn't know the future, right? Or you'll mess up the timeline. Or something."

Devon looked like he wanted to laugh at this foolishness, but instead he was scowling. Stanley could see it right then that he was berating himself for believing in such a foolish thing as time travel, even for a half a second. Time travel wasn't real, everybody knew that. Yet here Stanley was, sitting at the sturdy kitchen table in a French cottage on the edge of what had been a battlefield but was now a cemetery and memorial.

The war that Stanley knew to be real had ended, and everybody he knew was dead. Everybody who'd been alive then was dead, too, as a matter of fact, and Stanley was the only one left who knew what it felt like to type on an Underwood typewriter. This knowledge, added to everything else, rushed over him. He was swamped with overwhelming sadness, a grief so deep and dark and bitter that he found himself curled over his knees, gripping them hard and gasping sharp breaths, trying to stem his tears.

"Stanley."

Devon said his name, but it came from far away. Everything felt so far away that nothing could save him. He was adrift and alone.

Then Stanley felt something warm touching him. Stanley opened his eyes to see that Devon was half kneeling on the wooden floor. Devon's hands were on his knees, warm and steady. He'd pulled Stanley's chair out so that he could get close. His eyes were very green and kind and concerned, and Stanley knew that he was safe.

"Can you breathe a little bit for me, Stanley?" asked Devon. "Just breathe in and out. Look at me and breathe while you listen to me babble on about the war and about my paper. About how my thesis advisor is insisting that the overall theme should contain something uplifting, even though both you and I know that all war is futile and the only reason countries start wars is to help generate income and raise their gross domestic production—or is it product? I never can remember."

Stanley raised his head. He lifted himself up and allowed his hands to rest on Devon's, keeping them where they were while his heart slowed and the tightness in his throat eased.

"War is futile," said Stanley, nodding, as if he was the sage and Devon the student who needed confirmation. "It's not even glorious, you know? It's just mud and shit and blood and leftover shrapnel."

"I know it is," said Devon. "I know."

Devon didn't seem like he'd ever been in a war to actually know, but he'd probably done enough research, and his eyes said that he understood it'd been horrible. What's more, this was about the fifth or sixth time that Devon had mentioned his paper, and Stanley was such a bad guest, he'd never even asked about it. Which he should, not only because it would be a good distraction from his own woes, but also because he liked the way Devon's eyes lit up when he talked about it.

"What is your paper about?" asked Stanley. He pushed himself all the way up and made himself let go of Devon's hands. This caused Devon to stand up, though he didn't move away, and remained where he'd knelt, quite close and in that same steady way.

"My paper?" asked Devon, as though surprised by the brisk change of subject. Then he seemed to understand exactly what Stanley wanted. He rubbed his chin and traced a crumb on the tabletop, as though suddenly shy about the whole thing. "It's a thesis—a study—of the effects of the weather on the battle you were in. Not on the whole war, right, because that would be too broad. My thesis advisor says that it's better to go narrow, to focus on one or two things because that makes a thesis sparkle."

Stanley didn't know whether or not a thesis about war could actually sparkle. There was a bit of a derisive tone in Devon's voice as he said this, which meant that Devon was probably aware of the same impossibility, too. Which made Stanley feel like smiling, so he did. Which made Devon smile in return.

"Yeah, I know, right? *Sparkle*."

Devon began clearing the rest of the breakfast things, placing everything in the broad sink with slight clanking sounds. He seemed at home as he puttered, investing in Stanley the huge and overwhelming longing to have the two of them go on, just as they were, till time ended. Stanley shook himself and made himself pay attention because he wanted to and because Devon deserved it.

"If I wasn't getting my history master's," said Devon as he rinsed plates and cutlery, "I would have been a meteorologist. You know, a weatherman. The guy who measures the isobars and takes temperature readings and looks at the rain gauge. That guy."

"That guy," said Stanley, agreeing because it did sound like an interesting occupation.

"But I was too obsessed, so into the program I went, and marked the checkbox next to World War I faster than you could spit."

"One?" asked Stanley. There was more than one? Devon had said it like that a few times, *World War One*, like the war Stanley was in, *had* been in, had only been the first one, the first of *many*. He didn't want to believe it.

"More time travel stuff," said Devon, half to himself while he rubbed his forearms with his hands. Then, having decided, he wiped his hands on his blue jeans and blew out a breath. "I'm not sure I should tell you, in case you really are a time traveler and might go back to 1917 and shouldn't know, but there were two world wars—"

"*Two?*"

"Only two," said Devon. "I mean, there were other wars, local wars I guess you'd call them, but only two that involved the whole world."

Devon didn't seem to want to talk about it more than that, though, so Stanley didn't push it because the thought of it was making his heart race again. Even though he kind of wanted to know, there wasn't anything he could do about it. And besides, it was far more pleasant to look at Devon as he went about his household chores.

"I have an idea," said Devon. "Why don't we get some fresh air and walk along the trenches? Then you can show me what you know."

Stanley didn't know much about anything, it seemed, but he liked the way the suggestion made Devon smile, and that was good enough for Stanley.

CHAPTER TWELVE

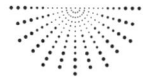

Devon had shared too much too soon, that much was obvious, but the suggestion of a walk had made a difference in the way Stanley was looking at him. Besides, he still felt conflicted as to whether Stanley was crazy or truly from the past. Either way, it was Devon's responsibility to do right by Stanley. That included not giving in to the impulse to grab him and hold him close simply because Stanley had such a sweet face and seemed quite eager, at a moment's notice, to listen to Devon babble on. So, putting on jackets and knitted caps, and after Devon grabbed the weatherproof map of the area he'd ordered online, they headed out.

He didn't lock the door, and noticed that Stanley didn't say anything about it. That only made sense, as, at least in Devon's mind, in Stanley's time, in 1917, the world had been a more honest place, and people didn't need to lock their doors. That might not be altogether true, but it pleased him to think about it that way.

They headed out across the wet grass as a mist was coming down, shrouding the green corduroy rows in wisps of grey velvet.

"Let's go this way," said Devon. He pointed to the edge of where the nearest trench began. When he'd first moved to France, he'd gone over every inch of every trench, starting from left to right, so it made sense, at least to him, to explore it that way now with Stanley.

When they got to the top of the first trench, Stanley stood there with his hands in the pockets of the dark pea coat that Devon had loaned him. The blue of the borrowed knitted cap was stark against his pale skin, the bones tightly drawn across his cheeks as he gazed across the rows of trenches.

"It's hard to look at," said Stanley. "When I see the memorial, all I can see is my failure."

"You did what you could," said Devon before he could stop himself, as it was too banal a thing to say when 200 men had lost their lives for nothing. "You volunteered. That was brave, and at least you tried. Right?"

"Maybe," said Stanley. "What is that?" As if to distract himself, he moved closer to Devon and pointed at the map in Devon's hand. "Is that a map?"

Nodding, Devon unrolled it and held it flat between his hands. He remembered finding the cartography shop online that offered reproductions of various maps from all the wars. Though it had been a bit pricy, the details in the map had helped Devon get a feel for what he was working on.

He'd looked at the map so many times that he knew it by heart, though it revealed something new every time he'd unrolled it. Had he been taken back to 1917, he really felt that he could have found his way around, would have known where to stop to get a cup of coffee or where to stop to get a new scarf from supplies, at least, had there been scarves on offer. Though, with Stanley right in front of him, the daydream that had occupied him for so long began to seem a little inadequate.

The unrolling of the map brought Stanley to his side, close and warm, his expression eager and interested, his eyes bright. Devon knew that he'd been waiting his whole life for this exact moment, where he could share this with Stanley and watch the expression on his face as he listened. Something bubbled up inside of him. He realized that it was happiness and he longed for time to slow down so they could stay this way forever.

"Okay, here's where we are," said Devon, doing his best to keep at least some of his excitement out of his voice so as not to overwhelm Stanley. He pointed to the lower left corner of the map. "The brown lines are trenches, shaded a little bit in the middle, there, and the green and blue X's are weapons, green for howitzers and blue for rifles. The gold cross is the chaplain's station. There's only one of those, you see. The circles are the canteen, the latrine, bunkers for sleeping, and supply caches."

He waited while Stanley squinted at the map and then looked up. His eyes were tilted down at the outside corners, and it made Devon want to throw the map to the ground and hold him close in the way he'd been resisting all morning. Except impulsive, physical contact was not how he wanted Stanley to know him. Besides, what Stanley was doing was attempting to determine where he'd been on that fateful morning when he'd volunteered.

Devon felt a little rush of excitement at the thought of what Stanley could tell him. Then he felt badly about it because why should he find any joy in knowing more about Stanley's demise, and the loss of his friends, not to mention the entire of the 44th?

"That's the cottage?" asked Stanley as he pointed to the edge of the map where a little bit of shaded grey area was.

"Yes, it's off the map and the church is too. I could only afford a portion of the whole map, as it was a limited edition. I figured I already knew where those buildings were anyway, so I got this one."

It was exciting to think that Stanley would be able to give him specific information. That he was standing there with an American doughboy and was able to ask him, in person, where he'd been during a crucial part of a disastrous military effort.

"These are the trenches," said Stanley. He ran his finger along the shaded area that was the low point of the trench they were standing on. "And these are the bunkers for the commanding officers—"

"Where were you, Stanley?" asked Devon.

As Stanley looked over the trenches, his eyes narrowed as though focusing on the middle distance, rather than actually looking, Devon thought for a moment that he should take back the question. Otherwise, he was asking Stanley to plunge back into a very dark moment.

"Stanley—" said Devon. Why was he so obsessed? Why did he have to push it all the time?

He reached out and put his hand on Stanley's arm, which seemed to wake him. He was about to tell Stanley to never mind. He had enough information for his thesis; he didn't need to drag Stanley through the sad mud of the past to get it.

"It just looks so different," said Stanley. "So peaceful."

With a last glance at the map, Stanley headed into the nearest trench and began walking along.

"This was the med station," said Stanley, pointing at a spot in the trench wall with a jerk of his thumb. "I never got sick, but there was one guy who got his leg blown off. They tried to cauterize the wound, but he didn't make it."

Devon followed close behind, thinking that he could take notes, or he could just let the statement soak into him. He looked at the spot where the soldier had died, one of many, and hurried to catch up to Stanley, who was marching as though he was on patrol. Doing his duty even though it might be painful, which was the last thing Devon wanted to for him.

Devon stared at the back of Stanley's neck, where the collar of the pea coat ended and where the knitted cap began. The line of skin there was pale and vulnerable. Devon wanted to kiss that skin and realized that his feelings had gone beyond his obsession with American doughboys. Even if Stanley turned out to be a con artist, or someone mentally deranged, when he pointed out where the solider had died, what had happened in the war meant something to him.

"This was one of the places you could get coffee any time of day," said Stanley, waving over an area of the entrance to a bunker that had caved in. "Of course, you couldn't get away from your post to go get it, but sometimes they'd have a private take a tray around. Like we were at a Sunday picnic."

Stanley was smiling to himself about this, and turned to look at Devon.

"Is that how it's listed on your map?" Stanley asked.

"Yeah, it's a circle," said Devon. He checked the map, Stanley close at his side. "But where were you when—when you volunteered for your mission?"

He almost hated himself for asking, and again was just about to take it all back when Stanley sped up and kept going. They were low enough in the trench that the world was rimmed by a dark green horizon under a misty grey sky, cutting them off from everything except what was before them.

At the point where the trench was cut through with the path to the memorial, Stanley went left, up two rows of trenches, and then to the right, down another trench. His movements were as sure as if he'd done it many times and knew the way, and the thought that he'd actually been at the battle sent a shiver through Devon's body.

Stanley didn't even look at the map, but led Devon to a point that was marked with a green X, and which was also marked with a circle for a bunker. When Stanley stopped, it was suddenly, with Devon tripping over his heels. He'd passed this particular point many a time, noting absently the sagging wooden frame, surrounded by grass now, that had been the entrance to a commander's bunker. Never in his life had he ever expected that someone from the war would be standing not half a foot from him, his hands in his pockets, on the verge of explaining it to him.

"You don't have to tell me, Stanley," said Devon, though he did want to know, and he wanted to believe that Stanley had come from that time, that battle.

"We're here anyway," said Stanley. "It's—it's not as bad as I thought it would be, seeing it like this. It's all gentled now."

Gentled was the word for it. All the hard edges and intentions of what the bunker had been built and equipped for were now a bank of earth softened by grass.

"This was Commander Helmer's bunker," said Stanley, pointing.

He reached out to touch one of the railroad ties whose edges were still crisp, though the lintel now sagged beneath the weight of earth.

"He was the one who deserted, right?" asked Devon. He knew all about the desertion and the domino effects that act had had.

"Yes. Lt. Billings took over, so it became his bunker. He wasn't in there for very long before he called for volunteers, and that was because—" Stanley's voice cracked to a stop, but he firmed his jaw and shook his head, blinking as though the battle was happening in front of him that very moment. "The explosion was right overhead, and the howitzer was blasted into the trench, still smoking and hot. The flying shrapnel ripped my friends to shreds, and the radio, too."

A large chunk of Devon's fascination with the battle melted right then and there because it wasn't more important than what was happening now. Stanley wasn't on the verge of tears, as he seemed to be made of something strong and resilient, but it wasn't going to be too much longer before he was a crumpled mess on the ground. Nobody could go through something like that and come out the same on the other side.

Devon had read plenty about the effects of war. He'd often remarked to his thesis advisor how the pictures of doughboys shipping out seemed happy and upbeat, but on the return voyage home, their faces were marked with the horror of what they had been through, what they had seen. In fact, there were very few pictures of homecomings, as if the soldiers wanted to put all of it in the past. The look on Stanley's face now, a reflection of that desire to leave it all behind, told Devon the same thing—there was nothing but futility to be found in war, and nothing but waste left it its wake. Nobody deserved to be forced to relive it. Devon raised his hand, but Stanley continued.

"My friends—" began Stanley, but his voice went all wobbly, so he stopped, set his shoulders, and tried again. "We were sitting just here on a little bench cut into the mud. I was sitting on a strip of canvas that Isaac had given to me."

He traced a line in the air with his hand, the flat of his palm level.

"The radio was there."

Stanley pointed to a spot just to the right of the bunker door. Though there wasn't much room in the trench now, Devon knew that the space had once been wider, and that sometimes there were tables for radios and sometimes there were spaces dug into the side of the trench. Either way, the radio would have been vulnerable to the elements and exploding mortar shells.

"If they'd been on my left, they would have made it, and the radio, too," said Stanley. "And after, their bodies were beneath a canvas, over there, to wait until we could bury them."

As Stanley pointed where the bodies of his friends had lain, the clarity of the moment rose up, a living picture of how it must have been, and Devon began to feel quite sick. This was exactly the information he would have wanted to know and include in his paper, so he had only himself to blame for Stanley's reaction. Stanley didn't deserve to be dragged through this again, and especially not for Devon's benefit. Devon needed to stop asking, stop obsessing over something that was so painful, so destructive.

"Stanley, you don't have to tell me any more," said Devon.

Devon rolled up the map and held it at his side. He reached for Stanley's arm, meaning to grasp it and give comfort that way. Instead, Stanley, seeing Devon's movement, must have interpreted it differently than Devon had meant it, for he took Devon's hand in his and gave it a squeeze, as though Devon were the one needing comfort.

Stanley's hand was warm, with calluses on the edge of his fingers. The calluses were just where they ought to be if he'd spent any time at all firing a rifle that wasn't an automatic, and that would need to be loaded and then fired with a fresh pull on the trigger each and every time. Everything about him, his hair, his eyes, his shy smile, was exactly as it ought to be, if he was who he said he was, a soldier from the war. He wasn't just a spitting image of an American doughboy, though, but a living human being who had survived a great deal.

Plus, soldiers needed to come home at some point, and not always be in the trenches. Maybe this was that time for Stanley. Devon held on to Stanley's hand and, for a moment, they stood there. The wind stirred the grasses around. The wet smell of the earth was rich in the air, and little points of creosote rose from the rotting railroad ties. Beneath it all was the scent of something old and quiet and still.

He liked holding Stanley's hand, the way the warmth of their skin began to turn into something more, something on the edge of excitement. He wanted to drop the map and wrap his arms around Stanley, and would have, except for the look in Stanley's eyes as he gazed at the edge of the trench. And finally, when he looked at Devon.

"A fellow's not supposed to care for another fellow," said Stanley, though he didn't let go of Devon.

"Maybe not back then," said Devon, giving Stanley's hand a squeeze. "But you're here now, and it's okay."

"So you believe me?" asked Stanley.

"I do and I don't," said Devon, a little relieved to be drawn out of his own darker thoughts. "Time travel is impossible, but there's something in your eyes that tells me you were there. When it happened. When it all went wrong, though it was wrong from the beginning."

"It didn't seem that way," said Stanley. "At the time, it seemed like a good thing everybody was excited about."

Devon knew exactly what Stanley meant. The pictures he'd been looking at since he could remember had contained exactly that sense of excitement and patriotic verve. The soldiers' faces had depicted an upbeat expectation about how it would be fighting the enemy and coming home victorious.

"It's getting cold," said Devon. He squeezed Stanley's warm hand and again fought the impulse to hug him. "And I think it's going to start raining."

"It always rained," said Stanley. "In the trenches, it was always raining, and the sky was the color of mud."

Stanley's face dropped back into sadness, as though he was being pulled into memories of the war against his will. Which made Devon want to take care of him all the more.

"Well, let's get you inside," said Devon, horrified at himself that he'd let Stanley go so far into his memories that he had an expression on his face like he did, one of sadness, despair filtering everything he looked at, every word he said. "Okay?"

"Okay," said Stanley, smiling to himself.

Devon made himself let go, and together they tramped along to the end of the trench. While it occurred to Devon that this was the direction Stanley would have taken to reach the commander on his mission, he didn't ask about it. Instead, he led them both back towards the cottage, cutting over the top of one trench, slipping down the other side to the path between the rows, getting to the cottage just as it began to rain.

"Some coffee to warm up with?" asked Devon.

"Yes," said Stanley, with as much passion as Devon had heard from him, as though he was unbelievably grateful for the opportunity to drink something warm. "Can I have extra sugar in mine?"

"Yes, of course," said Devon, pleased to be able, at last, to give instead of to take.

CHAPTER THIRTEEN

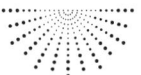

Devon made coffee using the French press. He did it as fast as he could, shoving the bowl of brown sugar in front of Stanley so he could have as much as he wanted. Then he took their damp jackets and rain speckled knitted caps and hung them up. He did not let himself think about the next thing that he wanted to do because he really should stop. He made himself sit across from Stanley at the kitchen table while the radiator oozed out warmth and the rain darkened the skies outside the windows and they drank their coffee.

"What I'd like to do," said Devon because he couldn't help himself, and maybe it would be okay. "I'd like to take pictures of you in your uniform to send to the history department at the university."

"Why?" asked Stanley, his eyebrows going up as he finished his coffee. "Why would you want to do that? Would that help them?"

Devon felt a pang in his heart because of course that would be Stanley's first concern. Not that it might make him uncomfortable, but that it might help somebody else. Which was why he'd volunteered even though his friends had just been horribly killed and no other soldier had been brave enough to go on what turned out to be a suicide mission.

"Never mind," said Devon, shaking his head, and he meant it. Putting that uniform on was the last thing that Stanley needed, and the last thing Devon wanted to put him through. "I'll just take pictures of it on the floor. It'll be easier that way anyway, and I can get good close-ups."

"I'll put it on," said Stanley. "And maybe afterwards we can burn it?"

There was a jerk of hesitation deep in Devon's gut because the uniform could be invaluable in understanding the day-to-day life in the trenches. Except the world already knew enough about that, and they wouldn't miss this one uniform if Stanley wanted to destroy it. Except as Stanley went into the bedroom to change into it, Devon's heart began to race, for he knew it would be like seeing not just his work, his thesis, but his dream come to life.

As Stanley came out of the bedroom, Devon's heart almost stopped. There was mud on the uniform, and the sweater vest had holes where the moths had gotten to it. But the boots were tight, and the laces new. Stanley looked like he ought to look, the pure vision that had been in Devon's mind since he could remember. Except it was better because the image was overlaid with Stanley himself, his smile, the brightness in his eyes, the willingness with which he'd put the uniform on *just* so Devon could take pictures.

When Stanley bent to put on his puttees, Devon raced over to help him. Impulsively he knelt at Stanley's feet to wrap the puttees around Stanley's boots with an anxious joy of feeling a live human being beneath his hands.

"There," he said, looking up at Stanley. "Is that better?"

"Yes," said Stanley. "But if you could hurry because there was a lot of lice in the trenches, and I think some of them came through time with me."

Devon couldn't tell whether Stanley was joking or not, but he got up, grabbed his cell phone, urged Stanley to stand in front of the fireplace, and took pictures.

There was no film to worry about, so he took pictures from each angle as it occurred to him, from the back, shoulder height, the front, the long view from the side. He even took close-ups of the buttons until he was sure that he'd used up almost all the space for photos on his phone.

Stanley's face began to grow pale beneath his shorn hair, his breathing becoming a bit sharp, and Devon knew he needed to stop.

He stood there, with the phone in his hand, and realized how dark the room had gotten, as it was starting to rain harder.

"I'm going to use the flash for a few more," he said, thinking too late that Stanley wouldn't know what a flash was. "Then you can get out of that."

Stanley nodded. He stood there with his rifle gripped in one hand, held at his side, with the canteen looped crossways over his chest. Just like a soldier ready to march in step with his fellows, or to slam himself to the earth to shoot at the enemy, whatever was called for.

With his ID tag glinting in the hollow of his throat, Stanley looked so young. There was still such a trace of innocence in his eyes that Devon almost hated using the flash. He decided it would be the last picture, and the best way to capture the details of the uniform. He turned on the flash, focused the camera, and tapped the dot on the phone.

The room was lit up by the flash and sudden jagged streaks of lightning. There was a stutter of blackness against the white as Stanley shrank back, his arms in front of his face as though he was attempting to protect himself from a blow. Then the whole room went dark.

"Don't worry, Stanley, it's just a power outage," said Devon. "The lights'll come on soon."

The lights came on a moment later. Devon stared at the spot where Stanley had just been, but there was nobody there. There was no trace of Stanley in the room. There was only Devon, his mess of papers, and two coffee cups on the table. Those could have been from Devon himself, leftover in his rush to get his paper done. He must have made everything up in some sort of feverish haze. His desire to meet an American doughboy had become a reality in his mind so maybe he was the one going crazy. Except—

"Stanley?" called Devon. "*Stanley?*"

He rushed into the bathroom where there was no trace that anybody had been in there other than Devon. There was a pile of clothes neatly folded on the counter, Devon's own blue jeans and long sleeved t-shirt, socks, underwear—all his. He went into the bedroom and opened the closet door, and when he saw the empty hangers, he reached up to touch them, his heart pounding. The hangers could have been used for anything, and were utterly still, giving evidence of nothing. Had he imagined the entire encounter?

No, he had not. He remembered the warmth of Stanley's hand, the impulse to hug him, how much more pleasant it had been to work on his paper with Stanley sleeping on the couch. How the dream of the American doughboy had given way to the reality of Stanley, the way he would smile at Devon as though he wasn't sure that it was okay to smile. How his eyes were the color of whiskey, and that detail, so sharp now in Devon's mind, wasn't anything that he could have seen in a sepia-toned photograph. All soldiers had black eyes in those, except for the ones with blue eyes, and they looked like ghosts. All of them were ghosts, now, only—

Devon went to the corner where he'd leaned the rifle to keep it out of the way. There in the plaster was the small gouge from the bayonet. Of course, the gouge could have been from anything, a past occupant of the cottage, say. But this mark, this cut in the plaster, was at exactly the height of the blade of a World War I bayonet on the end of a Winchester 1912 rifle.

The angle was such that only a thin object could have made that mark so close to the corner where the walls met. Devon traced it with his fingers, dug in with his fingernails, and watched the plaster sift over the coat of paint.

"You were here, Stanley," said Devon. "I remember you."

He wanted to cry and then he wanted to puke. He knew in his heart that Stanley had disappeared right before his very eyes. Except time travel was impossible, so Stanley could not have vanished into the past, but had instead run off into the night and probably needed help staying in touch with reality. It was crazy, but it was better to imagine that Stanley was a liar. Otherwise, Devon would never be able to find him because he couldn't reach back to the year 1917 and bring Stanley home.

It was dark and it was raining and Stanley needed his help. Whatever the truth was, Devon knew he loved Stanley and all he wanted was Stanley, safe and sound, with Devon.

He went to call *les gendarmes*.

LES GENDARMES ARRIVED PROMPTLY within the hour as the rain began to trail off. They arrived in their Peugeot automobile. On the passenger door, shining in the porch light, was emblazoned the emblem of the local village that shone in the porch light by the front door. Devon could see the light glinting off the usual gear for all police officers, the radio, the gun rack, the grill between the front seat and the back.

With great efficiency, the two officers, one young and one old, checked Devon's papers and listened patiently to his story about a young man, dressed as a World War I soldier, who had appeared and then disappeared.

"Were you the American who called the council asking for reports of any mentally unstable persons in the area, *monsieur*?" asked the older office, giving Devon the idea that everybody in the village knew everybody else, and that Devon's recent phone call was the talk around every coffee table.

"Yes, that was me," said Devon. "I wasn't sure who he was and thought I'd check."

"There have been no reports, *monsieur*," said the younger officer. "But we will investigate."

As they began to look around the cottage, Devon felt a rising sense of panic that they might think he'd either made the whole thing up or been involved in Stanley's demise. Either one of which would bring him under legal scrutiny of a most unpleasant kind. But what did that matter if they found Stanley?

In spite of the fact that they couldn't find him because he'd gone back to 1917, it was easier to believe that Stanley had just run out into the rain because the phone's flash had startled him.

Les gendarmes went outside to search the grounds. They did not allow Devon to come with them, in case Devon was complicit in some way, he guessed. While he appreciated them being quite thorough about the whole thing, he was beginning to think he'd have been better off not calling them.

When *les gendarmes* came back from their search in and around the trenches, they gave Devon their conclusion.

"We have found nothing out of the ordinary, *monsieur*," said the older officer as he closed his tablet. "Only your tracks in the mud we could see."

Which meant that the rain had washed away Stanley's footprints and left Devon's behind. Or not, because the footprints *les gendarmes* found had been the only ones to *be* found. Had Devon gone a little crazy? Had he been driven over the edge by his isolation, his focus on his paper, and the fact that he was so far from home without any friends that he'd imagine the whole encounter?

"Sign here," said the young officer as he held out an old fashioned clip board and a pen.

Devon did as they asked, his fingers numb.

"Call us if you need anything else, *monsieur*," said both officers at the same time, and with that, they tipped their French police hats, got back into their Peugeot, and drove away, splashing rainwater with their tires as they went.

For a long moment, Devon stared at the car until it disappeared into the copse of trees along the road that led to the village.

CHAPTER FOURTEEN

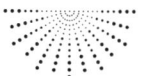

The next breath Stanley took shot into his lungs so hard that he choked on it, clutching his chest in a futile spasm, his mouth open. He tried to scream through the panic, as if that would help. It didn't.

In one twitch of his body, the hole he was falling into was black as pitch and so narrow he started to feel the coldness of the dirt and the dampness all around. With a mighty jerk, he found himself lurching backwards, his heels in the mud, as though he was holding onto the sides of a beast while it tried to buck him off. His head slammed back and his shoulders were shoved into a wall of mud so hard that he knew he'd be leaving an imprint there.

Then it stopped. When he opened his eyes and took a shriek of a breath, all he could see was the wall of mud of the trench opposite him. There was a scent of smoke and gun oil. In the dim light of what was the gloomy sun splashing like mercury behind the grey clouds was the spattered reflections of mortar shells exploding high in the air. It was raining, though the rain came down in a miserly thin way, like it didn't really want to. Like it would rather be someplace else altogether.

In his hands was a tin mug of coffee, the bitter dark brew that served in place of anything more civilized. There was not enough sugar and definitely no milk to soothe the ragged edge of the taste that Stanley took without hardly thinking about it. He blinked as he swallowed, disoriented in his mind, and unable to focus on any one thing.

What had just happened to him? Something bad, something that left him feeling his insides had been carved out, as though he'd been given a gift only to have it snatched away. There was a memory of a dark-haired, handsome man whose name Stanley could not recall. The sensation of his kind hands, his caring eyes, the warmth of his skin flitted about like the smoke wafting up from an overworked primus stove.

The harder he struggled to remember, the more evasive the memories became. He probably didn't deserve them anyway, except they lingered in his head, in his heart. They curled around like smoke from the barrel of a newly fired howitzer, with the blow-back coming at him full in the face, tasting of hard usage, and futility, and death.

"Are you all right, Stanley?" asked a voice between the sounds of shots being fired and mortar shells exploding.

Stanley turned to face the voice as the images of the dark-haired man trailed in and out of his head.

In the long trenches, there were bunkers for officers, where they could lay out maps and plan strategy, and little dug out places lined with canvas where soldiers could go to get out of the line of fire or if it was raining very badly. Most of the time, you were in the trench, either up along the battlements, ducking gunfire or mortar rounds, or lining up the howitzers. Other than that, you leaned against the opposite wall of the trench and smoked, or waited along the low, damp seats cut into the mud along the trench.

Sometimes the seats were covered with wooden slats, though usually they were just bare mud most of the time. Stanley was lucky because Isaac had found spare pieces of canvas to spread over the dirt, so at least they could be a little bit warmer, a little bit dryer, that way.

"Stanley," said Isaac. He held up his tin mug to Stanley in a mock toast, as if the mug held good, clean, crisp beer, as if the moment was something worth toasting.

Beyond Isaac were Bertie and Rex, who were looking at him as though he had the answers to everything and could possibly, perhaps by magic, transport them to the previous week when they'd gone into the village and been able to take a break from the horror of their daily lives. They'd gone into that pastry shop, and while it had sold the smallest pastries in all of human existence, each bite being about half of the pastry, the taste of sugar, the taste of normal, had been so delicious that they'd each vowed to fight to the last to preserve such a dignified and necessary establishment.

That had been last week, and Commander Helmer had, just yesterday, banned further travels outside of the trenches. In addition, Commander Helmer had disappeared in the night, and now they were waiting on orders from Lt. Billings.

"What are they doing in there?" asked Isaac.

From where Stanley was sitting, he could see into the command bunker. Lt. Billings was talking with the sergeant, who was in charge of the munitions supplies. The chaplain was also there, oddly out of place in his clean uniform, wearing a spot of white in the collar around his neck. With them was a scout, muddy up to his waist, his arms wrapped around himself as he nodded at the map on the plank table in the middle of the bunker.

Stanley could hear the sound of their voices, but could not discern the meaning, though by the look on Lt. Billings' face, it wasn't good. The officers were, as rumor had it, talking about planning a retreat. The shelling had been quite bad, with no new supplies, men dropping from gun fire, and constant shelling from the Germans. As well, a strangely powerful flu was finding its way through the trenches as winter neared. Overall, they were ineffective as a battalion, sacrificing themselves for nothing. Or so rumor had it.

Stanley remembered talking with someone, maybe the dark-haired man, about how war was futile. No matter how deeply the battalion dug their trenches and no matter how far they shot their shells and their bullets, no matter how hard they tried, the Germans kept coming closer. They would build an advancing trench in the middle of the night, and from their endless supply of weapons and ammunition would slaughter half a dozen men before breakfast. And then more before lunch and more before supper, and on it went.

The horrible weather was the key because it locked the battalion in place and prevented much needed supplies from getting in. If only they'd known in advance about the weather they could have prepared better, brought in more guns, more bullets, more food. If only they'd known—

"Stanley?"

Stanley turned his head and found himself looking at Isaac, studying him. Isaac had the collar of his jacket turned up in a jaunty way, like a pilot about to hop into one of those bi-planes. Bertie and Rex also had their collars turned up, as did Stanley. But only Isaac wore his in a way that made him look dashing, a brave young man who was fearless in his devotion to his country and his promise to protect his friends. Though as eye-catching as Isaac was, Stanley had the sense that his unrequited adoration of Isaac had been replaced by something else. But what?

"You can't hear anything of what they're saying?" asked Isaac, breaking in on Stanley's thoughts.

"No," said Stanley, but this with no rancor.

From where he was sitting, the trench took a little bend in either direction. To his left he could see the stretch of the trench, and to his right he could see into the bunker. Plus, he could see the radio on its sturdy stand. It was the cleanest, most intact thing in the whole trench.

Beyond the radio, the trench continued to his right, with his buddies from basic, Isaac, Bertie, and Rex, all lined up. The angle of the trench was such that he could see their faces quite clearly, for they were each leaning forward just enough, with Isaac in the front, and Bertie leaning out to peer around his shoulder, and Rex leaning out a little bit further than that. All of them were looking at Stanley.

"I can't hear what they're saying," said Stanley, clarifying. "But the chaplain looks pretty grim, and they're all shaking their heads. Now Lt. Billings is pointing at the map."

"Are they going to go out and look for him?" asked Rex. *Him*, of course, was Commander Helmer.

"In this weather?" asked Bertie in a joking way, as if the weather were the worst thing to be wary of.

Isaac waved their questions away, putting up his hand like they were on maneuvers and he'd just called a halt. This drew Stanley's attention to Isaac like he was sighting his rifle on the enemy. Except Isaac wasn't the enemy, he was Stanley's friend, the one who'd begun the friendship as they stood in line to get kitted up at the beginning of basic. *Hi, I'm Isaac*. He was also the one who professed not to care for chocolate, and who usually gave Stanley half of his ration, and then broke the other half to two pieces to give to Bertie and Rex.

The memory of Isaac's kindness brought more images to the surface of Stanley's mind. Of a young man turning from his work to make sure that Stanley had all the oranges he wanted. Who fed him steak and gave him fresh, sweet milk to drink. Who gave Stanley a warm spot to sleep, and who let him take a shower with an endless supply hot water. Who made Stanley feel safe. And whose green eyes looked at Stanley with something like fondness, no—it had been more like affection.

Where had he known this dark-haired man? What was his name? It was on the tip of Stanley's tongue—the dark-haired man had typed on something while the rain fell outside the thick glass windows and the air smelled clean and felt warm against his skin. But where was that place? Stanley shook his head because it was just a dream, all of it.

That place had never been. Before the war, Stanley had worked on a farm outside of Harlin, Colorado. Isaac had worked in a cannery in Brooklyn. Bertie and Rex had both delivered newspapers, working their way up through the ranks of newsies to be in charge of routes. Nobody had worked at a desk. None of them had come from gentle office work, so it couldn't have been any of them that he'd talked to that way, or interacted with that way.

Besides, all of them had believed that the war was necessary and useful, and that they'd win all the battles and come home inside of a month, decorated with medals, proudly wearing their crisp dress uniforms. Rather than the reality of it, which was the exact opposite. It had been over a year and they were covered with mud and no closer to winning. The truth of it was they were closer to losing everything, at the end of which their lives would be forfeit.

In Stanley's mind, a voice said, *It was such a futile thing, but they gave it their all.*

He shook his head, almost spilling his coffee, trying to locate and stop the buzz that rattled the bones of his skull. It was so loud he was sure Isaac and the others could hear it. He looked at them, questioning with his face as if they were under silence orders, but then the buzz disappeared like he'd snapped his fingers and stepped through an open doorway.

"What's the matter with you, buddy?" asked Isaac. "Why do you look like you're going to barf all over my boots?"

Stanley placed his tin mug on the canvas strip next to his thigh. The mud beneath it was lumpy, so he used his fingertips to adjust where the mug was set so that the coffee wouldn't slop over the edges. Why that mattered was beyond him; if the coffee spilled it would soak into the mud and become just another layer of ugly brown that nobody would notice.

The chaplain came out of the bunker with the scout right behind him, and both men turned and went to Stanley's left, along the trench toward the mess area and the kitchens behind that. He thought they were headed to get more coffee, though why he thought that, he didn't know, and besides the coffee was terrible anyway.

Lt. Billings remained in the bunker with his head down, looking at the map. His finger was on a spot near the edge of it. Stanley couldn't see whether that spot was where they currently were or where they'd be if they went into retreat. It wasn't his place to ask, and it'd be a far braver man than he to walk into the bunker just then and peer over Lt. Billings' shoulder to see if he could find out.

"I'm going to go in there," said Rex in that way of his, full of seriousness and intention, as he seldom said anything he didn't mean.

"No, you better not," said Bertie, who was as serious in his way as Rex was, having been in charge of a whole pack of newsies before the war. He talked and joked more, though, and seemed to enjoy getting Rex riled up because the more Rex resisted the more Bertie would try, and on it would go.

"No, don't bother the lieutenant," said Isaac. "We'll stay put until he comes out. If he asks us our opinion, we'll give it, and if he doesn't, we won't. Okay?"

Stanley turned his head sharply to look at Isaac, his ears ringing with the way he'd said the word *okay*. The dark-haired man in Stanley's memory had often said *okay* to him in just that way, like he wanted only the best for Stanley and wanted to make sure Stanley was on board. Stanley strained to hear the echo of the word in his head, but it faded away as though it had been said by a ghost.

Stanley shook his head. It must have been the fact that Commander Helmer had deserted in the night that was making him feel so strangely, looking at every act, every word his buddies uttered, as though it was an experiment he was doing, where any gesture by him, any movement, was likely to set off a chain reaction. It was as if he knew that Rex was going to say what he'd just said, and then Bertie would disagree with him, and then Isaac would have the final say. And there they would sit, waiting for the lieutenant to come out of the bunker, all in a row like the obedient soldiers they had trained to be, had signed up to be.

From these thoughts came an odd impulse that Stanley couldn't fully identify, but he knew there was something he needed to do to.

CHAPTER FIFTEEN

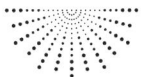

"Hey fellas," said Stanley as he wiped his upper lip clear of the nervous moisture that had suddenly formed there. "Why don't you come and sit on the other side of me."

"What?" asked Isaac. "We'll just be in the way when he comes out."

"No, it's dryer over here, I'm sure of it," said Stanley. He made a *come here* gesture with one hand while he patted the damp mud on the other side of him. He got up and tugged the strip of canvas from beneath him and spread it over the mud. "You can even sit on the canvas, so your asses will be a little bit more comfortable."

"Hey, I gave that to you," said Isaac.

There was mock dismay in his voice, but his eyes were sparkling, as though Isaac approved of Stanley giving up his own comfort for that of his buddies because in wartime, that's what you did. You looked out for each other. Except nobody was moving, and it felt urgent, somehow, that they should. Right now, this minute.

"Please," said Stanley. He moved his face into its most put-upon expression, his mouth in the shape of a pout, like he was three years old and having his buddies move to the other side of him his dearest wish. "I promise I'll give you all my next month's ration of chocolate."

"Does that include what Isaac gives to you?" asked Rex. He looked like he was about to stand up, but he hadn't yet, and Stanley felt his heart start to race.

"Yes," said Stanley. "All the chocolate that Isaac gives to me I will give to you and Bertie. Upon my honor, all of it, for the rest of the war."

"I'm in," said Bertie. He stood up and straightened his uniform like he was getting ready for inspection.

"Me too," said Rex, going through the same motion of pulling his woolen tunic into place while at the same time jabbing Bertie's ribs with his elbow.

"What about me?" asked Isaac. "I don't care for chocolate, you know that."

There was a twinkle in his eyes, but even as Stanley looked at him, he was drawn to another memory, another pair of eyes, so hard it was painful. He knew his heart was breaking, so he stood up to distract himself from the sinking feeling of loss and regret and having touched something so beautiful and sweet.

He reached out his hand.

"I'll find something special just for you, Isaac," said Stanley, attempting to put humor in his voice, his expression. "Just for you. Now will you please all move over here next to me?"

"We are next to you," said Rex, even as he started walking to go where Stanley wanted him to.

"On this side, damn it," said Stanley, pointing. "*This* side."

He could hardly breathe as they trooped over to sit on his left side, with Isaac right next to him, and Bertie and Rex on the other side of Isaac, all in a row. Isaac was so close that Stanley could feel the warmth of his body, the press of his thigh, and the smell of sweat on the back of his neck.

Stanley closed his eyes and wanted to place his palms over them to stay in the blackness where an image of a low light danced, illuminating the top of a stove, a tiny green dot in the darkness. A place where he stirred to get more comfortable so he could fall asleep on the couch in the cottage. The clean pillowslip rustled. Warm air touched his skin, and somebody was typing. There was the scent of dark coffee brewing, but it was so distant he could barely smell it. The harder he tried, the faster it faded until it was transparent in his mind and disappeared completely.

The loss formed an ache in his chest, but he had to ignore this and move on because there was something else he needed to do.

Stanley opened his eyes with a snap, and turned to his buddies.

"Close your eyes," he said. "Turn your heads, look towards the chaplain. He's coming this way, he's got news to tell, look at him, *look at him—*"

At the urgent, strident sound of Stanley's voice, and with their eyes wide, they all turned their heads just as a mortar shell exploded over the trench, sending black shrapnel digging into the muddy sides just where Bertie, Rex, and Isaac had so recently been sitting. Broken metal screamed as flak tore into the radio and spun into the air. Huge silver clouds descended, bits of metal pattering into the mud as left-over powder exploded, sending more metal flying.

Stanley felt his arm start to sting, and looked down. There were tiny holes in his uniform. Dark red blood began to soak into the brown wool, but it wasn't very much and didn't spread very fast. He'd keep the arm, and maybe he'd get some R&R to recover and maybe his buddies could stay with him and maybe they'd all walk into the village again, their boots clanking on the damp cobbles as they wandered about and listened to French voices.

Only the French voices had been silenced, and the village had been bombed to bits. Somebody had told him that, and also that a new community had been built around the foundations of the old village, left as a war memorial. He couldn't remember how he knew that, but the thought of it filled him with a growing sadness, and as he turned to look at his friends, he scrubbed at his face so they wouldn't see the tears.

Except as the chaplain went into the bunker and Lt. Billings came out to meet him, Isaac, Bertie, and Rex were all looking at Stanley with eyes round as saucers.

"We were *just* sitting there," said Bertie.

Rex was studying him as if he'd been a newsie who'd just sold all of his papers at full price in under half an hour. As for Isaac, he was as white as iced paper, his eyes the color of ancient moss that has grown over a stone.

"We were, Stanley," said Isaac, almost accusing, pointing at the place where they had just been, that the chaplain was gesturing to while he talked urgently to the lieutenant.

Stanley couldn't understand why he couldn't hear what the chaplain was saying when the chaplain was as close to him as Isaac was. But he couldn't.

"It was like you knew," said Isaac. "Did you?"

"You accusing me of being a German spy?" asked Stanley, jokingly serious to cover up the growing sense of panic within him.

"No, of course not," said Isaac. He shook his head, and reached out his hand.

"Please don't touch me," said Stanley, half-choking on the thickness in his throat. "I don't think I could bear it just now."

His friends were alive, and though the war would have continued with or without them, Stanley knew there was no price too dear to have them with him.

CHAPTER SIXTEEN

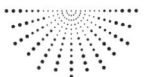

Heartsick, Devon stood in the middle of the cottage, looking at his laptop, his pile of notes, his old fashioned canvas notebook, thinking what a waste it all was with nobody to share it with. And how it had become, in a single moment, less important than it had been. He was tempted to take the whole mess and dump it in the nearest trash bin and just leave it all behind him. But that would be throwing away two years of work, which was ridiculous. What he needed to do now was to find Stanley.

The idea of a search was a distraction, he knew that. But he couldn't just sit there and keep working on his paper, not if Stanley needed to be found. The alternative was that he'd been dragged back in time and was now suffering through the war all over again. Devon didn't want to simply go on the internet and check the records because he was afraid that the truth of it would be more than he could bear. So he would search. But how?

He'd called *les gendarmes* and they'd been worse than useless. The act had only brought Devon himself into a circle of interest, where *he* was the lunatic escaped from the asylum, and Stanley his imaginary friend. No, not imaginary.

With a sudden thought, Devon pulled out his phone, tapped the Photos file, and thumbed through the images. There were pictures of sunrises and sunsets, and of the stones of the cottage etched by the morning's frost. The expensive bottle of wine he'd bought when he'd first arrived. The shop window that contained every kind of cheese imaginable. A few selfies that he'd sent, embarrassed, to his old college buddies; he never did take a good selfie.

There were no images of Stanley, only black frames, one after the other. The most recent photo had a white blob in the middle. That could have been caused by anything, probably the flash from the phone, and it was no proof that Stanley had been there.

Devon turned off the phone, closed his eyes, and was instantly flooded with the memory of Stanley, so close and so warm, so sweet, the last dregs of innocence clinging to his smile like the act of a desperate man. War hadn't destroyed him completely, but his last mission had come close. Or maybe he was mentally incapacitated and lost, and all Devon needed to do was to find him.

He knew he was retreating into his old, obsessive habits, letting one thought take over everything else. The urge to find Stanley held sway. His heart was breaking because it had been better to share things with Stanley than be on his own. Better to let someone else in his life than to always be buried in a book, better to find balance in Stanley's eyes.

He got his coat, still damp from his earlier walk, and his knitted cap. He put them on and brushed his fingers across the pea coat that Stanley had worn. It was bone dry, as if nobody had worn it in ages, with the second knitted cap sticking out of the pocket, also dry. With a shrug, Devon went out the door and began to walk along the trenches. It was raining, so the walk was instantly miserable, the cold drops going right into his eyes and down the back of his neck.

The ache of missing Stanley was almost choking him, but Stanley deserved better than to have Devon running around looking for him haphazardly, so Devon needed a plan. He needed a method to search so he could do it systematically, just like he'd do research for his paper. He needed to be able to cover a lot of ground, quickly.

He walked along the blacktopped road into the village, now desolate with the rain coming down hard. The car rental place, which also doubled as a garage, was on the edge of the market square. The fellow seemed happy to rent Devon a car for a few days. He sold him extra insurance for way too much, only Devon didn't care.

Once behind the wheel, Devon was shielded from the weather, and drove around the village. Up and down back streets and alleys he drove, covering the whole of the area in under half an hour. Then he went out of the village, and drove along the road that went by the side of the memorial. The green fields were now dark in the rain, the white crosses, row on row, gleaming in the low, grey light.

Devon pulled up in the little dirt parking lot, and left the engine running. He left the wipers going as they made little French sounding noises, *ksit-ksit*, as they wiped the rain from the windshield. He could see the tall humps where the trenches began and, beyond that, all the way to the memorial. The cottage was concealed from view from this vantage point, though he could see the bit of smoke rise up from the chimney, as he'd left the heater on. The cottage would be quite warm when he got back, but it would be empty with no Stanley in residence. Unless Stanley had returned in his absence?

Devon raced the engine and drove through the village at too high a speed for safety in any weather. He tore along the road through the small wood, and came to a screeching halt in front of the cottage. Leaving the engine running again, he bolted inside.

All was quiet, except for the rain on the windows, the hum of the radiator, and the slow, soft feeling that he was going quite crazy. Because he was. Nobody came forward in time, or went backwards through it, it simply wasn't possible.

He got back in the car, and drove around and around, squinting through the rain, looking for Stanley, for that shorn head and those straight shoulders. He pictured Stanley marching resolutely in the rain toward a destiny that would save his friends, regardless of the cost to himself.

Devon drove, searching always, only stopping once to fill up on gas. When it got too dark, he drove back to the cottage, parked the car, and turned off the engine.

He was tired, but he needed to take care of himself so he could search again in the morning, though he didn't know where he would look that he'd not already looked. Common wisdom said that insanity was doing the same thing over and over but expecting different results, and if that were true, which it was, he was well on his way.

Once inside the cottage, he stripped out of his wet clothes. He took a hot shower, and thought about eating. Though he couldn't really manage it, he had some toast and cheese, and sat at the kitchen table, staring at his laptop.

He hadn't wanted to do any kind of internet search, but perhaps it was time and, besides, he was desperate. He reached for the laptop and flipped it open to turn it on. His fingers were faster than his thoughts, and he typed in the combination of words to bring up the list of the soldiers in the 44th Battalion.

It was a list he'd found over the summer while idly looking for the names of scouts. Apparently it had been a scout who'd discovered Commander Helmer's body in a ditch near the village where he'd been shot by the Germans. The scout, who'd had the unhappy responsibility of reporting this to Lt. Billings, had lived a long and happy life. He'd gone on to own a garage in Memphis, and had eventually made a web page about it.

For an elderly man who'd been born so long ago, his web page design skills had been admirable. However, the list had the look of having been done without any sense of clean web design. The page had a splotchy brown background that reminded Devon of the color of the uniforms; the links were a faded green and hard to see.

The page displayed a list that was alphabetical but was not marked in any other way; it was just a list of names. Thus there was no way to narrow his focus to the lance corporals or anything like that. He had to scan the list, and went straight to the S's. There was a Sullivan, but it was Wilifred Sullivan, not Stanley Sullivan. Could he be Devon's Stanley? There was no proof either way, as some of the names had links attached to them, but those led off to descriptions of the function of that soldier, and contained nothing personal about them. The list was almost useless.

Devon scanned the list again, and found an Isaac. Was this Stanley's friend? The name didn't have a link from anywhere else, so Devon couldn't do any further checks except to note that Isaac and Wilifred and the other soldiers had been part of the 44th Battalion.

Devon wrote down Isaac's full name in his canvas notebook, and wrote down Wilifred Sullivan as well, though there didn't seem to be much point in it or anything. He buried his face in his hands, a gusty sigh punctuating his sense of futility, of loss.

He'd *not* had breakfast with a phantom, nor talked and walked and drunk coffee with a ghost. Stanley had been there, in the cottage with Devon. Otherwise, the only alternative was that Devon was going crazy. He most certainly was not going to do that because he had a paper to finish. He shut down the search engine, opened his paper and grimly began to type, determined to focus on what needed to be done, rather than on Stanley, who might never have existed at all.

His eyes kept going to the door, his ears cocked for any sound of Stanley coming home. He started to type slower and slower, and finally, when it grew truly dark out, and his eyes were too tired to focus, Devon put his work away. He realized that this was with the half hope that Stanley would come to the door, and they'd need the table cleared in order to eat on it. To have something sweet to share afterwards.

But the only person who came and sat at the table for dinner was Devon. Though he tried to eat, every act was tinged with sadness, every motion he went through with loneliness. When he gave up eating, he cleaned up and built a small fire in the fireplace. He poured himself a small whiskey, sat on the couch, and stared at the flames that leaped orange and gold and flickered long shadows across the walls.

If only he'd taken a chance and told Stanley how he felt, how he was drawn to Stanley not just because he was, or might be, an American doughboy, but because of Stanley himself. Stanley listened when Devon talked and seemed to care about what Devon cared about.

Stanley had actually been in the war. Or maybe he'd been nice to

Devon because Stanley was a shyster. Maybe he was crazy. Maybe none of that mattered because it had come down to the point where Devon didn't care. It was literally a dark and stormy night, and Stanley was out in it. And whether he was halfway to Paris, or he was huddled in a trench in the rain with mud up to his ass in 1917, Devon just wanted him back.

If Stanley came back to him by some fluke of time, or a burst of consciousness where he confessed his game, Devon would take that chance. He would stand up and tell Stanley how he felt, and wrap him in a hug so warm and safe that Stanley would never want to leave. Then he'd get Stanley the help he needed, or the papers required to get him into the States.

He wanted Stanley with him, and if Stanley was shy about being with another man, then Devon would be patient, though he didn't think it would be that hard to convince Stanley that it was okay. There'd been an expression in those whiskey colored eyes, a sparkle of hope that what Devon had said about being gay in the future was true. Besides, Stanley had gone on and on about Isaac, protesting too much when Devon had asked about it. Stanley had cared about his fellow soldier, but had never dared do more than that, it seemed. And if Isaac was left behind in the past—

Devon made himself stop thinking this way because it was cruel to hope that Stanley would never have Isaac just so that Devon could have Stanley. It was selfish and it was single-minded and downright creepy. Here Devon was sitting on his couch watching the dying embers of a pitiful fire wishing Isaac, a dead soldier, would stay dead in the past so that Stanley could come home to him.

He had the suspicion that Wilifred Sullivan was his Stanley, and didn't wonder that he went by another name. War was full of nicknames, some which were intended to hide deadly weapons of mass destruction, others of which were merely whimsy, meant to inject humor into a humorless situation.

And if he was analyzing his thoughts to this degree, it was beyond the point where he could make any sense of any conclusion, so he needed to go to bed. He would search for Stanley in the morning. When he went to the front door, he made sure the porch light was on, in case Stanley found himself in the middle of the memorial and needed to see which way was home.

CHAPTER SEVENTEEN

Devon did everything he normally did to get ready for bed, but after hours of pitching and rolling, and finally sending the blankets to the floor, he got up, turned up the heat, and made himself a cup of coffee that he did not drink. He sat at the kitchen table, his hands curled around the quickly cooling cup, and stared at the ash in the fireplace.

His eyes felt gritty and he needed to shave, but what if he were in the bathroom and didn't hear Stanley's knock? And then he remembered why he'd not slept—he'd heard Stanley's voice calling out to him in the dark, shouting to warn him of incoming shells, or, in a very quiet way, asking Devon to come get him and bring him home.

When Devon closed his eyes, he saw the trenches as he'd always imagined them before, full of soldiers, some young, some old. All of them were way too practical about it as they walked in the mud, carrying tin mugs of coffee, and singing songs while they stood around a glowing primus fire. Their faces were alight, their shoulders touching in a firm, warm circle, brothers in arms, waiting for death.

Burying his face in his hands, Devon tried to stem the faint strains of *It's a Long Way to Tipperary* from buzzing in his ears, but he was so exhausted that it was too late to keep the streets from being gold and everybody from being gay—

"Get up, Devon," he told himself. "Drink some coffee and go and look for him. You know you want to."

He did, he most certainly did, even though when he went to the door to look out into the freezing rain, he realized that it was not yet dawn. The rain cast silver shadows in the porch light, making the white crosses, row on row, look like they were being slashed through with bayonet blades. It was as if the rain meant to dig up the bodies, most of them unidentified, and bid them to walk so they could get up and help Devon look for Stanley. The fact that Devon was thinking this was a sure sign he'd not gotten enough sleep and was halfway to the loony bin himself.

Would driving around in circles looking for Stanley help? No, probably not, and keeping the car for additional days would eat into his remaining savings and would not be covered by the stipend. Nor could he claim it as a necessary expense: miles covered looking for ghost at twenty five cents per mile would not go over well with the IRS. Regardless, he needed to return the car.

Devon waited until the sun came up, then put on his jacket, grabbed his keys, and drove slowly into the village. His tires splashed through puddles, and if he drove slowly because he was looking for Stanley, it couldn't be helped. He would also look as he walked back to the cottage, and that couldn't be helped either. At least it wasn't raining anymore.

The owner of the garage looked surprised to see Devon returning the car so quickly, though he shrugged and took the keys.

"You didn't keep it long, *monsieur*," said the owner. "I saw you speeding through the village yesterday, though. That wasn't smart."

"No," said Devon. "I shouldn't have, and it won't happen again."

"You were also seen skidding into the parking lot by the memorial. What if you had broken down the sign? It's been there since 1920, you know."

"I know," said Devon, and it was true. If anybody knew when that sign went up and all about the ceremony surrounding its creation, it was him. "I was just—"

He stopped short because he couldn't explain any of it, though there was a sudden danger that he would open his mouth and all of his troubles would come tumbling onto the shoulders of the garage owner, a perfect stranger who couldn't possibly understand what had happened. How Stanley had appeared out of nowhere. How he'd disappeared just as quickly, so quickly that Devon was beginning to believe he'd imagined the whole thing, and just as he was beginning to feel that had they been able to share another moment together, he and Stanley—

He was in love with Stanley. Stanley who was gone.

That feeling was cut off so sharply that the pain of it was sinking into his bones only now, as though held off by a sense of shock and of loss, long delayed and smacking into him with the force of a runaway truck.

"Are you all right, *monsieur*?" asked the garage owner, in a very kind way. "There are ghosts in that memorial, my sister says, and if you wander unawares—"

"He wasn't a ghost, for fuck's sake, he was *real*!"

The garage owner took a step back, and appeared to be about one minute away from calling *les gendarmes* to come and take Devon away. If that happened and Stanley came back, then he wouldn't have any way to reach Devon, wouldn't know where Devon had gone.

It struck Devon then that he was picturing himself renting out the cottage for the rest of his days and nights in the hope that Stanley would come back. When he did, Devon didn't want the cottage to be occupied by someone else, or worse, deserted, as it must have looked to Stanley in the war, an empty hull with no life inside.

"I'm sorry," said Devon. "I'm tired, that's all. I've been taught better manners, so I'm sorry."

"*Ce n'est rien, monsieur*," said the garage owner with a jerk of his chin. "But please go away now."

Devon obliged him. He walked through the village with his hands in his pockets and his collar turned up against the chill, his feet thudding against the damp blacktop with every step. He kept his eyes peeled for Stanley, but that didn't make any sense because Stanley was gone. Gone back into the past where Devon couldn't find him, couldn't pull him close and hold him.

His dazed brain now believed that Stanley had been a time traveler. Why? Why now? Because he knew he wasn't going crazy, he couldn't be. The memories were too real, and his heart ached too much with missing Stanley. He had to be real.

As Devon approached the cottage and saw smoke from the chimney he had a sudden, bright, almost painful hope that Stanley had returned.

He opened the door to the completely empty cottage, and realized that he'd left the radiators going, wasting energy on the walls, on the empty rooms. There was only the cottage and Devon and a pile of papers that represented his work of two years. After which he would go back to the States and his perfectly normal life as a professor.

Never ever would he be able to tell anyone about his doughboy, his soldier, his Stanley. And never before in his life had he wanted to cry so hard.

But he couldn't cry; soldiers didn't cry so he wouldn't. He needed to finish his paper, needed to be doing something; otherwise, he'd stare at the walls or throw open the curtains or stand in the open doorway watching the damp wind whip the trees.

Which is exactly what he did now, imagining that Stanley would come home to him as he looked out over the green humped trenches. The view, once exciting to him was now desolate with the mist hanging low, a grey shroud on a hopeless terrain that, lifeless, gave nothing to Devon, not even hope. Finally, he closed the door and made himself get to work, unsure of whether he would search again later or just pack his bags and get the hell out of there.

CHAPTER EIGHTEEN

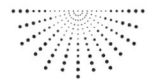

Dust and ash continued to fall, sifting down to the mud to be absorbed there in the footprints along the bottom of the trench. Lt. Billings reached out to the radio, one hand above the broken casing where a cake-shaped hunk of shrapnel had dug itself into the metal and wood. Just as he reached out, the shrapnel dislodged itself and tumbled into the mud with a splat.

As the lieutenant kicked the smoking metal away, Stanley looked at Isaac and the others and they looked at him, their eyes wide. Then Stanley turned back to the lieutenant, waiting to see what he would do.

Stanley had the sickening feeling that he should have known to save the radio, too. That if he'd moved the radio to the left another two feet, it would have been saved as well. He should have known, but why did he think that? Why did he have the sensation that the responsibility for the fate of the battalion rested with him? Because it did.

He'd known about the mortar shell, when it would come, where it would land, and the damage it would cause. Vague memories of a conversation about this very occurrence lingered in the back of his mind. He could have saved everybody, but he'd only saved his friends, selfishly. Not like a true soldier, not like someone brave who would deserve a medal at the end of all of this. Not like someone who deserved a quiet moment in a well-lit room, eating supper with a handsome young man, followed by an orange all his own.

Suddenly, vividly, all the memories and images marched front and center, and he knew exactly what had happened to him. He'd been in the cottage, only it had been occupied by the history major—Devon—who typed quietly away while Stanley woke up at his leisure on the couch, the soft pillow beneath his head and the warm air on his face.

There were traces of Devon's touch on Stanley knees, and of the expression in his eyes when he'd helped Stanley by telling him to breathe, slowly, in and out. There was the memory of sitting with Devon at the sturdy kitchen table, talking about that guy who could predict the weather, a meteor-something. And the memory of Devon's nearness, how he smelled, sweet like soap, with his smooth, tanned skin, like he spent days in the sun, and the way his chin was dark with beard growth.

"Stanley."

Stanley looked up to see Isaac bending close, as though to catch a word with Stanley before the lieutenant could notice that Stanley was making small, pathetic noises of distress. This was good of Isaac because soon Stanley *would* be babbling out loud about Devon and how he'd fallen in love with a scholar who knew all about the war and exactly how and when it would end.

More, Devon had rescued Stanley from freezing to death in a soaked uniform. He had taken Stanley in and talked him through his fears and anxieties, and had fed him. And who, for all his muscles and health, had been a soft-hearted man writing a paper about a war that he felt had been senseless.

"I'm fine," said Stanley, though he was anything but.

He sat up and spread his fingers across his cheeks as though wiping away the spray of ash from the mortar shell. Except his face was a little wet and the ash turned into streaks like black paint, as though he was about to step into the dark and needed to be disguised.

"What are we going to do about the radio?" Stanley asked to

distract everyone from his tears. "How is he going to call for retreat orders now?"

"He's going to call for retreat?" asked Isaac. Behind him, Bertie and Rex straightened up, staring at Stanley as though he was the second coming. "How do you know? Lt. Billings is in the bunker and we can't possibly hear him."

"I *can't* hear him," said Stanley as quickly as he could. "But that's what I'd do."

"Like you've had officer's training." Isaac made a friendly, scoffing sound.

How could Stanley know about the retreat? Because he'd lived through this morning already. Whether or not he'd been with Devon at a time when the cottage had been repaired and there were, once more, pastry shops in the nearby village, he'd already experienced the mortar shell, the explosion, and the death of his friends.

After which, Lt. Billings had determined they needed to retreat, as the Germans were getting too close and the battalion was running out of everything—he'd forgotten that from before—the reason they needed to retreat was because they were low on supplies. Even more important, the Germans had gotten a lock on their position and the bombs were exploding on target each and every time.

Another half a day and the Germans would be right on top of them. The whole battalion would be sacrificed to the war on account of a radio that had been in the wrong place at the right time. And all because Stanley had been focused on his friends and not on the bigger picture. He'd saved Isaac and the others so that he wouldn't be alone, rather than saving the whole battalion, which had been his mission in the first place. The reason he'd run along the bottom of the trenches to deliver the message.

He should have grabbed the radio, and maybe it would still be intact enough for the lieutenant to send out a signal and get one in return. Then within half an hour, the entire battalion would be packing up and heading over the back of the trench and beyond the frosty fields to safety.

Except now the retreat wouldn't be called in time because Stanley had failed. He didn't deserve the bit of happiness he'd found with Devon, in a world that was quiet and still and warm. Where there was food and hot water aplenty, and space and time to just sit and think. Where young men could have affection for—and fall in love with—other young men, or anybody they fancied. Even if that young man was a scholarly student tapping away at a bit of folded metal, his eyes on his work, but his attention on the fellow just waking up on his couch.

Devon had always been aware of Stanley, though he'd excused it as being interested in the uniform, Stanley's kit, the puttees. Instead, his eyes had gone to Stanley, time and again, a soft, gentle smile on his face.

While he'd apologized, embarrassed, for his obsession with the war, the first war, Stanley couldn't imagine chiding him for it, or becoming bored because Devon's eyes had lit up. When he would confirm this fact or that idea, he would smile as though he had something exciting to share. Stanley didn't like to think about those friends of his who'd grown exasperated or bored with Devon's favorite subject because they were missing out. Stanley would be happy to listen to him rattle on about uniforms and trenches and maps and escarpments until the end of time.

"Men," said Lt. Billings between the pounding sounds of mortar shells being launched. He made the gesture that they were to remain as they were, seated in a row, protected from the mud and damp by a bit of borrowed canvas. "The radio is broken, and I need someone to carry a message for retreat."

"Retreat, sir?" asked Isaac with a sideways glance at Stanley.

"Yes," said Lt. Billings. "The Germans are close and getting closer, and I need someone to go."

It was on the tip of Stanley's tongue, as it had been the last time, that in this dire situation where Commander Helmer had deserted in the night, if the lieutenant had assumed command on his own say-so, then he could call for retreat without permission, too. Lives would be saved, and precious time gained, for a retreat was a clumsy business, never smooth or orderly like it was described in the manual.

Time had folded in on itself. The morning was repeating as though to give Stanley a second chance. If time allowed him to be with Devon again, he would take that chance. If he could, if he ever could, he would tell Devon how he felt, he would take a chance at love instead of being afraid all the time.

"I'll go," said Stanley. He stood up. Isaac's hands reached to pull him back to the muddy, canvas-covered bench. "I'll take the message, sir."

"No, Stanley," said Isaac, desperation in his voice. "Somebody else should go, somebody faster."

He didn't mean that Stanley wasn't a fast runner; he meant that he didn't want *Stanley* to go because he cared for him, in spite of the fact that it was terribly illegal to have such feelings. If Stanley didn't come back from his mission, Isaac would mourn the loss. But what Isaac and the others didn't know was that if Stanley didn't come back there would be no battalion, and nobody to mourn for him anyway.

He couldn't tell Isaac that, couldn't tell anybody what had happened to him because they wouldn't believe him. Devon hadn't believed him, at least at first. He'd hardly believed it himself because all of it could have been some fear-induced dream. Except that Devon had been as real to Stanley as Isaac or anybody.

Stanley ached with missing the wonderful passion that filled Devon's face and spilled over his hands as he soothed Stanley with his fingertips. He was willing to do anything if it meant there was a chance that he could be with Devon in a world were love, no matter the shape, was *legal*.

"I'll go," said Stanley again.

"I need you to take the message and bring the rest of the retreat code back, as quick as you can, yes?"

"Yes, sir," said Stanley.

Lt. Billings gestured that Stanley should follow him into the bunker, and when Stanley stepped into the shell of mud-capped air, he cast a glance over his shoulder. Had this been before—before he'd met Devon—he might have been pleased with the looks of awe on his friends' faces, and a little cocky that he'd been invited into the bunker for a secret, man-to-man chat with the lieutenant.

With the taste of ash in his mouth, Stanley went up to the table where the map was and waited while the lieutenant tugged at one edge of it. Stanley looked at the map and did his best to pretend he'd never seen it before.

The last time, the lieutenant had been standing with the map in his hand, in the trench, just outside the door of the bunker. Stanley wondered why it was different this time, and why he was so calmly comparing the two, as if it had actually happened, as if he'd actually gone forward in time. But he must have done, otherwise, how would he have all these memories in his head?

There was more at stake. His friends' lives, the survival of the 44th Battalion, and most of all, being with Devon. It didn't matter where the memories had come from. Stanley was going to put them to good use for the greater good, and for Devon. For the chance at being with Devon once more.

Lt. Billings tapped the map with his finger, made sure that Stanley was paying attention, then traced the length of a wobbly line.

Stanley knew everything about the map because Devon had shown it to him and explained what everything meant. Even as the lieutenant was talking and pointing, Stanley knew that the dark brown lines were the trenches, and the small green and blue X's were various weaponry. Green X's were howitzers, and blue ones were rifles. The one gold cross was for the chaplain's station, and the circles of various colors indicated the mess area, the latrine, the bunkers for sleeping, the ramps to the supply caches.

"It's a death sentence, you know that," said Lt. Billings. "But you need to find the major and bring the code for retreat back or we're all going to die in this trench."

With a tap on the map, the lieutenant brought Stanley's focus to the area in the corner, where the major was holed up. Right on the edge of the map was a cross with a faint circle over it to indicate the bombed out church. Nestled beside it was the little cottage whose roof was falling in and whose walls were none too steady.

Stanley didn't let himself look at that, or think about Devon and the studious atmosphere that Devon had created with his work. Or think of how Devon had fed him and made him feel safe. Or how Devon had looked at him with that light in his eyes, as though Stanley was the most amazing thing he'd ever seen.

"Tell him I sent you," said Lt. Billings. "Here's your rifle, in case you meet up with any Jerries, and a canteen of water because your mouth will be so dry with fear that you'd drink out of a puddle just so you can spit."

"Yes, sir." Stanley took the rifle and slung the band over one shoulder, then took the canteen, which he slung over the other shoulder. Just as he turned to face the open doorway, where his friends were waiting to see what would happen next, he felt Lt. Billings' hand on his shoulder.

"Follow the length of the trench and stay low along the bottom," said the lieutenant.

Stanley nodded, though he knew better. Devon had said the damp weather had caused the air to be quite dense, which in turn had caused the mustard gas to sink quite low. Stanley had a chance to get to the major but only if he disobeyed orders. He would go along the top of the trenches, in spite of the risk of gunfire, because if there were any gas in the air, it would tumble to his feet, and he would be impervious to its effects.

He couldn't tell that to the lieutenant. He couldn't tell his friends, either, as he stepped out of the bunker and they gathered to wish him well. His body felt numb to their pats of reassurance and to Isaac's quick embrace. Everything fell silent as though the sound had been turned down on the radio. A low hum built up in his ears as he bid them all goodbye. He hefted his rifle and began walking along the bottom of the trench.

When Stanley rounded the first curve, he clambered to the top and began to run. Lt. Billings might see him or he might not, but Stanley was too far away for more orders, too far away to be stopped. He was on his own now, running along the top of the trench. The soldiers he passed seemed to understand his mission, that the code for retreat was being gathered. They fired off shots from their rifles to distract the enemy so that Stanley could keep running without fear.

He ran until his lungs hurt, but with the map in his head, his destination was quite clear this time. He wouldn't get lost or take a wrong turn because he knew where he was going, knew exactly where the command bunker was, thanks to Devon and his map. Devon who had unknowingly given Stanley all the information he needed to save every man in the 44th Battalion. It was as if Devon was helping him, and though he was far away in time, his voice was steady in Stanley's ears.

He ran on, imagining what the war memorial would look like if nobody died. But then he heard the zing of metal in the air and the ripping pop of a canister just above his head.

He looked up and tumbled into a trench. With the next breath he was inhaling it, the acrid taste of chemicals soaking into him from the inside. It burned and filled his body and his lungs, seared his eyes.

Stanley fell to his knees, spitting up, green mucus trailing in the mud as he braced himself with his hands, gasping for air as he sank down into the earth. The blackness took him just as it had before, with hard arms and a fierce intensity, a live thing riddled with animosity and hatred and fear. His whole body cried out with loss. He had failed. Again.

CHAPTER NINETEEN

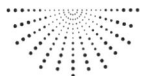

Stanley awoke with a gasp, inhaling dirt and grass, and found himself face down in a frost covered field, surrounded by white crosses, row on row. There was a barrier of trees that held back the sky, rattling their leafless branches as a wind picked up and whistled through the air. Grey clouds tumbled towards the earth, and it was cold, as cold as the trench he'd fallen into, except he was here, amidst the memorial for the 44th Battalion.

For a moment, he was quite still. He could not believe what had happened. What might have happened. Was he back where Devon was, in that future time? For all he knew, he was years too late or too early, but it seemed to be the same terrain as he'd held in his memories about Devon. Maybe time had granted him the gift of arriving at just the *right* time.

Crushed by desperation, he pushed himself to his feet and rubbed his eyes, then bent to pick up his rifle and his canteen. Devon would want to examine them, to include notes on them in his paper, and if the universe were kind, there would be a Devon to give them to. Stanley could watch him examine them with strong and careful hands. His eyes would light up as he talked about them, and then he would look at Stanley and smile.

Stanley took off running, canteen banging against his thigh, his rifle rattling. The cottage was in sight, though it looked silent and still. There was a growing wind that took Stanley's breath away and seemed to threaten his every step, as if it meant to take him back to the muddy trench and the smell of smoke and death. Back to the war. Stanley ran faster, right up to the door of the cottage.

His heart surging with hope, he raised his hand to knock, just in case it wasn't Devon inside. The door flew open and Devon was there. He flung his arms around Stanley and pulled him close and hugged him tight.

Stanley quickly propped the rifle and flung the canteen aside, and hugged Devon right back. He stood as close as he could to Devon's body, feeling the heat of him all up and down as warm air drifted through the open door. He squirmed to get even closer, his mouth open with everything he wanted to say to tell Devon how he felt.

"My god, Stanley," said Devon as he pulled back to look at him, his hands warm and sure on Stanley's arms.

Devon kissed him on the cheek, quick and brief, and drew him into the cottage. He did not let go of Stanley, but with one hand he picked up the rifle to look at it. Stanley picked up the canteen, allowing himself to be drawn into the peace and quiet of the cottage. There was a fire flickering in the stone-lined fireplace, and a sprawl of papers on the kitchen table.

"You've been gone for days," said Devon. He took the canteen and placed it and the rifle on the table, not paying attention that several pieces of paper drifted to the floor. "*Days*, Stanley."

"It was only an hour," said Stanley, feeling somewhat faint, as though he'd not eaten in ages, nor slept, nor had any peace. But Devon's touch grounded him, letting him know that he was safe.

"I saw you go," said Devon. He turned to Stanley and held his face, shaking his head. "With my own eyes."

"Saw me go?" asked Stanley.

"When I was taking the pictures, and turned on the flash—"

"It was like bombs were exploding in front of my eyes—"

"You turned like you were stepping through a doorway, an opening. I swear, I fucking swear, I could see the trench behind you, and the edge of the opening to the bunker, and the radio, I saw the *fucking radio—*"

"The radio's broken," said Stanley, horrified that there was a crack in his voice, as though he'd been split wide open with the realization of it. "I didn't make it through."

"You're here now," said Devon, all of his attention on Stanley, his arms around Stanley's waist. "You're here now and you're going to stay here. With me."

"I don't want to go back." Stanley trembled with the idea of it, of going back to the battlefield with the trenches and the mud and the exploding shells—and of leaving Devon, which would hurt most of all. "Ever. I want to stay here with you."

"And I want you to stay," said Devon. "So don't leave, okay?"

There was that word again. The way Devon used it bolstered him up, though Stanley swayed a little on his feet, feeling faint and hungrier than he'd ever been in his life. Devon had said he'd been gone days, though it had only been an hour to Stanley. Back in the trenches they'd long since finished their biscuits and coffee, and then Isaac had said—

"You're nothing like Isaac," said Stanley.

"Isaac?" asked Devon. "The one you liked, right?"

"Yes."

Isaac and Devon couldn't be more different, for Isaac was brimming with flyboy charm, and Devon was studious and intense. They seemed to care about Stanley in the same way, though if he were here, now, and wanted to be with Devon, was that being disloyal to Isaac?

"I never told him," said Stanley, startling himself with the realization. "Though even if I had, it never would have made a difference."

"Maybe it would have, but I'm glad you're here with me," said Devon. He hadn't yet let go of Stanley, and his embrace was warm and sure. "It's hard to live with regret, that I know. Never mind that, are you hungry? I haven't been to the store. I didn't want to leave in case you came back, but I have a frozen pizza I could heat up. Then we could go to the store, and you could see the village."

Stanley nodded, though he didn't know what a pizza was, except maybe it was something that Bertie had mentioned, that boys from the Italian neighborhoods would eat.

He felt as though he could fall asleep standing up. Devon brought him clean clothes and directed him to the bathroom, where Stanley went through the same ritual as before, taking off his uniform carefully so Devon could look at it while he showered. He knew all about the taps, now, and which was the hot water and which was the cold, so his shower took no time at all and, besides, he would rather be with Devon.

He got dressed in the clothes that Devon had given him and picked up his uniform from outside the door where he'd left it, a little surprised that Devon hadn't already unfolded the garments and spread them out so he could take notes about them. Instead, Devon was at the table, busy gathering up the papers that had fallen, collecting them into a pile with the others, and folding the metal—the laptop—so that it became even thinner.

He placed a large round circle of hot pizza on a wooden board and sliced through it with a circular blade.

"Come on while it's hot," said Devon. "I've got milk and I've got beer, so let me know."

"Milk," said Stanley. He was so grateful when Devon handed him a glass that he drank down half in one gulp.

CHAPTER TWENTY

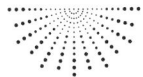

As Devon watched Stanley eat, shoving slices of pizza into his mouth till his cheeks bulged, he was reminded of a feral cat the guys in his dorm had found in a snowstorm. They'd fed the cat, left trays of dried food and fresh water in the alley all for a lark, though Devon privately thought that every one of them had serious intentions of being kind.

This had gone on for weeks, each guy trying to outdo the other by leaving toys, or catnip, or open cans of the most expensive cat food. Finally, one of the girls on the co-ed floor who was moving into her own apartment caught the cat in a box, took it home, and the last time Devon had seen it, it had been a sassy and sleek tiger-striped cat, sleeping in the sun on the arm of a couch.

Stanley should be that comfortable and happy, should be able to eat without looking over his shoulder. He should be able to have a second and, yes, third glass of milk without acting like he thought it would be his last treat until the end of time. Stanley should be sleek and well-petted and loved and at home, home with Devon.

When Devon opened his mouth to say something about it, it felt a little abrupt and too soon. He promised himself that before too long, he would be telling Stanley how he felt and about second chances and about saying things when you thought them. Also about love and about Stanley coming home with Devon to the States.

"Do you want to tell me what happened?" asked Devon. Not so much because he was desperate to get more information about the time period, though that was always interesting. More because Stanley was looking at him with large eyes, that deep whiskey color, his mouth curved as though he wanted to speak, but didn't know what Devon might like to hear. "Just to get it off your mind, you know?"

After a long pause, a hectic flush on his cheeks, Stanley began to tell the story. About how he'd found himself in the past, in that same morning, but earlier, before the bomb had exploded. How his friends had looked at him while trying not to listen when, in the command bunker, Lt. Billings discussed the issue of Commander Helmer's desertion. About how Isaac, Rex, and Bertie had all survived the shelling because he'd gotten them to move in time, though he'd neglected to save the radio. How Stanley had gone to discuss the issue of retreat, and how the lieutenant had needed the second half of the code. How the map showed Stanley the better path to take. How Isaac had practically begged Stanley not to go.

"But it was different this time," said Stanley slowly, drawing out the words as though drawing out a half-forgotten memory. "We said almost the same things, and did *some* of the same things, but it was different, though the outcome was exactly the same."

"How was it different?" asked Devon. He didn't understand any of what had happened, and he was horrified at the thought of Stanley having to relive that all over again.

"Well, before," said Stanley. "Before I was alone in the trench in front of the radio while Lt. Billings tried to get it to work. There was a piece of howitzer muzzle jammed into the mud behind me, and nobody else was around. The second time the chaplain was there, along with a scout, I think, and the supply sergeant. My friends were alive, and there was no howitzer muzzle. The radio still got busted though."

Devon got up and cleared the dishes, nodding at Stanley to let him know he was thinking about what Stanley had just said and not ignoring it.

He made them both some coffee in the French press. When he sat down at the table to drink his, he saw that Stanley didn't seem to want any. Maybe he was too full or too distracted. Probably a little of both.

Devon didn't press it. Instead, he drank his coffee black with just a little bit of the brown sugar, moved his chair closer to Stanley's so their shoulders were touching, and waited the silence out. Stanley could have all the time he needed, if he would just stay with Devon.

"The conversation was pretty much the same," said Stanley into the silence. "We all said the same things about Commander Helmer's desertion, and meant the same things, but we said them from different places in the trench. The chaplain was there, and the scout who had gone out to reconnoiter for Commander Helmer. Then there was the lead commander—"

Stanley stopped and lifted his hand in the air as though pointing out the lead commander, and Devon could almost see it take shape in front of him.

"The chaplain was standing there talking to Lt. Billings, and I think it was about our weapons supply. All those officers were all in the bunker together, though I know it hadn't happened that way the first time. But how would I know I'd not seen that before unless there'd been a *before?*"

"Because there'd been a before?" asked Devon. "Maybe you're remembering both versions, just like I'm remembering you being here the first time?"

He shook his head; it was all too much quantum physics for him to manage. He was just a history student with an obsession about World War I, a huge piece of which was sitting right in front of him: an American doughboy in the flesh. Who, as Devon could plainly see, was falling asleep at the table, his belly full of food, his mind full of an experience he could not comprehend.

"You look tired, Stanley," said Devon. He put his hand on the table next to Stanley's hand, close enough so that their pinkies touched.

"Like last time," said Stanley. He didn't take his hand away, but instead moved it closer. "I remember I could barely keep my eyes open and it's happening again."

"Coming through time must be tiring," said Devon, and though he was worried about how exhausted Stanley was, he was smiling, too, because Stanley was here with him.

"You could take a nap on the couch," said Devon, now. "I'll watch over you, make sure you don't go anywhere."

What Devon meant was that he would watch over to make sure Stanley didn't go backwards in time, though he had no idea how to manage that. What he *really* meant was that he wanted to watch over Stanley forever, to keep him safe and near, and help him forget about the war, which was, in its own way, one of the most ironic things he'd ever considered. His dearest wish was to help a young man forget the exact same thing that Devon had been obsessing over since he could remember.

Stanley got up, nodding, his borrowed clothes hanging off him in the same way that they had before. This time, he seemed less an object of study and more a real person wanting care, which Devon intended to give him.

He turned up the heat and grabbed the bedding from the closet, the same bedding Stanley had used before that he'd so carefully put away, and made up the couch. Stanley shuffled over and slithered in between the sheets. On impulse, Devon sat in the space near Stanley's waist and took his hand, which Stanley gave to him to hold, his whiskey colored eyes blinking with a little bit of surprise.

"I'm glad the map helped," said Devon, "and that your friends survived."

"Thank you," said Stanley. "I didn't want to ask, but would you sit for a while with me?"

"Yes," said Devon. "Of course, I'm happy to."

He wanted to say more than that, all the things he'd been thinking about that he'd say if Stanley came back. Only he couldn't say them now, for they might overload Stanley, cause him distress. He'd been through enough, and all Devon wanted to do was look after him.

Worst of all, he didn't want to point out that although Isaac, Rex,

Bertie, and a whole host of others might have survived the mortar shell explosion that morning, they'd not, ultimately, survived the German attack. They'd been outmanned, outgunned, out-supplied. Not to mention that the 44th Battalion had been made up of young, inexperienced men who'd enlisted just at the point when the Americans had entered the war with no idea what they were getting into and no idea how to get out of it. Except by following the rules, which Lt. Billings had diligently done to the demise of the entire battalion.

Wanting to lighten his own thoughts, as well as tender Stanley into sleep, Devon patted Stanley's hand and smiled as Stanley opened his sleepy eyes to look at him. Devon felt a surge of pleasure to have Stanley back with him, where they could be this way, quiet and content together.

"Is your first name really Wilifred?" asked Devon. He smiled a little wider when Stanley groaned and pretended to be glum that Devon now knew, his mouth moving into a lovely pout, his whole expression very put-upon. "I looked for you on the list because there was no trace of you in the cottage. I wanted to be sure that you really existed and that I wasn't going crazy."

Gone unsaid were Devon's faint but lingering doubts that Stanley had somehow come across the information about the war and used it to torment Devon, though Devon had had a difficult time finding the list of names himself, and he knew where to look. Stanley didn't, and probably nobody else in the world knew or cared about that list, except the person who'd made it.

"It is," said Stanley, solemnly as though confessing. "I hate the name Wilifred. Stanley was the name of a boxer I read about in a magazine. He knocked out Jack Johnson in 1909, and I thought he was swell, all the fellows did, but I did the most. I guess I talked about him a lot, so that was my nickname. Been mine ever since."

Stanley smiled at him, sleepy and warm, but then his forehead crinkled and he tugged on Devon's hand to get his attention.

"What did you mean, no trace of me?" asked Stanley. "I must have left a track of mud a mile wide when I came in that first time."

"It was funny, strange, you know?" said Devon. "You were gone, and I'd already put away the bedding, so there was no trace of you having slept on the couch. I thought I was going crazy because everywhere I looked, if I could imagine that you'd used a mug or a washcloth, it was just as easy to explain it away that I'd used those things. And the pictures I took, they were just black blobs, except for the last one, which was a bright white blob."

"None of them were of me?" asked Stanley.

"No, none," said Devon. "They were just pictures of blurs. The only thing—the *only* thing—that could prove you'd been here, and it wasn't very much, was the scrape in the plaster from the bayonet on your rifle."

Stanley stirred beneath the blanket, as though he wanted to get up and do something about it, like leave traces of himself all throughout the cottage. There was nothing he could have done differently, nothing anybody could have done, so Devon soothed him with long pets to his arm, tucking in the covers. He traced his fingers along the side of Stanley's face, a long, slow gesture meant to be calming, but which opened Stanley's eyes, though he looked exhausted.

"I have a second chance to get it right, this time," said Stanley. "I have a chance to be brave. With you."

It sounded as though Stanley meant being brave about the war, rather than about coming into the future and facing the unknown. Except he gripped Devon's hand in his and pulled it up to tuck beneath his chin.

"I mean about—" Then Stanley stopped, as if the words and the thoughts behind it were too much. "Having a second chance."

"Yes," said Devon. He wanted to say all the things he'd been feeling, but he tempered it because the last thing Stanley needed was for Devon to unload all of that when Stanley had just been through a harrowing ordeal that the last time had killed his friends.

"I'm glad you're back," Devon said. "I'm glad you're here with me because now I have a second chance, too." He carefully spread his hand so his fingers were over Stanley's, and his palm rested over the hollow in Stanley's shoulder. "You should get some rest, and then we'll go from there, okay?"

For some reason, this question made Stanley smile, but he obediently closed his eyes, and Devon waited with him while he fell asleep.

CHAPTER TWENTY-ONE

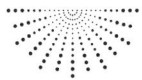

Stanley woke up on the couch where he'd fallen asleep. He realized that he could hear the sound of rain pattering against the thick windows as if fighting to come in the warm room with them. The fireplace was filled with low flickers of light, and at the kitchen table stood Devon. He had his arms crossed on his chest and he was looking down at the canteen with a scowl, as if attempting to decipher it.

When he saw that Stanley was awake, he uncrossed his arms and, smiling, came over to the couch.

"Did I wake you?" asked Devon. "I didn't mean to."

"I don't want to leave again," said Stanley with a croak as he sat up, pushing back the sheet and blanket.

"I don't want you to either," said Devon.

As he rubbed his eyes with the heel of his hand, Stanley struggled with the wave of dizziness that threatened to put him out flat on the couch, and clutched at the sheet.

He wanted Devon near him. He wanted Devon's warm steadiness. He wanted the weight of him on the couch so they could be together that way, even if just for a little while, in case the forces that had brought him out of the war suddenly decided to take him back to it.

None of this was real anyway, so it would be okay if he wanted what he wanted.

"Devon," Stanley said, a little desperate and a little vulnerable. He spread his fingerers across the edge of the blanket and tapped it. The gestured turned into a *pat-pat-paaaat* motion, which he hoped Devon would understand because he couldn't for the life of him articulate what he felt just then.

Devon's eyebrows flew up, black curves in his forehead, though instead of being shocked and drawing back, he seemed pleased. He sat down next to Stanley with enough haste that it threatened to knock Stanley over.

"I just wanted," said Stanley, attempting to start to say what he felt needed saying. Except he didn't know how to stop it rising up within his breast, didn't know how to say it out loud. He wanted a nameless, formless thing, a sense of expectation and need filling him.

But he didn't have to. Devon curled his arms around Stanley, warm through his thin cotton t-shirt, and pulled Stanley to him. Against Devon's broad chest, his eyes half closed, Stanley titled his head back with a wordless sigh. He felt a hand cupping his chin, Devon's strong hand, warm and gentle, and opened his eyes.

There was a question on Devon's face, a look of asking, and if Stanley said no, then Devon would move away. He didn't want Devon to move away, didn't want to be separated from Devon ever again, so he nodded. And then Devon kissed him.

It was not the forceful pushy motion that Stanley had experienced at the Bon Voyage dance. The army had organized the dance before they'd shipped out, where, to the rousing tunes of *Pack Up Your Troubles,* Stanley had his first kiss. The girl had been one of the blowsy types. She had been energetic and friendly, though her kisses had tasted of wax. Stanley had told nobody that he'd not enjoyed it, but instead had smiled at the jokes and the shoulder punches and nodded that yes, it had been the best fun.

All of that memory was nothing compared to the warmth of Devon's plush mouth, the tender moisture, the sense of Devon's breath on his skin. The feel of Devon's heartbeat speeding up in his chest, so close to Stanley's heart. And the way Devon held him as he kissed him, a bulwark against the fear of the unknown thing that was yanking him back and forth through time. Nothing could get at him, nothing could *take* him if Devon were near, of that he was sure.

He leaned into the embrace, sliding his arms around Devon's waist. He felt quite bold, shaking all over, for never before had he held another man with such an intent as he had, to get even closer, to somehow touch Devon's skin.

"Can I, Stanley, can I?" asked Devon, his voice rough, and Stanley realized that Devon was shaking too.

Not understanding what Devon wanted, but willing to give him everything, Stanley nodded, opening his eyes all the way so that he could watch what Devon was doing. Not because he was worried or needed to keep track, but so that he could memorize this moment and store it in his heart forever.

Devon took both of his hands and reached down to slide them up under Stanley's t-shirt. The motion, the sudden contact, took away Stanley's breath, but he was glad to lose it if he had this, Devon's hands on his belly as they curved upwards, tracing the line of his ribs, circling around his waist. Every movement tickled him a bit, but it was good, so good, to have Devon's hands there.

Stanley held very still, wondering, his whole body at attention, as to where else Devon's hands might go. Except that was a very wicked thought. Folks who weren't married didn't have relations, and especially not two *fellows*, whose mother neither of them had ever met, nor were likely to—all of a sudden, Stanley moved forward and flung his arms around Devon's neck, pressing close to his chest, causing Devon's hands to go all the way around his waist, sliding over bare skin.

"Can I touch you anywhere?" asked Devon, his breath warm on Stanley's neck.

"I'm not a girl," said Stanley, a little shy as his mind filled with all the places that Devon might touch him. "You don't have to ask."

"Doesn't matter," said Devon, and Stanley felt him smile. "No means no, and yes means yes, period."

He seemed so adamant about it that Stanley smiled in return. He tipped his neck, though without actually saying yes, Devon wasn't going to do anything else.

"Yes," Stanley said. "Yes, a hundred times, but I don't know what to do—"

Devon pulled back, his face flushed as he looked at Stanley with serious eyes. For a moment, he thought that Devon was going to stop altogether. His hands remained on Stanley's waist, though, and he didn't actually move away, so maybe it would be okay.

"Have you never—?" asked Devon. "Wait, are you a virgin?"

"I do know how to use my right hand," said Stanley, a sudden blush warming his cheeks. "I'm not a virgin *that* way."

"But you've never been with anybody, never been kissed."

"I've been kissed by the girl at the dance hall when we shipped out," said Stanley, somewhat defensively.

"Before the war?" asked Devon. His eyes lit up. Stanley could see that he wanted to get out his laptop and start taking notes about the dance hall, about the girl, about what it was like to be shipped to a foreign land to fight and die for one's country. Stanley was tempted to start whistling *It's a Long, Long Way to Tipperary*. Except that would distract Devon even more, and focus his attention in a direction other than Stanley.

Devon shook his head, as if shaking off his thoughts about his paper and his degree. Then he smiled at Stanley, looking a little chagrined.

"You wanted to take notes just then, didn't you," said Stanley, teasing because he could.

"I did," said Devon. "But it can wait till later."

It could wait till forever because Stanley didn't want to talk about the war anymore, although Devon, buried in a pile of paper and being excited about his notes, was terribly endearing. But not now, not just now.

Stanley leaned forward, sliding into Devon's embrace, and tipped his neck sideways, the ID tag moving to a new place on his skin so the metal felt cool.

"Please kiss me," Stanley said, the words coming out breathless. "Kiss me anywhere, touch me anywhere, I'm saying yes, do you hear? *Yes.*"

The yes turned into a soft sound that came up from the middle of Stanley's chest as Devon kissed him along the length of his neck. The sudden prospect of hands upon him that were not his own made his heart race. In the middle of his head was a space of quiet expectation, a waiting place, as if he'd been preparing for this moment all of his life. That through all the intervening years since the moment of his birth there'd been the knowledge that he'd be with Devon just like this.

Devon kissed Stanley on the neck again and then drew back to ease him onto the couch so he could kiss his mouth then circle his waist with strong arms and cover him with the weight of his body. Surround him with warmth. Still him into quiet with the force of his attention, which was so very focused that Stanley almost felt on display. He would have been startled when Devon began undoing the fastenings on the borrowed blue jeans, except that Devon's hand was so very gentle.

When Stanley opened his eyes, Devon's eyes were also open, and soft, and his eyebrows were raised as if he was watching Stanley and making sure of him.

"I missed you," said Devon, softly. "I missed you *every* day you were gone. I looked for you, all over. I even called *les gendarmes* in a panic, except they were worse than useless—"

"I'm here now," said Stanley. It made him feel strong to be the one to comfort Devon, strong and powerful. He surged up to grab Devon to pull him down so that Devon's body was all the way on top of Stanley. "Go on with what you were doing."

Devon huffed out a laugh and buried his face in Stanley's neck; his ink dark hair was silky on Stanley's skin, and smelled sweet. Devon's scent was warm and salty and filled Stanley with the sense that all was right with the world now, now that he was with Devon. Like this. On the couch with his t-shirt rucked up and Devon's hand at the waistband of his borrowed underwear.

It was good that Devon's hand was steady because it seemed to take a long time till it was all the way to where it ought to go, under the waistband and along the curve of Stanley's belly. There, where it tangled briefly in Stanley's pubic hair and circled around Stanley's cock.

Stanley took a sharp breath because Devon's hand was cool against the heat of his skin as he stroked and tugged, an urgency sharpening Devon's breath in his ear. When Devon raised himself up, pushing Stanley's underwear and blue jeans all the way down his legs. He eased his knee between Stanley's thighs, pushing them apart, rendering him open and helpless and lush as blissful tingles swept through him.

Stanley closed his eyes and let the feelings take him where they would. They rose up from his belly, clenching and unclenching inside his chest as he succumbed to the loopy, heady sensation of being brought close to pleasure without touching himself. His cock was as stiff as a rod, his spine swirling, sending little shocks inside his head. Devon's breath was in his ear, that hard knee between his legs, spread far enough so that Devon could stroke the length of his cock, pumping him, sliding up and down.

Suddenly Stanley's head jerked back and his hips jumped, pushing his cock hard into Devon's hand. Then Devon squeezed, just right, at the base, and Stanley came across the taunt skin of his belly.

With panting breaths, Devon settled next to Stanley. Stanley could feel Devon shoving into the space between Stanley and the back of the couch as he used Stanley's t-shirt to wipe at the come. Stanley didn't open his eyes right away to see any of this, but wallowed in the moment, at ease in a way that he'd not been since before the war. Before his Pa had gotten sick, before all of this had started, and the ill-realized dreams of the glory of war had not yet become the order of the day.

"How was that?" asked Devon, whispering in Stanley's ear, pulling Stanley away from the darker thoughts that seemed to be waiting at the edge of everything, as they always were.

"I've had better," said Stanley, smiling behind his closed eyes. "With my own hand, because you missed a spot."

"I did not," said Devon, insisting, whispering as he kissed Stanley's cheek and the corner of his mouth, tickling Stanley into a smile. "I didn't miss anything, not even how your breath quickened when I curled my fingers like this."

Devon reached down to cup Stanley's cock quite gently, now that Stanley's cock was soft against his belly. His fingers combed along the trail of hair that led down below Stanley's belly button. He pressed at the base of Stanley's cock, in the back where the flesh curved to become Stanley's balls. The touch was quite tender, and Devon stroked for a moment, then drew away.

"You like me touching you there, don't you. Just right there."

"Yes," said Stanley, a little breathless as his heart slowed. "I guess I do. Never had the patience to find out. Not when I had to be quick so the other fellows didn't find out what I was doing."

"They were probably doing the same," said Devon gravely, in a way that told Stanley that this was not something from a book or Devon's notes, but something Devon knew himself. "Or spending their money going to a red lamp district."

"We didn't have one," said Stanley. He opened his eyes and looked at Devon, who was concentrating on the path his hand was making on Stanley's belly. "The village was too small, and the fighting—well, there just wasn't any time."

"And you and Isaac never—"

"I never even told him." Stanley shook his head and reached to brush the dark hair back from Devon's forehead, in the hopes that Devon would look up at him. Which Devon did, his eyes green and dark. "I couldn't be sure of what he would say. I think he had a girl back home anyway, and besides, we both would have been shot. No court martial, just shot at dawn."

"Right," said Devon. "I keep forgetting that part. I'm only thinking that you might have been a little less lonely if you could have told him."

Stanley was coming to realize that Devon was like that, concerned about such things like having a friendship to offset the loneliness, the sensation of being adrift in the world without anyone to connect with, to be with. And that was because Devon himself was alone, alone with his books and his papers and his notes. His metal laptop. His goal of getting a master's degree in a field that nobody else thought was interesting in the least.

That made Stanley a little worked up about it. If anybody had ever paid attention to Devon while he was talking about his interests, his paper, they would have seen the light in his eyes and heard the passion in his voice and been instantly drawn in to how alive Devon was, how smart he was and how fine and good.

Stanley turned on his side so that he was inside of the curve of Devon's chest so that the only thing Devon could do was wrap his arms around Stanley to keep Stanley from falling off the couch. Devon obliged him with a deep-throated sigh, pulling Stanley close, his legs weaving with Stanley's in a way that bound them together in a steady, warm embrace.

Stanley felt a little sleepy now, which always happened after he came, but he wanted to let Devon know that he was interested in Devon, in Devon's work.

"Tell me about the war," Stanley said with half a yawn.

"You don't want to hear about that," said Devon. "Besides, you were already there, and know all about it."

"I do," said Stanley. "I want to hear what *you* know about it, and your theory about the weather."

"It's just isobars and isotherms," said Devon, his voice a little faint, as though he was prepared to defend himself if Stanley was teasing him. "Temperature anomalies and climate patterns. A cold front that stayed and stayed and stayed."

"Why did it stay?" asked Stanley.

"Because it didn't have anywhere else to go, not with the low pressure coming from the North Atlantic," said Devon. "That part's a fact, you understand, because the data proves it. My theory is about how that cold front affected what was happening at ground level on the battlefield."

Stanley was quite sure that Devon's theory was absolutely spot on. As Devon talked, he had a great many facts at hand, and described, in some detail, a chart he was developing that showed the various forces at work. And how though the chart might not be accepted as part of his thesis, it was definitely helping him work through the patterns in motion at the time.

Stanley wanted to ask what the weather had been like at the end of the war, whether the sky had been sunny and blue, or whether it had been raining and, indeed, when the war had ended, which it had. Devon had said it had ended. Stanley opened his mouth to ask, but the breath turned into a yawn, and the rumble of Devon's voice in Stanley's ear where it was pressed against Devon's chest was too powerful a lullaby to resist.

CHAPTER TWENTY-TWO

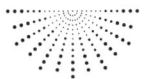

Devon woke up and got up from the couch carefully. Needing a distraction from waking Stanley, he puttered around the cottage, rinsing the dishes in the sink, straightening his papers and books so they weren't all over the place. Mostly, he kept his eye on Stanley, who was asleep on the couch, looking a tad more rested, his eyes closed, his lashes dark on his cheeks. The point of all this, of every bit of it, was to make it easy for Stanley to stay with him.

He hadn't quite told Stanley how scary it had been to watch Stanley vanish in front of his eyes. When he'd thought about mentioning it, the more important thing had been about how Stanley had felt about getting dragged back into the war, into the trenches, on the verge of watching his friends die all over again. Which they would have, except for Stanley's quick thinking.

That had taken guts and a steel nerve, none of which were visible now, or even when Stanley was awake. He seemed, then as always, an innocent youngster from a small farming community. He'd had no idea of the scope of the war, except that some foreign duke had been killed, and the idea of it had seemed glorious. Enlist, get a free trip overseas, kill some Germans, and come home again.

Devon wondered how quickly it had taken Stanley to figure out that this was not so. Probably only a handful of days, which had been driven home when the weather had turned sour in the middle of September. In Stanley's world, it was November 10th, the day the entire battalion had been wiped out. It had been raining, and Stanley had had no coat. This thought above all others was driving Devon crazy; why the hell had there been no thought to bringing in much needed coats for the men?

Against his better judgment, but with the thought of keeping himself occupied while Stanley slept, he opened his laptop and looked it up. He brought up a brand new webpage that he'd not seen before, and he read it, half sick at what the details revealed. The rain had flooded the nearby River Ornes, wiping out the bridge, thus preventing supplies from coming in. For weeks before that, the supply corps had been battered by German attacks, and unable to get their trucks across broad expanses. Even if the river hadn't been out, there wouldn't have been any supplies.

Part of him wanted to tell Stanley about this, as if it would make any difference to him. What did Stanley need to know about the war? Now that he was with Devon, he could forget about all of that. Except that Stanley deserved a medal for not complaining more, about the lack of coat, about the weather, about any of it. He seemed stoic in nature, and might have determined it wouldn't have made any difference anyway, so why waste the energy. Maybe the war had ground him down at that point to where his only defense was in pretending not to mind, until this had become engrained within him.

All of this was too much. Devon needed to do what was best for Stanley. Not telling him what had happened to the 44th Battalion because Stanley didn't need to worry seemed kind, but it was also a lie. Devon snapped the laptop shut and buried his head in his hands. Why had he ever thought that writing a thesis about the war, even from the distant vantage point of the weather, would be a good idea? He was an idiot, that's why. He'd had high ideals that none of it would truly affect him, that he would be immune to the ethos of it all—until

Stanley. Stanley who was like a dream come true and who deserved better than what he'd gotten.

Well, he was with Devon now, and Devon would make sure that he got all the good things in the world. He would take Stanley far away from the little village of Ornes so that time would not be able to yank him back into the past.

It all depended on how soon he could finish up his research, though to be honest, he'd been dragging that out just so he could stay in France, where the bread was better. Only now, that wasn't important any more. Once back in the States, they could have the bread shipped to them, or they could make it at home—if Stanley was willing to stay with him.

Stanley would have to overcome his own background. He'd have to become used to being gay out in the open rather than like it must have been in 1917, where you had to hide all the time. But, if he were brave enough to make his friends do weird things, like move along a muddy bench for no apparent reason, then he would be brave enough to face the future. But he wouldn't be alone, he would be with Devon.

Devon lifted his head and looked over at Stanley, who was still sleeping. Eventually he would wake up and need feeding. Only there wasn't a whole lot in the cottage, as Devon had been remiss in taking care of anything while Stanley had been missing. They needed to go to the village and get groceries, and Devon needed to finish his thesis so that he and Stanley could go home.

With firm determination, he got up to grab his canvas notebook, sat down, opened his laptop, and began working. If he could focus, it wouldn't take long to finish. Then, after that, it didn't matter. He would have completed his thesis work, and then he and Stanley could start their new life together.

When Stanley woke up, Devon was at the kitchen table with his coat on, and it looked like he had keys in one hand and his wallet in the other. Stanley watched, only half awake, as Devon put the items in his pockets and, with one quick gesture, pulled up the collar of his jacket just the way Isaac would do it. A quick flick of both wrists, his thumbs standing up to draw a line along the seam, setting everything just so.

Devon being Devon, he probably had no idea of the image he presented, how familiar it was, and the way it both warmed Stanley's heart and alarmed him. He didn't want to keep making these kinds of comparisons, and besides, any thoughts of the trenches, and the misery of war, or even of Isaac, felt like a threat that could yank him back in time at any moment.

"Are you going somewhere?" asked Stanley as he sat up, a repeat of the last time he slept on Devon's couch. A secret hope bloomed in his chest that the next time he slept it would be in Devon's bed, with Devon.

"Yes, I thought we'd go into the village and maybe have a little supper, then get some groceries," said Devon.

Devon came over to Stanley and reached to pull him up from the couch. He did a little wave with both his hands and shuffled his feet that, in a way, oddly reminded Stanley of a dance hall girl attempting to entice a customer into spending a dime. But Devon's smile made the gesture sweet and innocent.

"French wine, French cheese," said Devon with a laugh. "And French fries, too, though you probably don't know what those are."

"Yes, I do," said Stanley. He captured Devon's hands, folded them together in his own, and kissed them. He felt a little shy as he did this, not because it was intimate, but because he wasn't used to being so purposeful with his affection. "I've had them, though it was when we shipped over, not before."

"Ah, yes," said Devon. "Doughboys and their *pommes frites*."

"We just called them French fries," said Stanley, though he smiled rather than rolling his eyes because he didn't want to tease too much, not when Devon was showing off a little, sharing what he loved to learn about.

"So you want to go?"

"Into the village, yes," said Stanley. "I'll get dressed. Do you have a coat for me?"

As Stanley pulled on his socks and blue jeans, Devon promptly went to the closet by the front door and brought out the dark blue pea coat that Stanley remembered from before. He was glad for the pea coat because he did not want to put his uniform on, not even to keep off the rain. He wanted to leave the war far behind him as fast as possible.

When Devon opened the door, Stanley was almost surprised to find it was only afternoon, and though there were grey clouds sweeping overhead, the pale blue sky shone through in places, and it wasn't raining. It was, however, terribly cold, so Devon got them both knitted caps from the top shelf of the closet and as they put them on, Stanley grinned. He remembered the cap from before, too.

As Devon tugged the cap over Stanley's ears, Stanley put his hands over Devon's hands to keep them there a moment longer. He laughed out loud, glad to be where he was—with Devon on a cloudy, frost-speckled afternoon, far away from the thunder of war, the explosions of shells and mortar, and the smell of stale sweat.

"I don't have a car, but it's only about half a mile," said Devon as they started walking along the blacktopped road that led into a copse of trees. "Just through there and over a little hill."

"I'll help you carry the groceries," said Stanley, wanting to be of use.

"I'm counting on it," said Devon. He moved close as they walked and looped his arm through Stanley's so they could walk together that way.

It was on the tip of Stanley's tongue the entire distance to the village to tell Devon how he felt, to say out loud everything that was in his heart. How dizzy with happiness being with Devon made him feel. But as they walked through the woods and especially as the village, with the cluster of red tiled roofs bright against the dreary day, came into view, he felt that being with Devon was enough. Later, when they could share a private moment, he would tell Devon everything.

Also, as they walked into the village along the blacktopped road, Stanley was distracted by the number of cars and how fast they went, the motorized bicycles, and all the bright signs in the windows. Stanley could hardly believe the world he'd arrived into. What's more, even though he and Devon, two men, were walking arm in arm, nobody seemed to pay them any mind, except to nod a greeting or to let them pass on the sidewalk. It was only as they got near the village square that Devon dropped his arm, and that was only because he was opening the door for Stanley and gesturing that he should go ahead.

Instantly the smells of garlic and butter and grease greeted Stanley, the warmth of the place soaking into his skin. He remembered this smell from one of the times he and the fellows had gone into the village. They'd not had enough money for a full meal, but had gotten sausages fried in batter, one per soldier, each almost too small to make any difference to their hungry bellies. But the sausages had been good, and as they'd all walked back to the battalion, they'd licked their fingers and agreed on how delicious French food was.

Inside the restaurant, a host greeted them with a little bow, his hands spread across his snowy white apron. As Devon spoke to him, Stanley stayed politely quiet and then followed behind Devon as their host led them to a little table by a window.

"Is this good?" asked Devon. As if Stanley could find anything to complain about. As if it made any difference to Stanley, as long as he was with Devon.

"Yes," said Stanley. "Can we start eating now?"

"Yes," said Devon, laughing as he sat down, gesturing that Stanley should do the same.

The host came to take their coats and knitted caps. As soon as they were settled in their chairs, a waiter, thin, his hair oiled back the way Stanley was used to seeing, brought them a bottle of water and two narrow glasses. Someone else brought them a little cloth-lined basket of bread and a white china bowl filled with curls of yellow butter.

The menu that the waiter brought them was in French, of course, the words printed in silky black ink on the creamy paper. Devon slowly parsed the French into English, describing various options that inevitably involved a great deal of butter and garlic, and all of which sounded delicious.

Overwhelmed by such richness, Stanley could hardly decide. Besides, being with Devon, like this, in this clean, well-lighted place seemed enough of a bounty that he didn't need to eat. Though he did, he knew he did, so he thought about it and made up his mind.

"Which is the one again?" asked Stanley. He ran his fingers down the page to feel the smoothness of it. "The chicken in wine one? *Cock o' van?*"

"*Coq au vin*," said Devon though he could hardly manage for laughing at Stanley's mispronunciation of it. Not to mention that Stanley's was the naughtier version, and it filled him with a sense of joy that he'd found a way to make Devon laugh. Playing the fool when he didn't know the language was quite easy, and the result was Devon's bright eyes and handsome smile.

The waiter came, delivered the wine and bread, and took their order. Once he discovered that only Devon knew French, even if very little, he focused his attention away from Stanley. Which was rude, in a way, but Stanley shrugged, reached for the bread and butter, and drank from the glass of red wine that the waiter poured for him, happy to be where he was, happy to be with Devon. If thoughts of the war intruded, he would simply push them back; he wouldn't let time jerk him around anymore.

When the food came, Stanley's dish contained a mess of chicken parts in red sauce. He was dubious, for it looked like stewed chicken, which he'd had back home and didn't like very much. Except, when he ate it, the chicken was silky with butter and bursting with all sorts of flavors. He quickly inhaled the chicken and mopped up the sauce with more bread and butter, which the waiter disdainfully brought for them. Devon plowed silently through his steak and frites. To finish, they had sliced cheese and fruit. Stanley's stomach was so full he was never going to have to eat again.

"We can get groceries and go back," said Devon as the waiter brought him the bill to pay.

Devon took the bill and handed the waiter a thin bit of plastic from his wallet. He used the same motion someone might if they were handing over cash. Only there was no cash. Stanley stared, but no matter how carefully he watched, no money changed hands.

The waiter didn't seem to mind this, and went away. When he came back, he smiled with a bow as he gave the card back to Devon and gave Devon several slips of paper to sign. Then the host brought them their jackets and caps, and they stepped into the late afternoon street, the sunshine struggling to get through the clouds.

Several automobiles whizzed by them on the street and then two young men on a small, motorized bike. Again, Stanley had to work hard not to stare. He'd seen military vehicles, of course, but back home regular automobiles had been thin, black, spidery contraptions that belched smoke and bounced about. He'd ridden on the trolley car that you could get on for a nickel, which was a bit more reliable than automobiles.

He'd seen soldiers on motorized bikes before, too, but the young men were civilians, and it filled Stanley with the thought that if he stayed, if time allowed him to stay, he might get to ride one some day. With Devon in the front, and Stanley clinging on behind, his arms around Devon's waist, and the wind in their hair.

"Better hurry," said Devon, his words shaking Stanley out of his daze. "I think it's going to start raining again."

Devon led Stanley into a store that turned out to be a grocery store. The food was piled so high in every aisle that it was almost too much. Even in the middle of November there were all the fruits of summer, shiny and polished, row upon row of red and yellow and green.

Stanley followed Devon around, carrying the basket, being of use. He ended up looking at the floor a great deal because it became overwhelming, otherwise. The food in that store would have fed every man in the battalion for a year, and then some.

It was a little better when they got to the bakery section; the smells were familiar and the baker seemed happy to hand over samples. Devon dithered over his choices, and Stanley was content to breathe in the fresh baked bread smells, watching while various pastries and loaves were wrapped in silky waxed paper.

After they waited in line at the sleek looking cash register, the bored clerk took each item and moved it from one part of the counter to the other in a ritual that Stanley didn't understand. The machine somehow totted up a long line of numbers that represented what Devon had purchased, though as to how the machine knew that, Stanley could not fathom.

Devon again paid for everything with the thin card that he showed to the machine. Then they piled everything in the string bags that Devon had brought with him, stuffed in his pockets, and together they staggered out of the store and into the street.

"It's only half a mile," said Devon, as though Stanley needed encouragement. He couldn't wait to get back, to be alone with Devon in the cottage. In the warm, still air, where the war seemed far away, and where the modern world had yet to encroach.

CHAPTER TWENTY-THREE

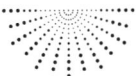

As they came through the copse of leafless trees and down the hill to where the cottage was, it began to mist. On the edge of the horizon, the sun was sinking low behind the clouds, arcing the light in streams of purple and blue dusk. The white crosses, row on row, shone brilliant against the dark, green grass. As they got closer, Stanley's gaze was drawn to them, again and again.

Isaac was beneath one of those crosses, or maybe he wasn't. The crosses didn't mark actual bodies, for the most part, but rather represented how many men had died. Some bodies were unidentifiable; other men's bodies had never been found. Over two hundred crosses had been driven into the earth to mark the occasion of the end of one battalion's futile struggle. Stanley's stomach turned at the thought of it.

"What's the matter, Stanley?" asked Devon.

He put his shopping bags down while he unlocked the door. When he saw where Stanley was looking, he quickly opened the door and ushered them both into the cottage and out of their caps and jackets. He bustled about, putting groceries away in the kitchen. Stanley lingered by the counter, wanting to help, but not knowing where everything went.

"You still look sad," said Devon. "Even with food in your belly and all this food in front of you."

The words started out half-joking, as though Devon had meant to jolly Stanley out of his mood. But then he seemed to realize that something deeper was amiss. He pulled Stanley to him and held him close. Stanley let himself breathe slowly in and out, his cheek on Devon's shoulder, his nose buried in the collar of Devon's shirt.

"Let me pour you some wine, and then tell me."

Stanley didn't want wine, and he didn't want to report on how he felt, as though this was something Devon could fix. As if this was something anybody could fix. But this was different; Devon's intention seemed to be that he only wanted to help.

Devon poured wine into jelly jars for them both. Together they stood in the kitchen, hip to hip while Devon fried onions and sausages and peppers in a pan, with the heat on low. Not because they were hungry, but because it seemed he liked having something to do with his hands and, besides, they had all the time in the world.

"I just wonder," said Stanley, enjoying the warmth of Devon's body next to his.

Devon looked up at him, his eyes dark and serious in a way that told Stanley that he was listening, really listening. That he probably wouldn't dismiss what Stanley was about to say.

"I just wonder if what I tried to do made any difference at all."

"What do you mean?" asked Devon after a swallow of wine.

"Well, I saved my friends, I saved *them*, but I didn't save the radio."

Stanley looked at his jelly jar glass, though he didn't really want to drink any. The wine at supper had numbed him a bit, but now his feelings were back, and they felt important enough not to drown out.

"In the end, I still had to go on my mission. Which then failed *again*. They died anyway."

Devon nodded as if he understood. Which he seemed to, and would, because he knew all about the war, knew how it had ended, and how peace had soon turned into another war.

"You never did explain what the mission was," said Devon. Stanley watched him put a bit of chopped garlic in the pan and, yes, more butter. "But I guess it was a secret mission and if you tell me you'll have to kill me?"

Devon's eyebrows went up like this was the tail end of a very old joke, one that Stanley had never heard before. The look on Devon's face made him smile, and he realized that he'd never fully explained what he'd set out to do on that fateful morning.

"Well, the first time," said Stanley, and you could have knocked him over with a feather if somebody had told him he'd go through that moment not once, but twice, and then end up taking about it in a kitchen in the distant future. "Isaac had died, along with Rex and Bertie. The same shell that killed them also destroyed the radio. The lieutenant needed somebody to go, to deliver the request for retreat—"

Devon made a sound, and Stanley could see that he was tempted to get out his pencil and paper and start taking notes. But then he shook his head as if chiding himself.

"Go on," he said. "Tell me more, tell me the rest of it." Devon paused to cup Stanley's cheek, gentle and reassuring, giving Stanley the strength to tell his story.

"The request for retreat," said Stanley, explaining it as though to a new recruit, "is half of the code. You find the highest ranking officer and you give him the first half of the code. Then he gives you the rest of the code, which is the approval for retreat."

"Why does it have to be in person?" asked Devon, stirring the food in the pan. "Oh wait, because the radio was broken."

"Yes, and the second time, I forgot about the radio, which if I hadn't—" Stanley's voice broke and he stopped, the full weight of his decision coming down on him so heavily he had to take a breath and start again.

"Right," said Stanley. "Normally, you could do this over the radio so that if the Germans were listening in, they wouldn't be able to crack the code. They wouldn't know that you were out of bullets and food, and that you wanted to head for the hills."

He felt his memory stagger back into that moment when he'd stood in front of Lt. Billings. He'd been full of dread, his stomach sinking, but he'd known he was the best choice for the mission because his friends were dead, and nobody back home would miss him if he failed.

"You did what you could," said Devon. Instead of this sounding like a platitude, it felt genuine to Stanley because the expression on Devon's face, with his turned-down mouth, made Stanley feel as though Devon truly understood.

"But I failed twice, Devon," said Stanley, half of his mind whirring at how bizarre that sounded. "Twice I couldn't get it right. *Twice*."

Devon looked at Stanley like he didn't quite know what to say to this, but at least he wasn't insisting that Stanley should just get over it. Instead, he turned off the heat beneath the frying pan and took out the crusty bread, warm from the oven, and pulled Stanley to the table and fed him. Food was a good distraction, even though he'd recently eaten. As they sat catty corner from each other, close enough so that their knees touched, Stanley made use of the moment to gather his thoughts while he ate the sausage and peppers, and warm bread with butter dripping off it. The wine, he left to Devon.

"If only you'd known the code when you went back the second time," said Devon. He tipped his head back to polish off his wine and plonked the jelly jar on the table. He looked at Stanley, his eyes serious, as though he had come to a decision. "You know, we could probably look that information up."

"We could?"

"Sure," said Devon. "It's not classified anymore. Right? It's in the records, at least it should be. There's got to be somebody out there obsessed with the small details. You know, like the train spotters."

"Like the what?" asked Stanley.

"You know," said Devon. "The guys who know every bolt and every button on every train on every line that ever ran. Guys like that."

Stanley couldn't imagine anybody with that much time on their hands, or access to that kind of information. They all must have their own version of Devon's metal laptop, though, where everything that had ever been known was available with a few taps on the keyboard. It made his head spin to think about it too much, so he nodded and licked his finger and poked at the breadcrumbs on the table by his plate.

"I could wash the dishes and you could look," Stanley said. He didn't think he could bear to scroll through the records for that kind of information.

Devon nodded and stood up, scraping his chair back, and together they cleared the table. Afterwards, Devon began researching, clicking on his laptop as Stanley began washing the dishes.

Stanley soothed himself by swishing his hands in the hot water, which was supplied by a never-ending source of more hot water from the tap. The suds were mighty as well, and the bubbles never seemed to shrink. In no time he was finished. He dried his hands on a towel and, leaving the dishes on the sideboard to dry, joined Devon at the table. He pulled his chair close to Devon's so their shoulders brushed.

"I'm not finding anything," said Devon. He moved his little roller mouse, which somehow knew how to communicate its position on the window, and scrolled the page down and down and down. "It's just not here."

Stanley shrugged. The code wouldn't make any difference now anyway, so there was no point in finding it. Devon was determined, however, and kept at it for another hour. Stanley stayed at his side, his shoulder pressed against Devon's, feeling a little lost.

Finally, Devon got up, and turned to Stanley. He kissed him on the mouth, and cupped his face in his warm hands, and Stanley started to feel a little better.

"Maybe it's in one of the books," said Devon.

"Maybe," said Stanley, and he couldn't keep his lack of enthusiasm out of his voice.

"I'll just look for a little while and then I'll stop, okay?" asked Devon.

He looked so hopeful, as though he thought it would help Stanley somehow to know a code that he'd been unable to complete on account of a broken radio and his lack of ability to run through a cloud of mustard gas. So Stanley nodded, put on a smile, and then realized that this was who Devon was. He loved to do research, and as the war was what his paper was on, he had a great many books to look through. As they both sat down on the couch, his hands went unerringly to a particular pile on the floor.

"*Life in the Trenches*, it's called," said Devon.

Stanley flicked a glance at the glossy cover and then concentrated on Devon's fingers as he turned through the pages. Devon talked to himself while he searched, and just when Stanley began to imagine that this could go on for quite a while, Devon straightened up.

"So you were in the 44th Battalion, right?" asked Devon.

"Yes," said Stanley. "That's the one."

His attention sharpened because it might be interesting to see his former world from an outsider's perspective; it felt objective and slightly clinical that way, and he could bear it if the information didn't reveal too much about the actual men who had died. Besides, the information was in a book, and printed words couldn't hurt him.

"Says here that there were a series of trenches built around village. It was Lt. Billings, not your Commander Helmer who deserted, who had half the code for retreat, and all the upper ranks, the ones who needed to know, had the other half."

Stanley nodded. He knew that much.

"What was your half of the code?" asked Devon.

Devon looked over at Stanley. Stanley straightened up, thinking for half a second that Devon might be a German spy who was tricking Stanley into revealing what he knew, and he was tempted not to tell him. Except that a wrinkle appeared between Devon's eyebrows, as though he was on the verge of realizing this, and Stanley could have kicked himself over it.

"You're going to laugh," said Stanley. "My half of the code was *There are penguins on the ice*."

Devon's straight white teeth came into view as he smiled, nodded, and bent over the book in his lap. With one finger, he traced his way down what looked like a list. As Stanley leaned close, hooking his chin over Devon's shoulder, he could see what it was. A list of codes of various sorts, all broken into their respective parts. If you knew the first part, you could find the second.

"This one," said Devon, tapping the page. Then he read the code out completely. *"There are penguins on the ice and they skate brilliant figure eights."*

A sense of sadness swamped through Stanley. If he'd known that phrase, he could have saved Isaac. The radio. He could have saved *everybody*. He could have saved himself, even. And then nobody would be buried beneath the green grasses topped row on row by white crosses. But he'd failed and didn't deserve his current happiness.

He barely heard Devon slap the book closed, but he did feel Devon's arms come around him.

"Don't be sad, Stanley, please," whispered Devon in his ear, his breath soft and warm. "I'm sorry, I didn't realize this would hurt you so bad. I shouldn't have kept looking."

"It's okay, Devon," said Stanley, his voice low. "Now I know at least what the code was, had I been able to make it through."

CHAPTER TWENTY-FOUR

"I shouldn't have told you," said Devon. He'd taken his research too far, again, as usual, and upset Stanley, which was the last thing he wanted to do. Stanley deserved better than to have Devon keep dragging him back into the past, when both of them knew that was the last thing either of them wanted.

He put the book down on the pile of books that belonged to the university and that would be shipped back home when his research was done. Scanning the room, he fought against the impulse to get up and tidy the piles, or to get to work. It wasn't a hard impulse to fight because, after all, he had an American doughboy sitting right next to him.

"I wanted to know," said Stanley, his whiskey colored eyes on Devon and that sad expression, as though all he wanted to do was to be of use. "I wanted to know if what I'd done had made any difference, and of course it hadn't. None of it mattered."

Then Devon did give in to the impulse to pull Stanley into his arms, to pet his shorn hair, to kiss his temple.

"None of it matters," said Devon. "After what you've been through, my paper, all my studies, they just seem stupid. I'm going to throw in the towel—"

"Throw in the what?" asked Stanley.

"I'm just going to stop," said Devon, dismissing the idea that Stanley should have known the idiomatic expression but didn't. "Stop everything and switch over to meteorology."

He felt a chill as Stanley pulled away and sat up straight, not touching the back of the couch.

"Why would you do that?" asked Stanley. "You're so close to finishing. Why would you *do* that?"

Devon wanted to ignore the question and to pull Stanley close and tell him how he felt, how he promised himself a second chance. How his dreams about American doughboys had turned into something more meaningful. How Stanley had touched the place in his heart he'd never told anybody else about.

"Why?" asked Stanley.

"It's stupid," said Devon. He got up from the couch, checking the thermostat to give his hands something to do, and to make sure that Stanley was warm enough.

"The whole thing is stupid," said Devon. "After everything you've been through. After hearing about it from *you* and having you show me the trenches, telling me about that guy who lost his leg—which isn't in the records *anywhere*—because you were there, and you suffered for it. For me to write a paper about it, it's like I'm benefiting from that without having paid the price."

The twisted feelings that had started when Stanley had shown up on the green grasses that were all that was left of a disastrous battle had risen to the surface, and he'd said them aloud. He could barely look at Stanley with this confession ringing in the air. His constant awareness about the futility of war was only the half of it. The other half was the loss that war brought, inexplicable and never-ceasing, and Stanley had been the one to go through that. Not Devon.

"But you're telling the story," said Stanley as he stood up and came over to Devon, so close that as he took a step forward, Devon found himself against the wall. "You're telling all of our stories, mine, Isaac's, everybody's."

"Nobody will care," said Devon. His voice broke on the last word because he realized that it was true. None of his friends cared, and his thesis advisor had strongly suggested he focus on another aspect of the Great War. In the end he was alone, except for Stanley, who could be dragged back through time at any moment.

"I care," said Stanley. "And you care. You can put the stuff that I told you in your paper, and then one day, somebody will read it. It'll matter to somebody, someday."

"You think so?" asked Devon.

"Promise me," said Stanley. He moved close and wrapped his arms around Devon's waist, as if he'd been hugging Devon all of his life and had no hesitation whatsoever about it. "Promise me that no matter what, you'll finish. It's important to finish what you start. And then you can go and study to be the weather guy, like you told me."

"Will you come with me back to the States?" asked Devon. He leaned into the warmth of Stanley's body, and echoed the motion of Stanley's arms, wrapping his arms around Stanley's waist, pulling him close. It felt warm and right to be like this, the question on his lips as Stanley lifted up to kiss him. "I'll have to start over and we'll have to live cheap for two years."

"I don't care about living cheap," said Stanley. "But what will I study?"

"Whatever you want," said Devon. He meant it as more than that. Stanley could study what he wanted, and Devon would help him in every way and support him. Show him the world. But maybe he needed to say that out loud.

Except that Stanley smiled and distracted Devon from his own thoughts.

"I want to learn how to get cats with spectacles on the screen, on the server. I want to do that."

"Computer science it is," said Devon. He returned Stanley's smile, and leaned down until he could see the lights in Stanley's eyes. See the faint shadow of Stanley's lashes against his cheeks. "I'll help you with your GED, with all of that, but first I want to tell you what I was thinking when you disappeared before."

"Tell me," said Stanley. His voice was hushed, and he leaned in and met Devon halfway, his lips brushing Devon's. "Tell me everything."

Devon lifted his arms until he was circling Stanley's shoulders. His hands were on Stanley's neck where he could feel the warmth of Stanley's skin, the low pulse beneath that echoed Stanley's heartbeat. He traced the length of hemp cord from which hung the ID tag that Stanley never took off.

"It's easy to take care of you," Devon began. "To get you hot coffee and to feed you and loan you my clothes." He paused to look into Stanley's eyes. He wanted to let him know that this was only the half of it; he needed to tell Stanley how he felt, like he told himself he would. "When you disappeared before, I promised myself that if I ever got another chance with you, I would tell you. I would tell you that I love you—"

"I made myself the same promise," said Stanley, his voice bright and clear and completely without fear. "When I was sitting next to Isaac, after I saved him but not the radio, I wanted the same thing. I wanted another chance with you, and if I got it, I would tell you."

"Tell me."

"I love you," said Stanley. "You're like the fellows back home, except you're not. And you make me feel safe."

Tears pricked Devon's eyes as he held Stanley's face in his hands and kissed him, very gently on the mouth. He could not bear the thought of Stanley feeling scared, of being in the trenches with black dust raining down from exploded mortar shells, or up to his knees in mud with the blood of his friends on his uniform.

He could not hold on too tightly, though, because if he did, he might startle them when they'd each just confessed their hearts. Time could not steal this moment; it could try, but it would fail, for Devon had Stanley in his arms, and when he kissed him again, Stanley lifted his face, his lashes long on his cheeks.

"Yes," Stanley said. "*Yes.*"

Devon blinked back his tears, not because he was ashamed but because he wanted to concentrate on Stanley who was standing in front of him, safe inside Devon's arms, warm and safe inside the cottage, and as far away from the Battle of Ornes as he could possibly be.

They were both still too near the trenches, though, and Devon vowed to finish his paper as soon as possible, and get a passport for Stanley so he could go home to the States, as he should have done, all those years ago. Home with his army buddies, where they all grew old and kept in touch, and yes, even Stanley's Isaac, who Devon wanted to tell, *You didn't want him, but I do.*

"Devon," said Stanley. It was a small reminder that it was now, not then, and that he was with Stanley. That his heart's desire had always been this, the quiet evening, and him and his American doughboy.

"I was just thinking how lucky I am," said Devon, and he meant it. "So lucky to have met you."

"Lucky that I died, then," said Stanley, his mouth curling into a smile as though he wanted to make a joke of it. As Devon's chest filled with a weight of something black and awful, Stanley's eyes opened wide.

"No, that's not what I meant," said Stanley. "I mean I *did* die, but I don't regret it, even though it was scary, because now I have you—don't I? I have you and your metal laptop, which maybe you'll let me use. I didn't mean it like it sounded, but sometimes the words they just—you know? They get away from me."

"As long as you don't get away from me," said Devon, and he meant it with everything he had. "I'm sorry you had to die—"

"Twice," said Stanley, though there was a sparkle in his eyes as he said it, a true joke this time.

"Twice," said Devon. He felt rush of passion within him, as though he was being lifted from the inside into a place of happiness and light, but if only he could be together with Stanley. "And never again."

"How do we stop time?" asked Stanley. "How do we keep it from taking me away again?"

Devon didn't know the answer to this, although he had a feeling that the question would remain an open-ended one.

175

"What I do know is this," said Devon. "We've been standing here for far too long, and you said yes to me before."

"I did," said Stanley. "I do."

CHAPTER TWENTY-FIVE

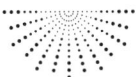

Devon turned off the lights in the living room, and the ones in the bedroom as well. He pulled Stanley to the bed and began to carefully undress him. He let the clothes fall where they might, and held up his arms so that Stanley could undress him in return. It was a good thing he'd turned up the heat, though his skin shivered as Stanley ran his hands along Devon's arms.

"You still have your underwear on," said Stanley, announcing this rather like a seven year old who had no restraint on saying what he thought. "And I do too, so what are we going to do about it?"

"Let's take them off," said Devon, laughing beneath his breath in a way that felt new and sweet. "I'll pull yours off if you'll pull mine."

He could see Stanley in the near dark, and traced the curve of his face with his eyes, put his hands on Stanley's hips, and tugged. With quick, jerking motions amidst a tangle of arms and wrists, they pulled each other's underwear off and then moved together in the dark. Their hips met and the long muscles of their thighs. Devon could feel the scratch of Stanley's pubic hair, the curly wiriness of it. Their hard cocks trapped between their bellies. The quick breaths that lifted Stanley's chest.

"You're not afraid of me, Stanley?" asked Devon, wanting to be sure, a tenderness rising in his throat; he would be willing to wait forever until Stanley wasn't afraid.

"I'm not afraid of you," said Stanley, kissing Devon's throat. Devon lifted his chin to let him. "But some of the fellas talked about how when they came through Paris and they went with the whores—"

"Did you ever go, Stanley?" asked Devon, though he could barely speak for the feel of Stanley's hands on his bare waist. "Did you ever go with one of those women?"

"I didn't want them," said Stanley. "What I'm trying to ask you is the fellas talked about taking a whore from behind so as not to get her, you know, in a family way. Are we going to do that, you and me?"

"Do you want to?" asked Devon. His face felt hot and his erection thumped against his belly, side by side with Stanley's erection as they stood in the quiet darkness. He knew Stanley was waiting for direction, not because he was a good soldier, but because he was practically a virgin, and a lovingly delivered hand job on the couch wasn't enough to make a difference.

"Do you want me to?" Devon asked now. "I'll be gentle with you, so gentle, Stanley."

"I know you will," said Stanley. "But I don't know what to do."

"I'll show you," said Devon. "Here, on the bed, like this."

In the dark, Devon used his hands to guide Stanley to the bed, petting the length of his hip, his thigh, to gentle him and ease him into the moment. Beneath his fingertips, Stanley was shaking, only a little, but it was enough for Devon to take a moment when Stanley was on his belly to make long strokes along Stanley's body, to kiss the back of his neck, to feel Stanley's heartbeat from the pulse of blood beneath his skin.

"I'm going to take it slow, Stanley," said Devon, his mouth whispering across Stanley's cheek. "So slow, okay?"

"Okay," said Stanley, and in his voice was a small, low quiver that pressed against Devon's heart.

"Lay like this," said Devon as he guided Stanley's leg, brushing it over and over, as though soothing a wild young thing. It was better this way, rather than having Stanley on his knees, which might feel more aggressive and certainly wasn't what was wanted now. "I'm going to pet you and push my fingers inside of you, and get you ready."

"And then we'll fuck?" asked Stanley, his voice a little shaky, but full of brightness and the sweetness that Devon always saw shining in his eyes. "Like the fellas talked about with the whores?"

Devon laughed, pressing kisses across Stanley's shoulders, running his fingers across Stanley's shorn hair.

"Yes," said Devon. "Like that, but only better because we love each other, you and I, and soldiers never love whores."

Stanley turned in a sudden motion, twisting backwards so that he was looking up at Devon in the near dark. His eyes shone in the half light, bright sparks that drew Devon to him. He bent close and kissed Stanley, sensing that Stanley wanted to tell him something important.

"Some of them did," said Stanley, and there was urgency in his voice. "Some of those soldiers loved the women they were with, even if they *were* whores. It was their last night on earth and they gave each other all the love they had. That's what the soldiers told me."

Devon went still, his throat tight. Thoughts of those moments filled him and the images flickered in his mind. The desperate gestures, the glad faces in the red lamp district that had hid the despair of the soldiers. The whores who serviced them welcoming the soldiers with open arms, the moment more pure than it might have otherwise been, each knowing that it might be the last time those boys knew anything gentle or passionate or good.

"Stanley," said Devon, feeling like he was choking. "Oh, Stanley."

"But we're not like that," said Stanley quickly into that mournful moment. "We're not like that, not like those soldiers and those women. Because it's not the war anymore, not our last night on earth. Right?"

Never had Devon more wanted to bawl like a child about the dark losses that war caused. At the same time, he had his American doughboy in his arms, naked, spread out beneath him like a beautiful thing, a poem, a prayer. Stanley trusted him, *was* trusting him, and

Devon needed to get it together and show Stanley how good it could be between two men who loved each other.

It was not the war. There was no sound of mortar shells, no whiff of mustard gas, no gurgle of mud, not even the sound of the lark to fill the deathly silence between attacks. There was only the feel of the clean sheets beneath their naked bodies, the warmth of the radiator, and the wholesome dark to protect them in the night.

"I love you, Stanley," said Devon. He bent to kiss Stanley on the mouth, brushing kisses all over his face and down his neck. He eased Stanley on his belly, tugging his knee up, and brushed Stanley's cock to make sure it was comfortable. "And I'm going to show you all the love that I have."

He reached for the lube that he kept in a drawer in his nightstand, lube he'd not used in a while, for he'd been too lonely, too distracted by his work. Which meant that the lid was a little stiff, but he managed to get the lube on his fingers and not spread it all over the place. Very gently he stroked Stanley's bottom, petted the small pucker there, and pushed in with one finger, just a little. Then he did it again, his forehead resting between Stanley's shoulder blades, breathing in the scent of Stanley as his sweat grew in the dark. Feeling the pulse of his heartbeat, the rise and fall of his chest.

"Like that, okay?" asked Devon.

"Okay," said Stanley. "Go on, I'm okay, go on."

Devon continued on, pushing in his finger and pulling it out in time to their slow breaths that echoed in the dark. Stanley grunted once, and Devon paused to let their bodies settle together, and then pushed a second finger in to the tightness of Stanley's body and eased him open. All the while whispering the words of endearment that only his heart knew, had known from the beginning of time, but which had waited for this moment to be spoken out loud.

In response, Stanley's body seemed to surge on the bed, as though he was opening himself up for Devon, opening up to him, and his legs spread, his limbs shaking a little, but he was ready. Very quickly, Devon slicked up his cock with the last of the lube on his fingers, and leaned forward to whisper against Stanley's skin.

"Take a breath and let it out slow, very slow."

"Okay."

When Stanley took that breath, Devon lifted up and pushed into Stanley's body, but only a little way. When Stanley let out that breath, Devon eased himself further in, pushing. Little by little, he joined them together until his chest was aligned with Stanley's back, their sweat making them slick together, a shivering eagerness joining them body and soul.

"Oh," said Stanley, though it came out as a sigh of wonder.

"Yeah," said Devon, agreeing with Stanley as the sensations ran through him, sparks of joy and the tumult in his belly of expectation. "It's like that, right? You okay?"

With a physical response that took Devon's breath, Stanley moaned and pushed back, sheathing their bodies together even more until Devon was pressed so deep inside the heat of Stanley's body that they were melting together, becoming one. Devon surged up and rocked his hips, curling them forward and back, shuddering with the intensity of it, of holding back until he could show Stanley the pleasure of it, the heat of it, how it could be when there was no war and only love to be found.

His whole body flushed with heat and desire. He wanted to make sure that Stanley could feel how good it was, so he reached around, stroking Stanley's cock in time with the movement of his hips, and was gratified that Stanley began moving with him, in time with him, as though they were one body rather than two.

Stanley half rose on his knees, drawing Devon's cock deeper inside of him. Devon pushed and trembled, his teeth gritted as he tried to draw out the moment, the ascent into the deepest vibrations along his spine. But his hand shook, tightening his grip for a fraction of a second, and Stanley spent himself on the sheets.

Devon, a moment later, pulsed into the deep heat of Stanley's body. Small cries escaped him as he came, despair for the brevity of the pleasure, and the poignant sorrow of the moment they shared. He wanted to weep, but instead drew Stanley into his arms and away from the dampness on the sheets. He hugged Stanley close, felt the life in his arms, the eager sweetness as Stanley turned to him and rested his cheek on Devon's shoulder.

Devon scrubbed at his eyes with the heel of his hand, kissed Stanley's damp forehead, and returned his hand to curve around Stanley's shoulder. Pretending all the while that he'd been doing something other than wiping tears away.

"Are you okay, Devon?" asked Stanley in a low, soft voice.

"Yes, I'm okay," said Devon, though the words came out like a frog's croak. "Being with you carried me away and I didn't know where I was."

"You're right here," said Stanley, quickly rising up and turning so that he was holding Devon in his arms. "I was right there with you being carried away, on account of I didn't know it would be like that. Sort of sweet and sad at the same time."

"It *can* be fun," said Devon, looking up at Stanley, seeing the dark line of shadow around his head and, unable to discern any of his features, focused on the brightness of Stanley's eyes. "Sometimes you can laugh, you know? But being here, so close to the trenches, it's making me—" Devon stopped to swallow. "It's almost too much, so I'm going to get us out of here and back to the States as fast as I can."

"Okay," said Stanley, petting Devon's shoulder, his arm, with long, sure strokes of his warm hand. "It's going to be okay, Devon, I promise you."

Promises in the dark such as Stanley had just spoken to him were the truest kind. Devon closed his eyes and allowed himself to drift into sleep with Stanley's arms around him. The warmth of the radiator filled the air, and Stanley's sturdy body was alongside his, letting him know he was no longer alone.

CHAPTER TWENTY-SIX

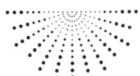

Stanley sat up in bed, feeling the pleasant ache through his body, memories of Devon kissing him, the warm air sifting over him.

Then he froze in the blackness of the room. The dream had been so real and Stanley's heart was pounding. The images of the trenches, and the sense of danger had been so real it was as though he'd been there, going through it all over again. The dream had been made up of a hundred versions of that moment when the shell had exploded, sometimes over their heads, sometimes in Stanley's face, sometimes at his feet, but always sending up shards of mud along with the metal.

Each time his friends had died right then, or they had not died instantly, but later. Each time the radio had been wiped out. Each time, the end of the dream was the same as the reality: Stanley had not been able to save Isaac and his friends or anybody in the 44th Battalion.

The devastation had been real, all of it was real. But the dream was not real, no dreams were. Perhaps not even the one he'd found himself in that he'd awoken to now. The one where he was with Devon, who lived in a world that was the furthest thing it could possibly be from

Stanley's world. The one where Stanley was not a soldier, the one where he was in love with a scholar.

It might be that he was meant to be here. However, the longer he was with Devon, the more he had the sense that he didn't deserve it. He'd tried to explain that to Devon, but he'd not done a very good job so, like with everything else, he'd fallen short. Just as he had on that day when fate had dive-bombed his efforts and destroyed everyone he cared about. If he stayed here without completing his mission, would the result be the same? Would he lose Devon anyway?

Very quietly, he slid out of the bed before he could think about what he was doing, making very sure not to disturb the blankets, the bed. Devon. Then he padded across the wooden floor and went to the closet where Devon had put his uniform. Very quietly he took it down, and went out into the living room, closing the door behind him. Then he got dressed.

Everything went on easily, even in the dark, for he'd put that uniform on more times than he could count without the aid of a lamp; in the war, you had to be prepared for discomfort. More importantly, you had to know how to button your trousers with blind fingers, and be able to lace your boots without seeing them.

The uniform was scratchy and smelled, oddly, like iodine and salt, though maybe that was because the mud had dried and now smelled like blood? Stanley didn't know, but he couldn't stop to think about it, or his heart would start pounding loud enough for Devon to hear. Which would wake Devon up, and then he would want to stop Stanley. As Stanley was on the verge of stopping himself with every other breath, he couldn't let that happen.

He left his canteen and rifle in one of the corners of the living room, though without them, he felt half naked. At the last minute he took off his ID tag. He hung it on around the bayonet blade for Devon to find as proof that Stanley had been there, so Devon wouldn't think that he was going crazy when he woke up in the morning to find Stanley gone.

For a second, he thought that he needed to find that book, *Life in the Trenches*, and double check the first part of the code and its accompanying second part. This was a delay tactic, he knew that. He knew the full code; it was right there on the tip of his tongue, and he could hardly move without seeing the words dance in his brain.

In the dark, with the vague ambient light slitting along the bottom of the curtains, he took a moment anyway to find the book. It was on the couch where they'd left it, and he touched it, a talisman, a good luck charm. He didn't know why he was worried, though, because what he was planning probably wasn't going to work anyway.

Tiptoeing in his heavy boots, he went to the door and unlatched the lock. Then he turned the knob and pulled the door open. Outside, the night sky was not black but instead a silvery grey. The faint stars were being covered up by swiftly moving clouds that smelled fresh and cold, and he realized it was raining.

The heavy, slowly spinning feeling that had been in his head all day sped up, along with his heart, his breath. He had one moment where he could go back on what he'd set out to do. The world would wag on, and maybe other wars would be fought, maybe peace would reign.

The truth of it was, his friends had not deserved to die, nobody in the 44th Battalion had deserved to die. It had just been bad luck about the radio, and maybe Stanley could go back one more time and fix it so they could live. Whether or not he'd be brought back to Devon, he didn't know, but he had to try. Otherwise, his life with Devon, in this time, would always be bittersweet, the sweetness strained because he'd done nothing to deserve it.

He closed his eyes and thought about Devon's sweet smile, the dark hair above his green eyes. The way he would get so focused on his studies, his work. How smooth his skin was behind his ear. The way he listened. The way he looked at Stanley, like Stanley was something special, and not just another soldier.

Except now, in this moment, another soldier was exactly what Stanley needed to be. He needed to do his duty, then he'd let fate decide whether or not he deserved to come back to Devon.

The rain pattered against his face, cold little dots that seemed not to want to cause him harm, but they were raindrops, after all, and their job was to fall. Just like his job was to save his friends.

He thought about the trenches and the mortar shell, and the acrid smell of old oil and blood mixed with mud beneath his feet. The sound of far away pounding, the babble of men as they discussed whether there was enough coffee, and who had hid the sugar. In that moment, he could almost hear it all, smell it all. If he reached out, perhaps he could touch it all.

He needed to do this. He needed to go back in time and the best way to do that was to recreate how it had happened before.

Closing the door against the rain, he went quietly into the bedroom and took Devon's phone from its cord. He closed the bedroom door, then went to the spot in the living room where he'd been when Devon had taken pictures of him. He'd been watching when Devon had used his phone, so he was able to figure out how to turn it on, and how to turn the camera around so it could take a picture of him. He took a deep breath.

"There are penguins on the ice and they skate brilliant figure eights," said Stanley to the night air. He aimed the phone at himself, tapped the face of the phone, and closed his eyes.

It seemed that nothing was happening, though Stanley kept his eyes closed. It was only his imagination that the air was colder and moving swiftly past him, as though he was running. Out of breath. Falling, the phone dropping from his numb fingers, a bright flash like an explosion lighting his brain.

And just as he wanted to open his eyes, his whole body was jarred to attention as his back was slammed against a muddy wall, and his boots were mired in mud. The same dizziness overcame him; he was going to throw up and, half choking, brought the back of his hand to his mouth. Drew in a breath. Smelled gun oil, burnt coffee. Iodine.

"Are you okay, Stanley?"

Stanley opened his eyes to look at who had asked him the question. It was Isaac.

He was sitting to Stanley's right, and on the other side of Isaac, as always, was Rex and Bertie. They each leaned out a little bit more than the fellow in front of him so that Stanley had a glimpse of all of their faces. They peered at him in an almost comical manner, eyebrows raised in the same way, mouths open to ask a question, or to share exciting news, like maybe a retreat had already been called.

"What were you saying?" asked Isaac. "You were mumbling just now and ignoring the fact that I'd just offered you my chocolate. You know I don't care for it, so won't you help a fellow out?"

With numb fingers, Stanley took the chocolate, still wrapped in a fold of greased paper, and put it in his pocket. He couldn't remember what he'd been about to say or do, only that there'd been something terribly important he needed to accomplish. Well, it would come back to him if he didn't worry about it too much. Maybe.

"Hey, thanks," said Stanley. He had the vague sense that there was something or someone he should remember. He couldn't seem to focus on it because there was too much going on in the trench.

"Ah, here comes the coffee," said Isaac. "Finally. If we missed breakfast, on account of them wanting to know about Commander Helmer, which couldn't wait, the least they could do is bring us coffee."

Rex and Bertie nodded in agreement as each took a tin mug from the rough-edged wooden tray that a lowly private was holding out to them. There was one mug left. It was for Stanley, so he took it, and it was with no surprise that when he tipped the mug to his mouth, the dark coffee was bitter with not enough sugar and definitely no milk. It was also hot enough to burn his tongue, and tasted like dirt. At least it was warm and filled his belly. He drank several huge gulps of it to distract himself from the odd sensation that there was something he needed to do.

The sky over the trench was a dull silvery brown, thick with smoke from exploded shells, and rippling with the golden light of the sun as it tried to batter its way through. Below that was the line along the top of the dark brown trench they were in, a close-up horizon decorated with howitzer barrels and the points of bayonets. Bits of logs draped with razor wire tumbled along the edges of the trenches like badly decorated and very ugly cakes.

In the bunker in front of Stanley was Lt. Billings, who was talking with the sergeant in charge of ammunition. The chaplain was with them too, though his reason for being in the bunker made no sense to Stanley. If they were all handing out death at the far end of their weapons, what good was a chaplain except to bury the bodies? Then there was the scout, a wiry fellow, coated up to his hips in mud, his arms wrapped around himself as he talked to the lieutenant.

"Can you hear what they're saying?" asked Isaac. "Can we go? We already told them that Commander Helmer hadn't told us anything about what he was going to do."

Stanley turned his head, holding his tin mug in front of his mouth so the other fellows wouldn't see that it was trembling. He watched Isaac put down his tin mug to turn up his jacket collar in the jaunty way that pilots did, except that Isaac wasn't a pilot. He was a lance corporal, third class gunner, one level below Stanley because, as Stanley had often thought, though Isaac's hands were always steady on the trigger, he didn't have the heart for it.

"Are you going to barf on my boots?" asked Isaac.

Stanley could see in his eyes that while he might pretend to be angry about it, he wouldn't be. Sometimes in the trenches, when things got scary, you simply had to throw up and there wasn't always a bucket.

"I'm going to go in there," said Rex.

The statement rang in Stanley's head, as if he'd heard Rex say that exact same thing a dozen times, and would have to make his weary way through hearing him say it another dozen if he didn't do something about it. But what?

"Better not," said Bertie, in a way that told Stanley that he expected Rex to obey him, just as he'd expected the young newsies back home to obey him.

"Hey fellas," said Stanley, suddenly moved by an impulse he couldn't identify and that scared him half to death. "Why don't you come sit on the other side of me?"

"Why?" asked Isaac. "We're quite close right now, aren't we, darling?" Isaac batted his eyes like a showgirl, and Rex almost splashed coffee out of his tin mug as he elbowed Isaac in the ribs, laughing.

"Right now, come on the other side of me," said Stanley, not hiding the urgency in his voice. "I'll let you sit on the canvas that Isaac gave me."

"Now?" asked Bertie. "They'll see us moving and think that we're trying to get close enough to hear what they are saying."

"They're saying that Commander Helmer deserted in the night," said Rex in a tired way, as though he'd said this many times already. "And they're deciding whether or not to go and look for him, or to report him. Or whatever it is that you do when a coward runs off."

"He was too young for command," said Isaac, shaking his head. "Just because his pop owned that shoe factory in Denver, and he was set to take over the board if his pop ever died—"

"Doesn't mean he was fit to lead," said Stanley, finishing for him, feeling yet again that this was a conversation they'd had not only once, but maybe *dozens* of times. "It's all moot now, as there's no way he could have made it to wherever he thought he was going. Not with the Germans getting closer every time we look away."

It had been like a game of Stop-and-Go for days. The Germans with their massive amounts of manpower had been able to build new trenches in the middle of the night, and now they were closer than ever. If you listened hard enough, if it got quiet enough, you could hear their voices saying German words that nobody could understand.

Well, except for Bertie, who knew that *Achtung* meant *attention*, and *feuer wenn fertig* meant *fire when ready*, and *kleines madchen* meant *little girl*, though how he knew that was anybody's guess. Rex had gone as far, that one time, as to accuse Bertie of being a German spy. They'd almost come to blows over it, until Commander Helmer had broken it up and told them that Bertie had been close to being accepted into cryptography training. Only they'd needed more warm bodies for the battle, and his paperwork had been stamped for the front lines.

Stanley looked at Bertie with his narrow face and wide blue eyes, his crop of flaxen hair now shorn so it could fit beneath the metal helmet. The way he squinted because he needed glasses, only he never asked Commander Helmer for them.

Stanley thought Bertie never wanted to draw any attention to himself because doing so back home had gotten him beaten up in a back alley somewhere. Bertie should have gone into the ranks of ciphers and coders, and he sure as hell shouldn't have ended up at the front with Stanley. In a trench up to their ankles in mud and who knew what all else.

Then there was Rex, who was big across the shoulders, enough to strain the seams of his uniform. He had tree trunk thighs, and wore huge boots, the biggest the army had to give him, but he walked with the grace of a dancer. He hated Germans so much that he was first up in the morning, and the last asleep at night.

His aim was quite deadly, so deadly that there had been mutterings by Commander Helmer that Rex might be transferred into sniper training. Only Helmer had deserted. Lt. Billings sure as hell wasn't going to order a transfer right in the middle of their current disaster when every man was needed in the trenches, so Rex was stuck with the rest of them, destined to fight in the mud, to die in the mud.

And then there was Isaac, who was still looking at Stanley as if waiting to answer an unasked question. It was a question that Stanley would never ask because as he looked at Isaac, he knew the answer would be no. It wasn't that Isaac would get angry and punch Stanley in the face. Instead Isaac would refuse and demur, then make a little joke, brush the scar on his chin with his thumb, and then they could go on as they always had.

Whatever private impulses Isaac might have, he hid them. He moved away and then close, whatever suited him, always the dashing young soldier more concerned with his uniform than he ought to be, given their situation. He always looked as though he was on the verge of hopping into a little wood-and-canvas biplane, a silk scarf around his neck, to fly up into the blue, blue sky. He was like a story that Stanley enjoyed reading, but it was a story only, and would always be so.

CHAPTER TWENTY-SEVEN

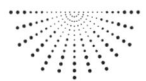

"You fellows ought to move on the other side of me," said Stanley, urgency rising within him, strong, like a punch to the gut. "I'll give you my chocolate for the rest of the war if you do it right now."

"Even the chocolate that Isaac gives you?" asked Rex, always on the lookout for what was right and decent, where every man got his share.

"Yes, even that," said Stanley. He stood up and gestured to the canvas, which was wide enough to cover the muddy bench front to back, and long enough to accommodate at least three soldiers, if not more.

"What about me?" asked Isaac as he stood up.

In his eyes was the expression that Stanley had seen a hundred times before, the one that had made him want to move close and to say things he'd regret in the morning. But that was just Isaac; he didn't mean anything by it.

"I don't care for chocolate, you know that," said Isaac.

"I'll find something special, just for you," said Stanley. "New shoes, maybe," he said, gesturing to their feet, where the mud was squishing over the toes of their boots. "Something you can wear to dance in."

"Suits me," said Isaac with a toss of his head. "Just make sure they're highly polished."

"Swell," said Stanley. "Now everybody move so I can grab this radio."

They were all in motion at the sound of his voice, which made Stanley feel the way commanders and lieutenants must feel. Stanley pushed away the heady rush as his friends sat down where he'd told them to.

When he grabbed the radio and lifted it up, it was quite heavy and bulky, and he was on the verge of dropping it. From behind him, without asking a single question, Isaac leaped up to help. Together they hauled the radio further down the trench and put it on the canvas, right next to Bertie. Bertie put his arm around it in a protective way, though he looked up at Stanley, a little startled.

"What did you do that for?" asked Bertie.

Without knowing why, Stanley took a step backwards, making sure that the radio, and Rex, and Bertie, and Isaac were all on the leeward side of him. They needed to be away from the danger he could hardly describe even to himself, a feeling of loathing and wariness. Of needing to be the bulwark against the onslaught that was yet to come.

Stanley opened his mouth to say *I don't know,* except that at that moment, at that *very* moment, a mortar shell exploded right over their heads, and pieces of metal slammed into the mud where his buddies had just been sitting. Another large metallic shard hit the table where the radio had just been, shattering the spindly wood to bits. Smoke billowed up in an ugly yellow-brown cloud, and leaves of mud pattered heavily down, a brown rain that smelled of gun powder and choked Stanley as he breathed it in.

"*Stanley,*" said Isaac. "You're bleeding."

Though he was yelling, Stanley could barely hear him after the defining roar of explosions. As Isaac yanked on Stanley's arm, he looked down. The upper arm of his uniform was darkened with blood that seeped into a bigger shape even as he watched, a cloud of spreading red and brown.

He looked up, startled, to see Rex coming at him. Rex yanked off Stanley's jacket, tossing it aside as he reached for Stanley, tearing his tan shirt, exposing Stanley's arm.

It could be just a scratch, as Stanley craned his head to see. Blood flowed in a line down his arm, like a thin, red waterfall. Or, it could be, as sometimes, happened, that a thin slice of metal had been driven into his arm by the explosion, so fast and sharp and quick, all the way to the bone, that he'd not yet started to feel pain. Rex was going to check with his hands. In another moment, either he'd wrap Stanley's arm and that would be the end of it, or he'd look at Stanley and mutter a prayer because Stanley was about to bleed to death.

The chaplain was quickly at Rex's side, and though he didn't take over as Stanley had thought he was going to do, he stayed close and watched as Rex ran his fingers along Stanley's bare arm. The blood coated his hands, but he was shaking his head and looking satisfied all at once.

"It's just a nick," Rex said. "Just a regular nick."

Stanley wanted to throw up on his boots, his gut churning because it could have been that the shrapnel had gone through his uniform, slicing all the way through his arm, and had that happened, Rex's ministrations would have yanked the arm all the way off. But it stayed in place, even when a medic came up, slopped iodine all up and down Stanley's arm and wrapped it in a bandage.

"There are no clean shirts, I'm afraid," said the chaplain. "You'll have to put on your bloodstained one until our situation changes."

Stanley was about to open his mouth to say that he was fine with that, especially since he got to keep his arm, but his head felt woozy at the sight of his own blood being churned into the mud below everybody's feet. Rex helped him back into his shirt and brown jacket while Isaac and Bertie watched with wide eyes.

"Who the *hell* moved this radio," bellowed Lt. Billings.

Stanley swayed on his feet, a little unbalanced. Everybody moved out of the way, though he couldn't blame them. Lt. Billings never raised his voice unless the moment was imminent and dire.

"I did, sir," said Stanley. He did his best not to reach for the bump on his arm where the bandage was. But his arm ached, and he couldn't help himself, which drew the attention of Lt. Billings and pretty much everybody within earshot and eyeshot.

"He moved it before the bomb hit it, sir," said Isaac.

"Yes," said Bertie. "Just in the nick of time, sir."

"You might have broken it," said the lieutenant. "And just when I needed to use it."

He didn't say what he needed to use the radio for, but then, he didn't need to. He was the officer in charge, and anything he might say was on a need-to-know basis. Besides, as he shoved his way over to the radio, Stanley had a sinking feeling that he knew what the radio was about to be used for, though how he knew this, he couldn't explain, even to himself.

Lt. Billings turned the radio on. The radio squawked to life with one long, shrill sound that warbled up and down. Lt. Billings adjusted the dial next to the compass. He tapped one of the vacuum tubes, at which point the noise of static went up, and the warble went down. Which meant that although the radio was working, there were no other radios within range that were on or functional.

The full awareness of being the officer in charge fell away from Lt. Billings, and just for a moment, he became a man faced with a very difficult decision that could not be written up in a report and then forgotten afterward. No, Stanley could see it in his face that what he was about to say was going to alter the lieutenant as a human being for the rest of his life.

"The radio is working, but we can't reach anyone on it," said Lt. Billings. The air of being a commander settled over him as he straightened up from the radio to address the small group of men, the chaplain, the scout, and Stanley. "I would call for retreat, but I need the other half of the code to do that. However, I can't reach anyone, so I can't get the code."

Any lesser man in charge would have left it at that, and used the force of suggestion or the enormous blank silence that grew in and among the soldiers in the trench. Lt. Billings wasn't that man, which Stanley knew even before he cleared his throat to speak.

"I need someone to volunteer to go to the major's trench and deliver half the code and bring the other half back," said Lt. Billings. "Then I can call retreat for the 44th Battalion. Otherwise, we are in danger of being overrun by the Germans."

Stanley stepped forward before anybody could speak because in spite of being a battalion made up of young men, there was more than one soldier who would have been willing to take on the task that had no chance of success and that would surely be a one way trip. But Stanley knew he needed to be the one to go. He had a mission to complete, and he had made promises—

In that moment, Stanley remembered. *Everything.*

He remembered Devon. He remembered tripping over Devon in the rain. Being taken inside the warm, dry cottage, and being fed marvelous food. He remembered the hot shower, the clean clothes, and the piles of papers and books that occupied various shelves and spots on the floor.

He remembered Devon sitting at the heavy wooden kitchen table, typing away at his metal laptop, or scrolling to search for information to include in his thesis. The way he would look at Stanley and smile, as if in amazement that Stanley was listening to his ideas about his paper, that Stanley was interested. Which of course Stanley had been, it had been his own life, after all, that Devon was writing about.

More than that, when the passion would light up Devon's eyes and his face became animated, it had been more than Stanley could do to resist him. Devon's gentle hands in the dark, bringing Stanley to pleasure, was a sensation that Stanley would never forget, as long as he lived. What's more, he remembered Devon telling him the code. In any other regard, it was useless unless complete, until, at this moment, when the 44th Battalion needed it most because Stanley knew the full code.

"I'll go, sir," said Stanley. He drew his hand away from his arm and stood as straight and steady as he could.

"But you've been wounded," said Lt. Billings.

"A scratch, sir," said Stanley, and he meant it. Before Devon, he might have played it up, limping like a wounded bird dragging its wing across the dirt, but now he needed to finish his mission. He needed to save the entire battalion to be worthy of Devon's love. "I can make it, just tell me what to tell them."

Lt. Billings placed his hand quite gently on Stanley's arm and pulled him, alone, into the bunker.

"Where's your rifle, son?" asked Lt. Billings. "Where's your canteen? You're going to get mighty thirsty running between bullets, scared enough to piss yourself."

Stanley thought about how he'd left both of those things in the cottage so that Devon wouldn't think he was going crazy when he woke up and found Stanley gone. But it was worth it, all of it.

"They got hit by mortar fire," said Stanley, ducking his chin to hide the fact that his ID tag was also missing.

With a sigh and a grimace that seemed to reflect a sense of desperation, Lt. Billings tapped the map that was spread out on the table. He drew Stanley's attention to the upper left corner, just beyond where the cottage was, the cottage where Devon would one day live and write his paper about weather and how it affected the war.

"It's the far corner, here, do you see?" asked the lieutenant. "You can run along the bottom of trenches for the most part, except for here, where you will have to go over two of them."

As he looked at the map, the lieutenant's face was grave and still. Stanley knew that he would have to disobey orders and run along the top of the trenches the entire way to avoid the mustard gas. He also knew in his heart that the lieutenant would rather have gone himself than to send someone in his place. But he was the officer in charge and needed to stay with his men.

"I understand, sir," said Stanley.

He had the way memorized, and almost turned to go on his mission before he remembered that the lieutenant had not yet given him the first half of the code. It would look odd if the lieutenant remembered later that this had not happened, but that Stanley had been able to come back with the rest of the code just the same.

"The code, sir?" asked Stanley.

"Yes," said Lt. Billings, and with a little sigh, he raised his head to look at Stanley. "Tell the officer this: *There are penguins on the ice*. He'll know what it means, and he'll give you the other half."

"Yes, sir," said Stanley.

He straightened up, gave Lt. Billings a smart salute, and then, exiting the bunker, touched his forelock to his buddies, and smiled at Isaac. Then he ran at a dog trot until he reached the place where he needed to decide whether to go up along the top of the trenches or down along the bottom, as the lieutenant had ordered. Both directions had meant his death by mustard gas, as the last two missions had proved to him. Maybe this time would be different, or maybe it would be the same. Either way, he was going to do his best and prove that he deserved Devon's love. To the world. To time itself.

CHAPTER TWENTY-EIGHT

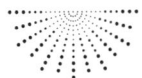

When Devon woke up, he had a crick in his neck that was demanding ibuprofen and a hot shower. Except that as he sat up, rubbing the muscles on the back of his neck, Stanley wasn't in the bed. The sheets and pillows smelled like Stanley, warm and reminiscent of the night before. However, the bedclothes were messy enough so that right away Devon began to doubt his own sanity. Just as with the last time he'd woken up alone, he could have tumbled the sheets himself, and left the clothes puddled on the floor.

The light coming through the half drawn shades was a silvery color as though it was raining again, with the sun struggling through the clouds to light the day. Only instead of being comfortable with the thought of the weather being outside and him being inside with his papers and notes, it felt strange and funereal.

Where was Stanley?

Devon got up, pulling on his jeans, dragging on a t-shirt inside out, and stumbled around the cottage. Stanley wasn't sleeping on the couch, nor was he in the kitchen attempting to make coffee on his own. He wasn't in the bathroom taking an everlastingly long shower and using all the towels. He wasn't anywhere.

Devon's heart began to race, his mouth dry. Stanley wasn't there now, but he'd *been* there, right? It couldn't be happening again, or Devon would know, would finally know, that he'd dreamed up the whole thing, dreamed up *all* of it. That he'd completely imagined Stanley's shorn hair, the curve of his smile, his innocent face, or his bright eyes when he would gaze up at Devon through his dark lashes. The way he'd looked at the oranges the first day, wanting them, but not daring to ask.

Devon would give Stanley a hundred oranges every single day if he would just show up right now, but he didn't. He wasn't anywhere. And Devon was alone.

Except there in the corner of the living room, in the shadowy light from the curtained windows, was something, an object that looked out of place. Devon flicked on the overhead light. In the yellow gleam of brightness, he realized that he was staring at a Winchester 1912 rifle with a bayonet attached. There was a canvas-shrouded canteen dangling from it, with the dot-to-pull fittings gleaming silver. And from that—

Devon walked right up to the rifle and reached out, and before he could think he had Stanley's ID tag in his hand. The round disc with etched letters felt so heavy, reflecting the bleak trace of Stanley's name and rank.

The braided hemp cord was not new. It had been gnarled and twisted from weather and from wearing it in the shower, as Stanley never took it off. Only now Devon had it. When Stanley had left before, there'd been no trace of him, and Devon thought he was going crazy. Because Stanley cared and had listened and because he loved him, he'd taken off his good luck charm and left himself vulnerable for Devon.

Devon turned to survey the empty cottage. There, in the middle of the living room floor, was Devon's phone. He was sure he'd left it plugged in to charge during the night, so Stanley must have used it for some reason.

Picking up the phone, Devon saw a diagonal crack the shape of a lightning bolt going up its middle. Devon tapped on the screen, and though it was cracked, the phone brightened into life.

On impulse, Devon thumbed to the photos, and saw there was an additional image of a bright, explosive light. It was the last image on the camera; the time stamp indicated the photo had been taken just after midnight.

That Stanley had left on purpose was now obvious, and that he'd gone to finish his mission was even more clear. He was a soldier and could not allow himself peace from war until he'd completed his mission. He'd gone back the same way he had the first time, by scaring himself with the phone's flash, which to him looked like exploding mortar shells.

Devon's mouth opened with an almost silent cry of despair, and he gripped the ID tag in his fist so tightly it hurt. If he could go back in time and find Stanley, could he bring him home before the worst happened and the mortar shell actually hit Stanley this time? But how could he? He didn't know. He'd only ever seen Stanley disappear the one time, and when Stanley had come back, he had been running across the green grass and into Devon's arms. Everything was beyond his control. It was *all* beyond his control. The only thing he could do was search, like he'd done before, just to be sure.

As fast as he could he got dressed. He stuffed the phone in his pocket, pulling on his jacket even as he was opening the door. He raced out into the rainy morning.

In that first moment, it became obvious that his search would be for nothing, and that nothing would be the same.

Beneath the grey sky the trenches were still the same, grass covered corduroy rows of melted earth that backed up to the church. In between was the same shoulder-high trench that led to the memorial. Except now instead of white crosses, row on row, there was a wide field of rain-wet green grass and a single tall memorial of the purest white marble.

As Devon got closer, shoulders hunched, hands in his pockets, he could see that there was a knee-high fence of white-painted concrete posts around the memorial. Chain links had been welded into place between the posts and were also painted white, though the paint was chipped so that rust showed through, as though it had been there a long time.

As he read the inscription, Devon knew the truth of it. Stanley's mission had been a success. He was the only soldier to have fallen because there was only one name that was listed: *Wilifred Sullivan*, and the date *November 10, 1917*.

It was clear to Devon that he had two distinct memories, both of yesterday, when the memorial had included a graveyard, and of today, right now, when the memorial was only for a single soldier who had given his life to save everyone.

This memorial, the way it was now, meant that Stanley wasn't coming back to Devon, for Stanley had completed his mission and had died. Whether he'd been buried beneath the memorial or his body had been shipped home didn't matter. All that mattered was that he was gone. Forever. Devon was alone with only memories, with emptiness, and the ghostly feel of Stanley's hand on his face, as though saying goodbye.

He felt the tears slipping down his face before he could stop them; they left tracks of cold that mixed with the rain on his cheeks. His mouth trembled and he turned away from the memorial. He made a sound that came out like a dog's bark, an animal cry, and he knew that the pain in his heart would never heal.

It wasn't just his own loss, it was Stanley who'd given his life to save his buddies, the radio, and the rest of the 44th Battalion. Devon had an idea that if he went to check the records, the story would be different from what he remembered. The inclement weather, the cold front that had lingered and affected the turn of events, would matter still, but only up to a point. The village of Ornes would no longer have a sign memorializing the senseless disaster because the roads were too muddy to truck in supplies to allow any comfort in the trenches. Yes, it would have been miserable, but on November 10, 1917, the 44th Battalion, by some miracle, by Stanley's carrying the message, had gotten out.

Leaving Devon alone, forever.

By the time he got back to the cottage, it was raining even

harder, the pounding of raindrops on the slate roof sounding out high notes and skittering sounds. Devon shoved open the door, and walked to the rifle he'd left on the kitchen table. He picked it up, holding it in his hands, letting the moment linger as the wood warmed against his skin. The rifle he'd once drooled over now only represented the horrors of war, the loss of innocence. The waste of it all.

He lifted it and smashed it against the stone fireplace until it was nothing more than tinder and pieces of wood on the floor. Then he hurled the canteen against the wall, for what did it matter? The sturdy canteen dented with a low thunk and fell to the floor.

The only thing left was Stanley's ID tag, and this Devon picked up with shaking hands. He fumbled with the knot and tied it around his own neck. The hemp rope twisted in places and was rough on his skin, but he clenched his hand around the tag until it hurt and willed himself to stop crying, to be still.

He saw the pieces of rifle on the floor, the canvas-covered canteen with a dent in its middle, the remains of a life nobody would remember but him.

Through the open doorway to the bedroom, where the light was still on, he could see the rumpled bedclothes. If he squinted, he could see the scratch the bayonet's blade had left. The cottage was an empty echo of its former self, as though the rain pressing down intensified the loneliness that had been a part of it long before Stanley had arrived. Now that he'd gone, Devon was alone, swamped by the ache in his heart, tears drying on his face.

On the counter was his work, his laptop, his canvas notebook, and his spreadsheets, printed with weather data so essential to his thesis.

He stilled the impulse to chuck everything in the fireplace and set a match to it, for not only would that be a futile and wasteful gesture, he'd promised Stanley that he'd finish. That he'd tell the story the soldiers who had been in the war could not. Except now that story was different, so his thesis would have to be adjusted. But he would do that because he'd promised Stanley. Stanley, who had listened while Devon had gone on and on about his paper. Who'd looked at Devon with whiskey-colored eyes and seemed happy to be with him, listening with a smile on his face.

Shucking his jacket and wiping his nose with the back of his hand, Devon moved everything to the table, spread out his papers, opened his laptop, and with one last tug on Stanley's ID tag, got to work.

CHAPTER TWENTY-NINE

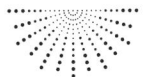

The thing of it was, Stanley already knew the second half of the code so there was no point in running all that way to the major and risking certain death. No point at all in taunting fate. He was halfway up the side of an empty trench where a miasma rose from the dead bodies beneath the mud when he realized what he needed to do. He needed to wait in hiding for the appropriate amount of time, and then return as if he had, indeed, gotten the second half of the message.

He crept over the top of an unmanned trench and tucked himself behind a howitzer that had been blasted into lumps. The smell of fuel that had leaked into the earth made the reason for the lack of soldiers clear. One single match would have caused a huge fire, igniting cloth and men and all the fuel within reach.

Stanley didn't have a match, didn't even have his rifle or his canteen. He'd left everything for Devon. Closing his eyes, he sent all of his hopes and dreams and love as fiercely as he could into the future. Then he hunkered down and prayed that nobody would come upon him, find out his mission, and consider him a coward for hiding out instead of running all the way to the appropriate trench. There was no way he could explain how he already knew the second half of the code. Just no way.

He counted to one hundred, thoughts of Devon in his head, and counted to a thousand, imagining every smile on Devon's face, the touch of his hand on Stanley's skin, the whisper of his breath across Stanley's mouth. There had been a kind of freedom in loving Devon, a sense of having come to a safe place that he could call home. If his mission were successful, then maybe time would let him go back there. And if not, then at least Stanley would have done some good in the world to have been worthy of the time he'd been able to share with Devon.

In the silence of the space between volleys from the Germans and the returning fire of the American soldiers, Stanley heard the larks singing. A spindly, frail series of notes rose into the pewter-colored sky with the braveness of the mightiest soldier, and the poignancy of those who had already fallen. Along the trench in front of him was a stand of three bright red poppies. They were the last of the season, tumbled by the wind and torn by the poison in the air, but still so red and vibrant that to look at them made Stanley want to cry, but he didn't.

He needed to be like the larks and the poppies and he needed to finish his mission to save his battalion, to save his friends. He suddenly laughed at that because when he saved everybody, what would Devon have to write about? There would be no lost battalion, no tattered remains in the trenches, and no cold front to have caused the disaster. Well, the cold front would still be there, but since the 44th would have gotten out before they were decimated, nobody would care, and the rain and the frost would go unnoticed, unwritten about. Unremarked, except by the poppies coated in a delicate curl of ice.

Stanley shook himself and counted out the moments.

It had begun to rain by the time Stanley determined enough time had passed, and he clambered to the top of the trench. He rolled down the other side until he was covered in mud and soaked through. And then he ran, straight as an arrow, back to Lt. Billings, who was waiting in the command bunker with Isaac, Rex, and Bertie. Behind them was a small group of officers that Stanley knew had not been there the last time. But then, he'd never returned from his mission with the second half of the code before.

Panting expansively, Stanley threw himself down at Lt. Billings' feet, as though exhausted by his toils, white faced and shaking from his supposed trek across the war torn fields.

Isaac, who must have been waiting terrified this whole time, hauled Stanley to his feet and embraced him, heartfelt but briefly, before letting him go.

"The code, soldier," said Lt. Billings. His face held no expression, as if he was completely prepared for Stanley to tell him that he'd failed in his mission.

"There are penguins on the ice," said Stanley. "And they skate brilliant figure eights."

Before Stanley had gotten half way through the second part of the code, Lt. Billings' eyebrows flew up in his forehead. Stanley realized that the lieutenant had always known the second part of the code, but that military order dictated a second, separate source.

"It's good having it confirmed," said Lt. Billings. He turned to the group of officers who had evidently been in the know, and who had been waiting for Stanley to return. "I'm giving the order for retreat. Pass it along, run if you have to. We're taking only what we can carry with us. Nothing is more important than a man's life; everything else can get left behind. Tell them to go over the top, and head west, and we'll muster at the river by the old mill."

Mud sprayed up at Stanley as the officers, the chaplain, the scout, and Isaac, Rex, and Bertie sprinted into action to spread the word to the rest of the battalion.

Soon, like ants, soldiers charged over the top of the trenches, headed west in a swarm of legs and arms and white faces. Once, when Rex ran past him, hauling a wounded soldier beneath each of his broad arms, he winked at Stanley. Bertie, close behind, leading a line of soldiers, attempted to pat Stanley on the arm, but missed and had to keep on going.

As Stanley went up the trench to check for stragglers, he saw Isaac out of the corner of his eyes by the opening of the bunker. When Stanley turned around, he discovered that almost everybody was gone. He was alone at the back end of the retreat, and smiled, pleased that finally he'd been able to complete his mission.

He looked at Isaac, and went toward him, wanting to share the moment with him. From overhead came the crack of a canister, the smell of acrid smoke pelting down, deep into the trench around Stanley. He was in the middle of it, and the first breath he took sliced right through his lungs as he tumbled at Isaac's feet.

In the next moment, Isaac was at Stanley's side, gripping his hand as though he was trying to pull Stanley out of a deep well. Even closer was the white faced Lt. Billings, his eyes urgent and wide. His mouth was open. He seemed to be shouting at Stanley, as though Stanley had made a mistake, and was getting yelled at for it.

He sensed the chaplain waiting not too far off, and beyond that was the blankness of an empty trench. All the soldiers were gone, and only these three remained to tend to Stanley in his last moments.

Stanley was sorry, honestly he was, for how things had turned out. He opened his mouth, wanting to tell them what an honor it had been to serve with them. To have eaten dried bread and drunk bitter coffee, and to have shared laughter about it, because that's all you could do, sometimes, when things were as bad as they had been. Beyond this moment, Stanley had the certainty that the 44th Battalion would not end up beneath a grassy field decorated with white crosses, row on row, but would go on to survive the war, and lead happy lives.

As for himself, he had known the greatest love of his life, a love that had returned each gesture, each word, and that with joy and acceptance and passion. In some distant year, when the cottage across the fields was whole once more and heated by sweet, warm air, Devon would write his paper about how weather had affected the last battle of the 44th Battalion. Perhaps, in one way or another, he would think about Stanley, the strange young man who had visited for a while, but who had gone back to save his fellows. Or maybe he wouldn't remember because it had never happened, and this was all in Stanley's mind, the last fevered imaginings as he struggled to breathe and large black spots formed in front of his eyes.

CHAPTER THIRTY

There was nothing but layers, layers black as pitch, hot like the sun. Stanley felt them all, his arms spread wide, his head tilted back, though whether he was moving forward or backward, he didn't know. Only that he was dizzy and still all at once, and that his fingertips felt frozen, and that the cold might be creeping closer to his heart with each moment, each eon, that passed.

He landed face down, his whole body slamming against something solid and cold. With a start, he opened his eyes, blinking against the damp. Slatted rain was falling on the still-green grass. Within moments, he was dotted with wet, flat flakes of snow.

Pushing himself up, he reeled as though he'd been tossed for hours. Then he was still, sitting with his hands braced behind him. He stared across the field to the cottage, shocked that there was no smoke coming up from the chimney.

A silver-colored car was heading out of the driveway and along the road to the village. In the back of the car was Devon's dark head, which was turning back to the cottage, as though for one last look.

Stanley opened his mouth to shout.

"Devon."

It came out a croak; he couldn't find his voice to stop Devon so he had to find another way.

Stanley stood up and started to run, except the grass was slippery. His legs felt like rubber, and he stumbled to his knees. He got up again and ran as fast as he could, though he felt like he was going in slow motion, mouth open as he searched inside of himself for the sound that simply wouldn't come.

He ran anyway, his arms up, reaching for the car that was about to turn the corner into the copse of trees. At which point, Devon would be out of sight and out of reach, and Stanley would be alone. He wouldn't know how to contact Devon in this land of small, portable phones, and metal laptops you could carry, and cups of coffee that tasted smoky and good.

His heart began to break, and his knees trembled.

Suddenly, to Stanley's astonishment, cutting through his fog of desperation, the taxi spun to a halt on the blacktopped road. Devon got out, jacketless, and began to run. He ran straight for Stanley, and within a moment, his arms were around Stanley. He was with Devon, *finally*, and Devon was protecting him from the cold, the snowy rain, a bulwark against the uncertainty of time.

"Stanley," said Devon, his face buried in Stanley's neck. His nose was cold, his lips were warm, his breath sweet and soft on Stanley's skin. "I waited and waited, but was leaving—"

"I saw you," said Stanley. He could hardly believe he was here with Devon, in the future, the war a faraway thing in his past. "I thought you didn't see me."

"Oh, I *saw* you," said Devon, and he was shaking all over as he held Stanley tight. The edge of the circle of Stanley's ID tag glittered on Devon's neck. Stanley admired it for a second before he kissed it, and kissed Devon's neck as he was held.

"One moment, there was green grass," said Devon. "I wanted to cry at the emptiness—but then you were *there*. I couldn't believe it, and then I couldn't get the driver to stop because I'd forgotten all of my French—"

"He's waiting." Stanley lifted his head. The driver had parked in the driveway in front of the door of the cottage, and was standing next to his taxi, looking at his watch.

"I'll tell him—" said Devon, and then he stopped. "But first I need to show you something. You need to look behind you, just look."

Stanley resisted. He didn't want to look because behind him was the past that could snatch him back at any moment. Behind him was mud and trenches and barbed wire and exploding mortar shells. Behind him was the war and he wanted it to stay there.

"No, it's okay," said Devon. He lifted his hand and gently turned Stanley around, away from the grey cottage and toward the soft, rippling humps that were the remains of the trenches built by the 44th Battalion.

And that was all that was there. Gone were the white crosses, row on row, stark against the green, snow-flecked grass. Standing solitary at the far edge of the field stood a single narrow monument of smooth white stone. Devon ignored the cab chuffing in the driveway, the driver standing next to it, and dragged Stanley through the wet grass to where the monument stood, a single reminder, a sentinel to the war.

"Look and see," said Devon as Stanley scanned the words inscribed into marble, the flare of stone bunting on either side a small shield from the snow. "From the moment you left the second time, it said this. I looked at it a hundred times while finishing my paper. You did it, Stanley, you saved them all."

"Is that me?" asked Stanley, though he could hardly believe what the words said.

Dedicated to Wilifred Sullivan who died November 10, 1917.
In honor of the brave soldier who saved every man in the 44th Battalion.
He gave his life so that others might live.

"Yes, that's you," said Devon, his arm solid and warm around Stanley's waist. "You completed your mission."

"I hid," said Stanley as Devon led him across the grass and back to the cottage. "Then I went back and gave Lt. Billings the code. He ordered the retreat. I stayed behind to make sure everybody got out and then—the mustard gas got me anyway."

"But you're here now," said Devon. "You're here now with me."

When they reached the driver, Devon talked to him in French. There were hand gestures on everybody's part until Devon handed over a small fold of bills, and helped the driver unload Devon's things. After which, he waved the driver away, which left them both standing at the door of the cottage while Devon fumbled with the lock, and then drew Stanley inside.

"Your things," said Stanley. He breathed in the sweet, warm air, and as Devon pulled him close and wrapped his arms around him, Stanley knew there was nothing better than this feeling, this moment.

"Screw my things," said Devon.

"Your papers," said Stanley. "Your metal laptop, you need those."

"I need *you*," said Devon. "Besides it's all done now. I sent everything to my thesis advisor yesterday. I was waiting till today to leave in the hopes—"

Stanley closed his eyes and buried his face against Devon's chest, and thought about staying there forever. Even then, he couldn't get enough of Devon's scent, the sound of the low pulse of his heartbeat, the solid feel of his arms, the way he swayed slightly back and forth as though rocking a child into a peaceful sleep.

Stanley opened his eyes and looked out at the falling snow, at the white flecks on Devon's suitcases, his boxes, the black cloth satchel that held his metal laptop.

"Where were you going?" asked Stanley. He pulled away and looked up at Devon.

"I was headed back to the States early," said Devon. He took his hand and traced the curve of Stanley's cheek. "I finished my paper like I promised you I would, so there was nothing for me here. You were gone forever, Stanley."

"Well, I'm back now," said Stanley. He meant for his voice to be firm and assured, but it shook. "And I want to stay with you, I want to stay."

"You can stay with me in the States," said Devon. "I'm going to make phone calls."

Standing in the open doorway they were both getting wet, and snow threatened to cover Devon's things with thick, damp layers. Stanley let go of Devon to bring Devon's things inside. Devon closed and locked the door while Stanley dusted off the snow and carried the suitcases back to the bedroom, and the satchel with the metal laptop, and the box of papers, back to the kitchen table where they belonged.

Each moment he'd been in the war, he'd thought of this cottage with its small rooms, the thick curtains that kept out the world, and it was important, at least for a moment, that everything was as he'd remembered it.

He realized that Devon had not moved from the door, and that he was staring at Stanley as though he was starving. His expression reflected how Stanley felt.

"I'm afraid time will take me back," Stanley said, admitting his biggest fear.

"It won't," said Devon. "You've done what you set out to do. You've completed your mission, so take off that uniform and have a hot shower. I'll make you something to eat, though it's only frozen pizza again, and we're out of milk."

Stanley smiled at the mundane concern about there being no milk to drink when they could easily go to the store and get more. He peeled off his jacket, now stiff with mud and blood. He'd forgotten about his wound until Devon made a sharp sound and was at his side.

"What the fuck, Stanley," said Devon, his hands on the bandage that the medic had so carefully wrapped only hours ago. "Are you wounded? Is that blood on your arm?"

"It's not bad," said Stanley, his hand going to test the edges of the bandage, as he would have done in the trenches to make sure that no dirt was getting beneath the edge. "It's only a little blood. The medic put iodine on before he wrapped it; a bit of shrapnel got me. It missed the radio, which still didn't work, which was why I had to go—"

"Take everything off and get into the shower," said Devon, making a slicing motion with his hands. "I'll unwrap your arm and after you shower, I'll get *real* antibiotic for that wound, and a clean bandage."

Devon began to peel off Stanley's shirt and was unwinding the bandage, though he was slowing down with every turn of the cloth, his eyes wide.

"This is a bandage from World War I," Devon said, his voice low with awe.

"Yes," said Stanley. He had to smile because Devon's face was lit with excitement, and it was okay now that Stanley was here and in one piece. The wound was a mere scratch, something to share with Devon. Maybe Devon could add something about the bandage to his paper, although he'd already handed it in. Or maybe he wouldn't add it, since it had nothing to do with the weather. "Rex checked that shrapnel hadn't gone all the way through to the bone and then the medic wrapped it."

"Rex was one of your army buddies, right?" asked Devon. His concentration was on the pile of muslin in his hand, which had little red lines from where the blood on Stanley's arm had soaked through.

"You remember. He was one of the fellows I went through basic with," said Stanley. "Him and Bertie and Isaac."

"Isaac made it out?" asked Devon, though the answer was obvious; every man had made it out alive because of Stanley. Unspoken was the question that Devon had asked before, whether Stanley had been in love with Isaac, and whether Isaac was like Stanley and Devon in that way.

With his chin tucked low, Stanley looked up at Devon through his lashes and, for a moment, both of them were still.

"He couldn't have loved me back," said Stanley, gently. "He wasn't afraid, he just didn't want it. But he was kind to me, always."

"He might have loved you in his own way," said Devon.

"Yes," said Stanley. "He was with me when I died, holding my hand."

"Stanley," said Devon in that soft way that told Stanley everything he needed to know. That Devon was glad he was there, was glad he made it through, and that he never wanted Stanley to leave. It strengthened him to be so loved; with Devon at his side, he knew everything would be good.

Devon kissed him, and brushed some of the mud from his face as he put the bandage on the table. Then he walked Stanley into the bathroom, and helped Stanley out of his uniform. He tossed each piece aside in a casual way, as though the uniform didn't mean as much to him as Stanley did. Later, perhaps, he would examine the garments, though Stanley really didn't want to see any of them again.

Devon turned on the shower, and as the hot water ran and Stanley stood naked on the bathroom rug, Devon checked him over.

"Look at the amount off mud that soaked through your uniform," said Devon. "And the bits of shrapnel that made their way through the cloth. And where did you get all of these bruises?"

Stanley shook his head and let Devon fuss over him. He felt a little tired by the journey through time, but it was different, in a way. Devon felt more real, the cottage more familiar, and though he was worried about time changing its mind, he knew he had finally earned this time with Devon.

"Shower now," said Devon, pointing to the water. "I'll make food."

While Stanley soaked in the shower, the warm water washed away the numb, cold feeling in his bones. As he was getting dressed in the t-shirt and baggy cloth pants that Devon had left for him, he opened the door to let the steam out. He could hear Devon on the phone talking in a loud voice to someone about papers for Stanley. Then came the sounds of Devon puttering around, the sounds of a frozen pizza box being opened.

In a moment, Devon came into the bathroom and pushed up the sleeve of the t-shirt. He bathed the slender wound in something that looked like jelly from a packet, but which quickly numbed the pain. Then Devon unpeeled the wrapper from something that looked like a pre-made bandage, and carefully laid it over the wound.

"We'll check that in the morning," he said. "If it's infected, I'm taking you to a doctor, you got it?"

"I'm not arguing with you," said Stanley. Although he was confused by the fuss, he could easily see that in this future time, first aid was taken very seriously. Plus, Devon kissed the edge of the bandage and smoothed it with his fingers, as though his love would surely be the healing of the cut, which Stanley, on the receiving end of all that care, was sure would be the result.

CHAPTER THIRTY-ONE

When the air was warm with the smell of garlic and pepperoni, they sat at the table to eat. Dressed in soft, borrowed clothes and wrapped in a fluffy blue robe, Stanley ate a slice of pizza and drank the soda pop that Devon had poured over ice. It was a great combination of flavors, though he wasn't very hungry. He just wanted to sleep in Devon's arms forever. Wanted sleep to take him away from his thoughts about time taking him back to the war.

He felt Devon looking at him with dark eyes.

"What's the matter, Stanley?" asked Devon. He leaned forward and took Stanley's hand.

"I'm afraid that time will take me back at any moment," said Stanley, allowing his worries to surface. "I'm so tired, but I'm afraid that if I fall asleep, when I wake up, I'll be back there."

For a moment, Devon looked at the slice of pizza in his hands, examining it the way soldiers in the trenches had, as though looking for mice droppings or flakes of mud before eating something. Stanley could see that Devon was thinking this through with as much concentration as he might a section in his thesis paper. Then Devon looked up at him, determination making his jaw firm, his eyes bright.

"We're going to test it," he said. "I'll take pictures of you in your uniform like we did before. And then the second time when you took pictures of yourself."

"I wanted to go back," said Stanley, though he hated the thought that admitting it might hurt Devon's feelings and wound his tender heart. "I had to finish my mission or I wouldn't deserve being here with you. So I put on my uniform, recited the code in my head, and took a picture of myself with your phone. Like we did before. I think it was the flash that did it, that sent me back."

If he'd thought that Devon would get angry in any way, Stanley couldn't have been more wrong. Devon put down the pizza, got up, and came to Stanley's chair, and hugged Stanley very tight. Stanley pressed his cheek to Devon's belly, and circled his arms around Devon's hips, and then they were still, together like that.

"You were so brave," said Devon, his voice thick with emotion. "I can't believe how brave you were; you saved everybody, and you still came back to me."

"Time let me, I think," said Stanley, though he couldn't say how he knew this. "At least I feel like it did."

"You've got good feelings," said Devon. "And I'm so, so glad you're here, I can't tell you."

Stanley stood up in the circle of Devon's arms, feeling a little warm in the blue robe now that they were so close. Devon slipped his arms inside the robe, and it was as though they were both wearing it together. He could feel the warmth of Devon's skin, and taste traces of garlic on his lips as he kissed him.

"I am glad that I'm here," said Stanley. "But I want to be sure, too, at least more sure, that nothing's going to happen, that I won't be taken from you again."

"We'll repeat what we did," said Devon. "Then we'll be sure."

With some reluctance, Stanley got dressed in his uniform, hopefully for the last time. The wool was scratchy. It smelled of mud and blood and the sad mildew of age, as though it was very old and nobody had touched it in a long, long while. Which was odd, since he'd just taken it off.

He took the wrapped chocolate out of his pocket and put it on the table, as he didn't want the lump ruining the line of the uniform. He took the ID tag from around Devon's neck and let Devon tie it on him.

Devon knelt at Stanley's feet, lacing his boots with the 48 eyelets, and wrapped the puttees in careful layers. Devon handed him the dented canteen to sling over his shoulder, but there was no rifle. Stanley didn't ask about the rifle because he really never wanted to see it again.

When Devon posed him in the middle of the living room, Stanley made a point to stand in the same way he'd stood before. His heart beat fast with the fear that the war would open up behind him and he'd be there once more.

Except it felt different. He'd completed his mission, and it didn't have the same feel, it just didn't. Yes, he was a little tired, but he wasn't experiencing that bone-deep pull of gravity in the same way, the way that reminded him every minute that this was not his world. He wasn't feeling that, but it was scary just the same. Especially when Devon turned on the flash with a flip of his thumb and took the photos.

The brightness of the flash stung Stanley's eyes, but nothing happened. The photographs had been taken and Stanley was still standing next to the sturdy farm table.

Devon looked at him with questioning eyes.

"Anything?" asked Devon, his voice full of hope.

"No," said Stanley. "It's different than the last time. It's strange. I don't have any of the same sensations."

"Okay, okay," said Devon, as though to comfort Stanley as much as himself. "Now let's try the other thing you did—didn't you say you said the code? So maybe do that."

"I opened the door first," said Stanley. "To look at the rain."

"Okay," said Devon, nodding, his eyes wide with nervousness. "Let's try that."

Stanley went to the door the way he had that one night, when deep in the darkness he'd awoken with a pulling desire to save Isaac and

Rex and Bertie and everybody, to save them all from certain death. To do the right thing.

Then, it had felt as though his whole body was buzzing, being pulled into the past. But as he opened the door, now, the mist was coming down. His face was wet, as with before, but his body felt the same as it had only a moment ago. He did not feel any urgency, nor any fear.

He turned from the open door and said the code, the whole of it aloud. The words resonated with only a shadow of their former power as Devon took another flash photo of him.

His heart was beating that he'd be taken from Devon and shoved back into the muddy trenches. Only nothing happened this time either. He looked over at Devon's tight body all drawn up as though in anticipation of the most mortal of pains, his face still and grave, no light in his eyes.

"Anything?" asked Devon. His lips barely moved. "Is anything happening?"

"No," said Stanley, shaking his head. "It's not the same at all. I just feel a little tired, but normal, like it was any other day."

"Maybe it is just another day," said Devon. "Maybe you'll get to stay with me now."

Stanley wanted to peel off his uniform and get Devon to build a fire in the fireplace so they could burn everything from the vest to the trousers to the puttees. He wanted to put the past behind him, but it was that same past that had brought Devon here, to the village of Ornes, where the last battle of the 44th Battalion had been fought. So maybe some part of that past ought to be preserved, to mark the moment when their two lives had become entwined.

"I feel like I've always been with you," said Stanley. He half expected that Devon might pull back at the heartfelt sentiment.

Nothing could be further from the truth. Devon came close, pulled Stanley to him, and hugged him. A whiff of mold puffed up from the uniform, which was crumbling on his shoulders as though tearing with the pressure of Devon's arms.

"What is going on?" asked Devon. He stepped back, his hands on Stanley's shoulders. "Take that off, it's falling apart even as I look at it."

The whole of the uniform was falling into flakes, into tatters, the leather of Stanley's boots crumbling and shrinking, the collar of his shirt worn to the thinness of an autumn leaf.

As he stepped out of his uniform, the seams on his trousers spilt and every piece blew away into a puff of dust. The strap on the canteen disintegrated and the canteen fell. The hemp around his neck withered into a strand that melted on the faint draft from the radiator, and the ID tag, more rusted around the edges than it had been before, clattered to the floor.

Devon grabbed the blue robe and threw it around Stanley. He tied the sash at his waist, then bent to pick up the ID tag. He held it in the curl of his palm and looked up at Stanley.

"Maybe time is letting us keep this," he said, his eyes hopeful as he searched Stanley's face.

"And the canteen," said Stanley. He pointed at it. The canvas case around it was gone, but the metal, a bit dented in the middle, shone like dull nickel beneath the overhead light. "But what happened to the rifle, Devon?"

He meant the question as a joke, but was surprised when Devon blushed and looked away.

"I smashed it because you were gone."

"What?" asked Stanley, his mouth open.

"I couldn't bear to look at it anymore," said Devon. The corners of his mouth turned down, his eyes dark with sadness. "I couldn't bear to think of you suffering through the war, and every time I saw the rifle, well, it got to be too much. So I destroyed it."

This, as if Stanley needed it, was evidence of how much Devon cared about him. Not his experience, or his uniform, his soldier's kit, but *him*. Stanley Sullivan, ex-soldier, and soon to be returning to the States with his scholar, whom he loved.

"Please don't worry about it," said Stanley. "We'll get a new strap for the canteen, and we'll make you a necklace with a piece of ribbon you can loop through the tag so you can wear it forever. Okay?" He said the word as Devon always said it to him, as confirmation and an expression of care.

"Okay," said Devon as he reached into his pocket for his phone. "But I'm going to worry until we are away from here, you know? Put some clothes on, and we'll pack, and I'll call the airlines—Stanley, what is this?"

Huddled in the fluffy blue robe, Stanley hurried to the table where Devon was picking up the chocolate that Isaac had given him. The three or so squares were wrapped in waxed paper, which had the oily look of having been stored someplace where the heat had gotten to it.

"That's the chocolate Isaac gave me," said Stanley. "He was always doing that because he said he didn't like chocolate, but I always thought it was because he wanted me to forgive him for not, you know—"

Stanley waved his hand in the air as though conjuring up an explanation. The floppy sleeve of the robe slid back from his wrist as he reached to take the chocolate from Devon, who surely wouldn't want it.

"Isaac gave you that?" asked Devon, his voice hushed. "On that last day, on November 10th, 1917?"

"Yes, he did," said Stanley. He didn't really understand the question until he saw that light of passion in Devon's eyes. Then he cleared his voice and told the story, laying out the scene as it ought to be done so that Devon could enjoy the moment to its fullest.

"Normally, we get our chocolate ration on a Thursday, after supper. It was always bully beef and rice, and the rice was usually undercooked, you know?"

Devon nodded his eyes wide as he listened to Stanley, rapt with attention like a child preparing to hear a beloved story.

"You know that what they gave us had to last a week, right? Well, none of the fellows could last that long, and usually they had races to see who could finish first. There wasn't much point in holding back if you knew you might die before the end of the week."

With a shaking hand, Devon started to put the chocolate on the table, but Stanley went to him and put his arm around Devon's waist.

With his other hand, he cupped Devon's hand, and lifted their joined hands so Devon could see the chocolate.

"Normally, Isaac gave me his chocolate ration on a Thursday, and I'd eat it all up before bedtime, and that's just how it was. But this this time, Isaac gave his chocolate to me on the 10th. I never had time to eat it and so now I'm giving it to you." Stanley unwrapped the waxed paper, pushing back the flap with his thumb. "Now, you do want to taste what it was like to be in the trenches on November 10th, 1917, don't you? Go on, you can."

"Can I?" asked Devon, looking at Stanley with all the hope in his eyes, his obsession for the war and everything about it a wild, passionate spark. "Really, can I?"

"Yes," said Stanley. "And I'll have some too, so we can share it together, a gift from Isaac to us."

The thought of Isaac and his generous nature and what he might say if he ever learned about Stanley and Devon, made Stanley feel a little sad because they'd never again meet. But it was more important to focus on feeding Devon chocolate that had come from the very war he'd written his paper about.

Still holding on to Devon's waist, Stanley laid the chocolate on the table, the waxed paper beneath it, and with tender fingers broke off three even pieces. He lifted a piece and fed it to Devon, who took it on his tongue as though it was something holy. With a dreamlike expression in his green eyes, he let the chocolate melt for a moment, and then began to chew. Stanley could sense him taking notes the whole while.

Stanley popped a piece into his own mouth, the familiar gritty taste of the chocolate melting on his tongue. When he swallowed, he fed Devon the last piece, taking no refusal, and watched with all of his concentration as Devon devoured it.

"It's not as sweet as I'd thought it would be," said Devon, then he shook his head as though dissatisfied with his explanation. "It was more like dark chocolate than I expected. You know, like you would use making a cake from scratch."

"Scratch?" asked Stanley, completely confused. "Do you buy it in a store?"

"No, no," said Devon with a little laugh. There was a smear of chocolate on the corner of his mouth, so Stanley leaned in and licked it off and stayed close while Devon explained. "It means—well, you make it from the ingredients, rather than a boxed mix, which is what we have nowadays."

Devon's world was filled with amazing things, like cake ingredients that came premixed in a box, and oranges in the middle of winter, and radiators that made chilly rooms warm. But the best thing was Devon himself, who was looking at Stanley with hopeful eyes. He seemed to need reassurance, and giving it to him would help Stanley feel more steady, which he was with every passing moment. Nothing was impossible now, and there was nothing to fear.

"You'll take me back to the States with you, right?" asked Stanley, doing his best to give Devon something to focus on besides the fading taste of World War I chocolate in his mouth. "You won't leave me here, right?"

"I will take you anywhere you want to go," said Devon. "And we'll be together for the rest of our lives."

Stanley tucked his face in Devon's neck, and reached out to clasp the fist that Devon had made around Stanley's ID tag. He clenched tight and let go. Devon placed the tag on the table next to the waxed paper that, oddly, looked as new as it ever had, and hugged Stanley very tightly.

"I love you," said Devon, his voice a hushed whisper across Stanley's temple.

"And I love you," said Stanley, equally low, lifting his chin to kiss Devon's jaw. "I think I always have. I think I've loved you since forever began."

He was trying to say something about time, and how time had gifted them each with the other, but he wasn't making any sense, not even to himself.

As Devon had so often understood him, he seemed to do so now, for he pulled his hand back and cupped his palm against Stanley's cheek.

"Forever begins now," said Devon, solemnly, like a vow. "Forever begins with you and me, right now."

The End

JACKIE'S NEWSLETTER

Would you like to sign up for my newsletter? Subscribers are alway the first to hear about my new books. You'll get behind the scenes information, sales and cover reveal updates, and giveaways.

As my gift for signing up, you will receive two short stories, one sweet, and one steamy!

It's completely free to sign up and you will never be spammed by me; you can opt out easily at any time.

To sign up, visit the following URL:

https://www.subscribepage.com/JackieNorthNewsletter

- facebook.com/jackienorthMM
- twitter.com/JackieNorthMM
- pinterest.com/jackienorthauthor
- bookbub.com/profile/jackie-north
- amazon.com/author/jackienorth
- goodreads.com/Jackie_North
- instagram.com/jackienorth_author

AUTHOR'S NOTES ABOUT THE STORY

The first book in my Love Across Time series is called *Heroes for Ghosts*, and yes the title is from the Pink Floyd song, "Wish You Were Here."

There's something about the tragedy of World War 1 that always spoke to me. Sure, all wars are terrible, but this one seemed more terrible than most. That is because so many young men signed up, having no idea what they were getting into.

In the time of their father's, wars were fought with guns and cannons. In comparison to the mustard gas and shrapnel and disease riddled trenches, the young men were overwhelmed by violence and death.

Oh my. So how do you make a romance out of something like that? And how would it even occur to me to do so? Well, you look at their faces, their sweet young face, and tell me there's not an angsty story to be told.

Some might say that you can't tell a romance set in war time, or you can't set a romance set in a tragedy of any kind. Well, in my mind, that's when we need the gentle touch of a story about a couple falling in love.

AUTHOR'S NOTES ABOUT THE STORY

This story is also inspired by two videos I saw on Youtube, and the dream that I had after watching them both.

The first video is a 2014 Sainsbury's Christmas Ad that is set in December 1914 in the trenches of WWI. In it, the Christmas Truce occurs, meaning that all the young men come out of their respective trenches and share some sports, games, shaving, and, of course, Sainsbury's Chocolate. This ad is a perennial favorite for me, as I watch it every year around Christmas to remind me what is important in this world: love, peace, and chocolate.

The second video is one by the One Voice Children's Choir, called "When You Believe." I stumbled across this video while looking for something else, and found myself entranced by their sweet, young voices, and the story they were telling that wove together the tragedy of war and loss, and the brave innocent soldiers who went to battle. Later viewings taught me that the video was actually about WWII not WWI, but I was still inspired to write a story about those white crosses, row on row. The video still sends shivers down my neck when I watch it. I later discovered that the children's choir was singing a cover of the song from the movie "Prince of Egypt."

After watching these two videos, I had a dream about a young soldier running across a muddy battlefield. Where was he going? What was his mission? Put that together with Pink Floyd's song "Wish You Were Here," and my mind insisted on this time travel story about young Stanley, his bravery, and his beloved scholar, Devon.

A LETTER FROM JACKIE

Hello, Reader!

Thank you for reading *Heroes For Ghosts* from my Love Across Time series.

Please take a moment to write a review of *Heroes for Ghosts* on Amazon and Goodreads. Reviews help with the rankings of my book and can bring them to the attention of other readers who might enjoy them.

Best Regards and Happy Reading!

Jackie

- facebook.com/jackienorthMM
- twitter.com/JackieNorthMM
- pinterest.com/jackienorthauthor
- bookbub.com/profile/jackie-north
- amazon.com/author/jackienorth
- goodreads.com/Jackie_North
- instagram.com/jackienorth_author

ABOUT THE AUTHOR

Jackie North has written since grade school and spent years absorbing mainstream romances. Her dream was to write full time and put her English degree to good use.

As fate would have it, she discovered m/m romance and decided that men falling in love with other men was exactly what she wanted to write about.

Her characters are a bit flawed and broken. Some find themselves on the edge of society, and others are lost. All of them deserve a happily ever after, and she makes sure they get it!

She likes long walks on the beach, the smell of lavender and rainstorms, and enjoys sleeping in on snowy mornings.

In her heart, there is peace to be found everywhere, but since in the real world this isn't always true, Jackie writes for love.

Connect with Jackie:

https://www.jackienorth.com/
jackie@jackienorth.com

facebook.com/jackienorthMM
twitter.com/JackieNorthMM
pinterest.com/jackienorthauthor
bookbub.com/profile/jackie-north
amazon.com/author/jackienorth
goodreads.com/Jackie_North
instagram.com/jackienorth_author

Made in the USA
Middletown, DE
16 July 2021